# With Grace Under Pressure

*A Novel*

*by*

M. Rae

ISBN-13: 978-1502838162

# DEDICATION

To my mother, Rose, and my children, Jessica, Sheila, and Timothy.
Through you, I have found strength, patience, courage, love, and a reason
to keep on running.

*"Limitations live only in our minds. But if we use our imaginations, our
possibilities become limitless."*

*Jamie Paolinetti*

# CONTENTS

# ACKNOWLEDGMENTS

Thank you to my editor, Ann Creel, for her guidance.
Thank you to my friends and family for their encouragement.
Thank you to the many women who have inspired this story and the many
men who have run alongside us in our journey.
Thank you to the organizations which extend their heart and hands to those
in need of friendship and support.

# 1  JAPLO

The heat rises from the earth in unending waves, bringing with it a cloud of dust that enters every crack in our homes and every orifice in our bodies so that we are never completely distinct from this land.  I pull a forest of weeds from the garden behind our house, the beads of perspiration clinging to my neck, my lower back, and the creases of my legs.  It is slow and tedious work, but satisfying and peaceful and productive.

Not everything is, these days.

I hear the rumble of the school bus from over a mile away, and it leaves behind a foggy trail of exhaust and dust.  There is enough of a clearing between our house and the main road that I can see this signal of my children's approaching return, so I finish for the day, throw the drying weeds into a pile by the fire pit, and go into the house to clean up.

Our home is small and simple, compared to some of the grander villas of Monrovia, but it is not as puny as the ghetto shacks that line its roads either.  Our home is not stuffed into the city; instead it is about twenty-five miles to the south in a lush green valley that hugs the bay.  Visitors cannot even see our house until they have crossed over several bush-covered hills and then there it is, a small white box, nestled into the deep jade of the trees and the dark blue-black of ocean as its front yard.

My husband's family has lived here for several generations, but now Tambo is the only one still living in Liberia.  His parents were both dead and his only brother, Jahn, had moved to the United States only a few weeks before Tam and I met, so that just left Tam, as a bachelor, living here alone some weekends, renting a small flat in the city most other days.  He is a legal consultant for one of the largest steel shipping companies in Liberia, one of the few men here who have achieved that high of status.  This was before the conflict had begun, when we had opportunity, even if we had little money.  Tambo's family had money — more than most — so he and

1

Jahn attended university. When he married me, I was finishing classes to become a teacher, but I did not have a job lined up yet. So we thought about moving to the United States, to settle somewhere that is not so tight with conflict and violence, but this home is all that is left of his family, and to abandon that would be a betrayal of his blood and his entity.

So we moved in, bringing our baby girl, Kai, and soon two more children entered our family--our son, Saa, and the little one, my baby girl, Donyen. Kai is a good girl; she studies hard and has plans to go to the university to become a lawyer like her Da, even though she is just fifteen years old. Saa is like any other nine-year-old boy of the Lone Star country-- he runs and plays and dreams of being a futbal player who travels the world and gets rich and famous. That is okay. Let him dream for now. He is still a boy and does not need to make any life decisions for quite some time. Donyen--Yeni I call her--has just started school with her siblings, and although she is smart as a whip from practicing with her sister, she is every day tired when she walks into the house, falling into my arms like a baby once again. I do not stop her because I am not really ready to let go.

It was a good decision to settle here, especially since the civil conflicts have increased and protests are rampant in the cities to the north. Pockets of rebellion pop up every few days and the news shows trucks of rebels, angry young men, clutching rifles and shouting into the air about freedom and revenge. I wonder how those two concepts can go hand in hand, but in their world they do. Some days when Tam returns home from working a case in Monrovia, he talks about moving away for a little while.

"Japlo," he says to me, "I am worried that the violence will spill into the Capitol and then we will be trapped. Perhaps we should take a long holiday to visit my brother soon. Get out of here until the Peace Talks have concluded."

I see the worry in his eyes, and the pain in his heart, so I will agree with whatever he chooses to do. I love my husband, and as long as I am with him, and our children are with us, I am content.

This home is simple and quiet and clean and full of love. How could I wish for anything different?

From the window over the kitchen sink I can see their heads appear one at a time. Kai's is steady and bent forward slightly. Probably reading a book as she walks. Her black hair is wrapped into a braid and wound around her head like a crown. Proud, beautiful and intelligent young woman! Saa bounces from side to side, disappearing then reappearing somewhere else. His movements are quick and erratic, and his shiny blue and red jersey floats around his slim body. Sure enough, an empty water bottle suddenly shoots into the air and he twists to the side to kick it over a shrub.

Where is Yeni? I do not see her but I am not worried because I know she moves slower than the tide, especially lately as she is so tired from school.

I fill three glasses with clean water and slice some rice bread, slathering jam on each. I can hear Saa's imagined commentary describe his athletic power, talent, and the joyous "He shoots! Goal!"

My spirit swells as they walk nearer, feeding me a joy that only motherhood can.

A crack of gunfire suddenly pierces the air, and in an instant my world shatters.

Kai is screaming.

Saa is pinned to the ground, a boy not much older than him kneeling on his chest, the tip of the rifle jammed against his jaw. He is gasping and struggling, too young to understand the danger of fighting back. Two young men, maybe twenty years old, have grabbed Kai's arms and they are pushing her to her knees, her face pressed into the dirt.

I scream and leap onto the back of one of them. I dig my nails into his face; I claw at his throat and from deep within me a growl rises up in such protective fury that I am afraid of myself even. I glare straight into the eyes of the little kid who is pressing the breath from my son and I howl, "Get off of him! Now!"

I see him jerk back instinctively, the pressure lifted from Saa, but then he looks at the man I am fighting with and his eyes narrow. He lifts the rifle and pounds the butt of it against Saa's jaw and then shoots wildly into the air. Saa cries out and calls to me while his assailant shouts and grins like a little boy playing with rocks and sticks and empty water bottles.

A sharp heaviness blasts into my skull and I am blown headfirst into a thicket of sticks and thorns. A blur of people, of children, of smoke. The two men who are holding Kai mumble something and laugh and grunt huskily. Saa is choking on his tears, his blood, on the pain of his jaw and the helplessness of his mother. I can see him searching for me, but my head will not let me move. Kai screams again as the gunmen hold her legs and pull her face up by the braid of her hair. I see skin and torn clothes and ripped flesh and blood and mud and mucus and vomit and semen and whiskey and tears. So many tears. My cheek is bathed in its own pool of blood as it runs into my eyes, my ears, and my throat. I am drowning and my children are being murdered...and there is absolutely...nothing...I can do...

Bits of feeling seep into my consciousness, but a door keeps slamming closed, keeping me in the dark emptiness. A mad shaking pounds against my limp body and as awareness returns my stomach lurches and my throat fills with bile. I try to spit it out but I can't so it sits there and burns. The pounding enters more of my body until I finally slip into the dark again.

I hear a familiar voice and an unfamiliar wailing. Thin strong arms are wrapped around me and I realize I am being carried. His cry is so out of character with the calm strength I know as my husband. I force my voice to awaken, reach for the will to call to him and can barely stumble out his name. "Tam."

He quickens his step and now lifts me through a doorway and onto the hard floor of our home. Our lovely and peaceful home.

He hurries to the sink and brings a bowl of water and my kitchen towels back with him. He pours the water over my head and the coolness stirs my alertness so that I am remembering Kai and Saa and Yeni.

I try to ask where they are but my mouth will only manage a weak, "Whe--" But he knows and his bloodshot eyes fill with tears again and his body shakes with grief.

"They passed me," he said, "while I was driving home. I didn't know. I didn't know it was you." And he buries his face in his giant hands.

"Kai.....Kai....Kai..." I demand.

He finishes washing the blood from my hair and face, picks at the bits of rock embedded in my skull. He wraps long strips of cloth around my head, a torn sheet I guess.

I am waiting for him to tell me where they are. I have abandoned them when they needed me most so I am prepared to hear the worst. But he is silent.

As soon as he has finished wrapping my head in cloth, I kick my feet under me and I roll onto my side. I push myself up onto my elbows and then drag myself to a chair. My head is dizzy and pounding, my vision blurred. My genitals are ripped, bloody and raw, but my legs work, so I stand up, leaning on Tam and I feel his strength pour into me. I turn to the door, but he holds my arms and says, "Don't." His voice is filled with pain, but I know that I must see it for myself. I pull away, but he stays next to me as I step outside.

The darkness hides much of the terror from today, but I know the twisted lump in the road is my Kai. Her body is naked and crumpled and torn. I step closer, but Tam stays behind now and he punches his anger and grief into a filthy pile of rags and cigarettes left behind by these monsters. My hands caress her shoulders and her back, and I pull her onto my lap, a cold lifeless shell. I pray that she was unconscious to the brutality inflicted on her and while the grief is overwhelming, part of me is grateful that she will not have to live with these memories.

"Saa?" I ask Tam in a whisper.

"No, he is gone. They have taken him. Yeni too is gone."

"Taken? Where?"

We hear the rumble of a truck from down the road. Gunshots again and I start to shake.

"Quickly!" Tam orders. "You must hide. They think you are dead. They know I am here and they think you are dead. You must leave. Can you run?"

I nod, and kissing my baby, grief suspended, I roll her sweet body back into the dust. Tam grasps my elbow and we move to the front of the house, toward the bay and the groves of trees. I don't know what time it is, but it is dark, and the trees are a good place to hide. Tam helps me along, gently holding me, pushing me and as we reach the grove he pulls me toward him and kisses me softly on my cheek and then on my mouth. I taste the salt of his tears, which makes me sad, but strong.

"You must go to Monrovia," he says. I shake my head, confused.

"They will search here first. I will distract them." He holds his car keys in his hand. "I will meet you in Monrovia."

He hurries back to the car and turns on the engine. The truck is approaching, so, keeping his lights off, he inches onto the side of the road. As the truck pulls near he suddenly spins out in front of them, a gun held in front of his face. They still do not see him as he fires into the face of the driver. Gunfire explodes around him and I can hear him shouting above all of it.

"Japlo! Run! Run! Do not stop!"

A small hand reaches out from the bushes. Yeni wraps her tiny fingers around mine and pulls me into the trees.

"Run," she whispers.

And so, clutching her hand, I run.

It is so dark now that I can barely see where we are heading, but I can smell the ocean in the salty night air, so I know we are heading away. I clutch Yeni's hand and I lead her deeper into the grove. I pray that the gunmen will not follow, and so far I hear nothing but our own feet hurrying across sticks, leaves, rocks. I try to see if Yeni is hurt, but she seems to be a moving blur. She is not crying. Nor is she acting scared. But she is only seven years old, and no child can watch such horrors without being terrified. How could they? But still, she steps one foot after the other, following me, leading me, next to me. She doesn't ask questions or tell what she saw and I am afraid to ask her.

There is no time to ask her, anyway.

My body demands rest, and though I try to push ahead, I must stop and rest again and again. Yeni rests only when I do, sitting close to me, but she must know that I am too weak, too beaten, to hold her in my lap.

In confusing bursts, we zigzag through the grove. Sometimes I feel we are getting close to the ocean; other times I think we have completed a circle and are back to the large rock or bend in the path. We push on nonetheless.

Suddenly the air around us becomes thin and light and I sense that we have walked into an open space. My stomach clenches in fear. I pull Yeni low to the ground and then crawl through the dirt until I feel a thorny tangle of vines that hang from a new grove of trees. We must have been walking at an angle, so instead of going directly to the cliffs at the shore, we have crossed over a tiny trade route that Tam's family and neighbors used years ago. This route is primarily untraveled now though, due to the lack of neighbors and the rise of commercialism. Crops and crafts are no longer valued, since cheap plastics and giant bags of junk food infiltrated Monrovia. Certainly, rural families are still mostly self-reliant, making their own food and household items, but this close to the city, there is no need to work that hard. Instead we work for foreign companies that pay us just enough to buy the junk we make.

Tam is an exception. He used to say he was lucky to have been born to educated parents who valued intelligence as much as they valued family. He said he was lucky to have attended school both in Liberia and in England, at a time when most children barely learned to read. He said he was lucky, but I always told him that it was more than luck. He was a man with a gift. He knew how to think. He knew how to plan. He knew how to face challenges and not run from them, turning them into opportunities instead. I was so proud to be his wife and to be the mother of his children. But that has all been destroyed in a day.

I am heartbroken again.

I pull Yeni into the brush and pull myself up from the dirt. I want to keep moving while it is dark, but I also wish I had more light so that I can see. I see shadows or maybe they are bugs or swaying branches or the movement of a nearby gunman or rapist. This uncertainty keeps me bristled with fear, and I whisper aloud, "I wish the sunrise would come soon."

Yeni stops and tugs at my dress. I reach back toward her, still walking, and hear her whisper back to me, "It did."

I turn around. "What do you mean?"

"Mama, the sun came up a long time ago. It's sunny right now."

The shadows, the darkness, the fading figures are not created by the midnight sky, but by my own eyes. I look directly at Yeni now, and through my left eye only, I see a blurry shadow of her little girl figure, but the details of her face, her hair, her limbs are just darker and lighter splotches that move in rhythm with her voice.

"How long?" I ask. "How long has it been light?"

Such a difficult question for a seven-year-old girl, to whom time is defined by sleep, play, school, and meals.

"Since the braided tree."

Ah, the braided tree. This old, gigantic tree is actually a confused mess of crowded branches that have grown around each other for decades, creating little tunnels and hiding spots for kids playing in the grove. This tree is near our home, maybe a quarter mile away only. We have been walking for at least two hours, albeit slowly, which means that for most of our walk, when I thought we were safely hidden by the dark night sky, we have been open and visible to anyone within several yards. My frantic crawl across the dusty old road must have looked ridiculous to anyone witnessing it. But no one has called out, or attacked, or killed us, so either we have remained unseen, or those who saw us are uninterested. This realization leaves me feeling cold and vulnerable, but then the deeper meaning settles in -- I am almost completely blind.

And I have been leading us in a pointless maze going nowhere.

We need to get to Monrovia. I try to remain focused. But the hope of sunlight has vanished, replaced by a dark, paralyzing panic that screams in my head. I need Yeni to be my eyes, to look for danger, but she is too young, too innocent to be alert for the evils around us. She is slowing down, and her breath is becoming more rapid and shallow. I place my hand on her left shoulder and feel her body relax and she pats my hand softly. We walk like that, she leading me, and I give up trying to see. I am powerless, which leaves me no choice but to place this burden of survival on a child.

I smell smoke. The smoke of a fire burnt days ago, but kept alive by the heat of smoldering debris. Like an animal, I tense and halt, listening, sensing movement around me. Yeni's shoulders lighten and pull out of my reach. As she slips away, I cry out to her, and a large dark shadow appears in front of me.

"Welcome." The strong voice of a woman. Two large arms wrap around me and a cool towel is gently folded across my neck. "My name is Kara. You are safe here. At least as long as any of us can remain safe here."

She leads me into a room that smells of fire and blood and women.

"Here," she says, helping me find a space on the floor. "Rest."

"Ma." Yeni lands beside me. "Ma, I got bread. I got you some too!"

I am sitting amongst a group of women that murmurs and hushes and freezes in silence at the smallest of noises.

"Ssh!" I try to quiet her before we are sent away.

"It's okay, honey," a deep smooth voice pours over us. "She's a child. Let her be child-like for as long as possible. I'm afraid it won't be very long."

She has shifted closer to me, turning my face up to her with her giant hands. But she is gentle, so I do not pull away. I can feel her move close to

7

my face and the blur of her figure fills the space in front of me. I sense her staring into my eyes as she runs her hands along my face. I do not think she can see my blindness any more than I can see her.

"Can you see me?" she asks.

Aggravated I tell her, no, I am blind.

"Oh, now I understand!" She touches my eyes with the tips of her fingers. "But you do have your eyes, and that is something to be grateful for."

I slap her hands away from me. "Grateful? You think I am, or can ever be, grateful for this? My children gone, my husband gone, my home gone." Tears have flooded my eyes and I feel them cascade down my cheeks.

"Yes, I know," she says, kissing the tears on my cheeks. "I have lost my children too. And my husband too. My home too. But you have your eyes, and that is good."

My hands reach out toward the large shadow of a woman who thinks that a set of eyes that do not see can somehow make up for the loss of everything I love. I try to push her away, but instead my hands land on her cheeks. They are rough and scarred. She holds my hands to her face and draws my fingers just a few inches higher. The empty sockets ooze with mucus and loose tissue.

I pull my hands away, and cover my mouth, as my stomach lurches.

The women have been talking. They say the Peace Talks have stopped. There is nothing more to discuss. The government says they will not negotiate with rebels.

And so the violence spreads.

Yeni seems immune from the fear we all feel. Violence has never been a part of our home life. Tam was the most gentle of fathers, and Yeni was coddled and spoiled by her older siblings from her very earliest days. Were we foolish to have kept ourselves so remote? Should we have faced the country's rebellion with our own anger and defense? Should I have taught my children to fight? It seems like the answer now is yes, but I cannot shake the image of our peaceful home, our quiet evenings together, the love that filled our hearts each day. To have brought an acceptance of war into our home would have been to destroy our home altogether. That is not what I wanted. It is certainly not what Tam wanted.

And so, even with the tears and dirt all around us, Yeni is still my peaceful little dove. I hold her to my heart as often as she will let me, hoping that her peace will spread.

Kara seems to be in charge here. She orders the women in and out of the house, and sets them to work on making food, writing letters, bathing the incompetent, and clearing out the blood. Yeni is the only child, yet she works as hard as the women, which makes me feel better about offering so little myself, but I feel guilty that she is still carrying a woman's work in her little hands.

"Shah!" Kara dismisses my worries with a light-hearted laugh. "You baby that child. Look at how strong and capable she is! No reason to keep her from --"

She stops herself. I know why. As much as I would like to look at my daughter, at how strong and capable she is, I cannot. This is not Kara's fault, nor should she feel bad about telling me to "look" at her. But I am bitter and sad, so I turn away from her all the same. I can feel her move away from me, and dropping her voice she says, "The floors need to be rinsed. It is your turn now."

I bolt awake and stare into the darkness. Yeni is warm and relaxed in my arms, a little sigh in her breath as she sinks deeper into sleep. Around me the sounds of women's gentle snoring and sleepy mumbling creates a backdrop of tranquility. I bury my nose deep into Yeni's hair. The scent of your own child never seems to change. When I held Yeni in my arms at her birth, she smelled of earth and trees. Kai had smelled of the sweetness of flowers and pastries, and Saa was salty and sweaty, even freshly bathed. Tam said he couldn't tell the difference, but I am their mother, and when they were born they took from my body the earth, the ocean, the bouquets of lilies that I had living inside me.

Crickets and night owls punctuate the quiet in a random, but rhythmic tune that almost lulls me back to sleep. An unexpected snap of a twig interrupts this night tune and my back and throat tighten. I pull Yeni closer and edge the two of us closer to the wall. Another twig snaps and now I know why I awoke in the first place. When my back touches the wall, I begin to inch us along its edge, trying to make us both invisible.

I can smell him before he enters the room, so I quickly place my hand over Yeni's mouth and hold her tightly. As I do, I hear the muffled scream of one of the women across the room, then a thud as she is silenced. Cries rise from the floor as a young male voice shouts into the female crowd, huddled and helpless.

"Shut up! All of you! I will--I will--kill each one of you and---and--your daughters too, if you don't shut up, now!"

A sharp gasp, harsh and incredulous, hisses, "No! Peter!"

I recognize her voice as one of the small quiet ladies who helps to feed the newcomers, making loaves of bread out of almost nothing. Then his voice again, only small and confused. "Mama? Mama...?"

Why, he must be no more than a child, perhaps ten or eleven years old.

"Peter! What happened to you?" I can hear her moving between the women, perhaps crawling, creeping toward the boy. "Peter, put that down. Peter, put...the gun...down..."

Her voice is steady, but cautious. I don't know why she doesn't fly across the room, grab him in her arms, hug him safe and tight to her chest. I ache to hear my own Saa's voice, and I feel the tears start up again. Then a growl seems to pour out of some demon lurking within him as he cries out, "I don't know you! I don't know you! You are a whore! I do not know you!"

The struggle is loud but short. In just a moment, the women have pulled him to the ground and he howls, "Get off of me! I can't breathe! Come help me-e-e!"

The women's voices stay low and someone muffles the boy's voice with a cloth so that his cries break my heart, but also ease my fear of drawing more viciousness into this home.

Kara cuts through these sounds with swift direction.

"They are waiting for him to return. They will be here soon, if not at any moment, to see if he has passed their test." She spits the word into the darkness, at them.

I feel her lift my arm, signaling me to stand, and then as we gather in fear and in strength, she commands us, "Hand on shoulder. Do not break the line. Step in time, quickly, quietly. Trust your sister in front of you."

My hand is placed on Yeni's tiny shoulder, and her arm reaches up and forward onto the shoulder of someone I do not know. Trust? How can anyone trust, or be trusted?

We move silently toward the door, our intruder behind me, now tightly held by two giant women who do not flinch under his tantrums and tears.

As we step into the night air, our feet slide rather than step, and they move rapidly and rhythmically, a frightened conga line. I am afraid to move faster because I cannot see, and eventually my fingers fall away from Yeni's shoulder. But she reaches back, grabs hold of my hand and once again whispers, "Mama, don't worry. Just run!"

We are a snake, gliding between trees, over rocks, along empty streets. I can feel the sun as it rises over the Sahel in the distance, its heat growing stronger since the days I first ran away from my home. I stumble, of course, but I also learn to read Yeni's movements in an instant, so that the lift of her shoulder means to step up, and when her right shoulder dips, we turn to the right. She dips low to avoid branches, which means I need to dip even lower, but my body soon responds instinctively, and I am miraculously able to keep our line from falling apart.

The boy has tired, and is flung over the shoulder of first one woman, then another, as they take turns carrying him for his mother.

I learn that he is like so many other young boys who have been taken from their homes, who have been shot full of heroin and bathed in whiskey until their addiction erases their memories of home and family and makes them rely only on the bastard rebels who offer them a steady narcotic supply. These boys, these children, are handed rifles, brainwashed, broken of all love and poisoned against their families, their morals, their own mothers. It is through violent attacks on their own villages, homes, and families, that these boys are welcomed into their new "family" of rebels -- and their future--our future--is destroyed.

Peter, though violently angry, is nearing exhaustion and is overcome with a narcotic crash. His body grows weaker, but hallucinations and paranoia grow stronger. The women behind me need to pass him back and forth more often as we wind deeper away.

I hear a rumbling in the distance and I know they are following us. I tap Yeni. "Faster."

She passes along the message, and as it reaches the front of our line, our steps veer off of the road and onto a grassy area. Yeni suddenly stops and I almost run into her, but a large arm shoots out in front of me.

"Get down, here," Kara directs. She puts her hand on my head and pushes down, lower, lower, until I am flat on my belly, my cheek on the dirt. She pushes my head through an opening, and I can feel her flinch as her hand hits something above me. Once through, I begin to lift my shoulders, but they catch on a sharp barb that digs into my skin. I try to suck my body deeper into the earth, but the barbs claw their way down my back, ripping my skin. As my legs wiggle through I reach an abrupt drop -- a cliff, perhaps, and I freeze. A hand reaches up, pats me, and pulls my arm down. I follow the arm, crawling steeply down and am finally drawn into a deep ditch with several other women. We crouch in a river of slimy water, the smell of sewage and stagnation circling our ankles. I reach out for Yeni. She falls into my arms, silent but quivering.

The familiar yet frightening roar of engines approaches, with shouts of "Capt'n! Capt'n!" calling out. Peter moans, a weak moan that fades quickly in the crunch of tires that spit gravel into the embankment above us.

We sit here until they are gone. And then we continue to sit, through the heat of day and through the dewy chill of another night. Finally, we are called to move on. I unfold my body painfully, and slowly follow these incredibly scared and strong women down the embankment and onto a path that seems to have no end.

Yeni has never seen the city. There was turmoil brewing before she was born, and we have stayed happily, peacefully, tucked away in our home for the past seven years. But that peace is gone and today Yeni meets Monrovia for the first time.

11

We have crawled like lizards, like weasels, along the riverbank for two days. Peter has vomited and cried and shaken with the removal of poison from his small body. Today he curls into his mother's arms and stares at nothing, speaks about nothing. When we begin to crawl again, he is terrified of losing hold of her, so she ties one of her long scarves around her waist and another around his waist so that they are like one creature crawling through the mud. It is good that he is no longer fighting against us, but now he has bigger, invisible devils to fight.

We walk together now as a group, like women who belong here, like this is our city. I can see the flashing of shadows and bursts of light as trucks and buses lumber past us. Gravel shoots out from under their giant wheels, spraying my ankles with tiny shrapnel. Kara directs us to move to the side. As we do, I hear city chatter fall to silence as we pass. A woman calls from a window above us, "Peace, sisters! Bless you, sisters! Power to you, sisters!"

More voices call out, and then the shuffle of feet — quick, soft feet— surrounds us, which makes me pull Yeni close to me.

"It's okay, Mama; they are walking with us."

"Who? Who is walking with us?"

"Ladies. Lots of ladies." I can feel her turn to look back. "It's a big parade, Mama!"

In the distance I can hear a woman's voice floating across the city from a loud speaker.

Kara places her hand on my shoulder. "We are not alone. There are hundreds of women here. Listen! They are all together, Christians and Muslims."

*Are you sick and tired of war?* asked the voice from the speaker. *Women of Liberia, it is time to protest! It is time to fight war with peace. It is time to demand peace. Nobody is going to deter us!*

"Oh, Mama! The park is full of women. It's so pretty! They are all wearing white dresses!" Yeni pulls on my hand. "I want a white dress too!"

I hear Kara laugh softly. "Japlo, did you bring your white dress?"

And then clothing is pushed into my hands, and I can feel others around me grabbing for clothing. Kara chuckles again. "You didn't need to bring your white dress, after all. Yeni, help your Mama put her shirt on. Put yours on, too."

"What is this?" I ask.

"Japlo, do you want to end this war with us? There are hundreds and hundreds of women here. They are praying, they are protesting, they are fighting for their children. And all of them -- all of us -- wear the color of peace so that our message is clear. No more war!"

Of course I want to end this war, but how can women -- injured, weak women -- end this war if our own government cannot end it?

"Put this on -- it is your uniform of peace.  It is the uniform of the women's army. We fight for peace, with peace."

Yeni has pulled a large T-shirt over her head.  I pull the same over my own head, and Kara wraps my head in a scarf, as well.  She leads me carefully around body after body, women on their knees praying, bowing to their god, their leaders, calling on the compassion of one and the reason of the other. Their prayers make a soothing chant that must be reaching some ears, somewhere.

The voice on the speaker continues, *This is the last chance for Liberia! The peace talks must end.  The talks are not a vacation for these leaders!  The peace talks must bring peace.*

Kara finds a spot for Yeni and me to sit. The voice is loud now, and I can tell it is reporting on the Peace Talks in Ghana.

Kara whispers to me, "There are more women in Ghana, at the Peace Talks.  They have taken over the embassy. With any luck, their leader, Leymah Gbowee, will not let them out until they have ended this fighting. Until our country is safe again."  She squeezes my hand.  I think she believes the women will win. I do not tell her that my faith is not as strong, that some things are impossible to fight. I do not tell her that it will take more than luck to turn the heads of these powerful men.

Over the speaker, a chant begins, *We want peace! No more war!*

Yeni picks up the chant, and adds the song of childhood to it.

"We want pe-e-ace!  No more wa-a-ar!"

Her song spreads through the park, and soon the chorus of voices reverberates through the city, bouncing off the buildings, rising to the heavens, and ringing deep into my heart.

Perhaps a little bit of my faith remains after all.

# 2  GRACIE

Running tests the limits of what is humanly possible. Over the years the limit of that possibility has been nudged further and further into areas previously decreed impossible. And we continue to ask ourselves if we can run faster. When, on May 6, 1954 Roger Bannister proved that, in fact, it was not impossible for humans to run a mile in under four minutes, it was as if a door was flung open to the rest of the competitive running community for them to follow in his wake and eventually out run even this miracle of speed.

I was born the next day, May 7, 1954, and my father was still talking about the four-minute breakthrough in the hospital as he held me, his newborn daughter. He has told me the story so many times, and like many stories that start out as a simple recounting of the day, it grew to hold meanings and premonitions and legendary lessons that clung to each retelling.

"You see, Gracie, your mother and I weren't expecting you for at least another month or so. The doctor said June, so we believed him. I was just finishing my last year at Harvard, and we were both excited about the changes that lay ahead. Ah, so young and ignorant, your mamma and me."

I recall listening to this story while I was peddling my tricycle in a small circle around my father. He was sitting on the ground of a dusty park, leaning back on one arm, the other one pointing at me as I pumped my legs as fast as I could, curving precariously, yet trying not to tip over. He started his story the same way, but I remember slamming my feet into the ground, bouncing to a sudden halt at these words of his. I leaned over the handlebars, arms dangling, and waited to learn more about this ignorant man in front of me.

"Therefore," Daddy continued, "I had no hesitations about accompanying the Harvard track team to the Heptagonal Track Meet

14

scheduled for May 15th against such strong and reputable threats as Yale, Cornell, and the ever-formidable Army, not to mention the less threatening rivals of Princeton and Columbia. We had had a fierce season, and were picked to win several events and most likely the whole meet. That alone was exciting, and it might have been enough to push us, but the real motivation was for The Mile. The Mile was going to be a special race, created for Josy Barthel himself, in order to test the limits of his strength, and therefore the strength of us all."

A group of teenage boys, who had overheard the mention of those Ivy League schools and paused their own game to keep listening, plopped down next to me.

"My best race was always the 880, two solid laps around the track, a true measure of strategy and stamina. Too fast, and your legs will crumble beneath you in the last straightaway. Too slow and the pack will lose you in no time, with no hope to catch up. I had a quick start and a keen sense of pace which led me to several top three finishes and a few victories as well, usually when Josy was only focusing on the 1500 meter. But at the Heptagonal Meet, the Mile was going to be run for one purpose only -- for time.

"Josy was my hero — I mean it! He was smart, tough, fast, and most of all, European! But he was running for Harvard, and he taught me what it meant to believe in myself. He was one of those men who believed that all limits are mental, and that we create those limits ourselves. So when the widely accepted belief that humans cannot physiologically surpass a four-minute mile, that doing so would result in cardiac arrest and respiratory failure, when that belief was suddenly questioned and studied and experimented with, well Josy put himself in that small group that said 'Prove it'. And I am proud to say I helped him."

A murmur rumbled through the boys, and behind them a young couple, hand in hand, leaned against each other and kept listening too.

"You see, in order to push himself beyond what he had ever achieved, beyond what had ever been achieved, he needed to run faster, longer than it was believed possible. So, along with the rest of the rabbits on our team, I paced him through his training runs, sometimes the first two laps to get his legs moving quick and steady from the get-go; sometimes the last two laps to keep him from fading. And it was always so close to four minutes that we knew it was only a matter of one longer stride, one deeper breath, one more twitch of muscle and he'd pass under that limit. He was confident in himself, and therefore it was easy for me to be confident in him, too.

Ten days before that meet, in the dark coolness of evening, with no lights or crowds or starting guns or photo finishes, a few of us went out to the track and jogged easy for a while. Usually when we were at the track we were focused and quiet and into our own mind-talk. But this night we just talked about other stuff. We talked about what we were going to do after college, where we wanted to live and work. And we talked about you."

Here, and in every retelling since, my daddy would tap me on the nose.

"I told my buddy Sal how much I loved your momma and how excited I was that I was going to be a daddy, but also how scared I was. I told him all the things that worried me about taking care of someone who was so tiny and helpless and who needed me for everything. I told him I was worried that I wouldn't be able to give you everything you needed, since I was working only part-time and finishing grad school. And honey, I told him I was afraid that once you were born, I would not be able to run anymore."

At this point he paused, because it was clear that of all his worries, this was the greatest, and the one of which he was most ashamed.

The young couple had been joined by a father and toddler son, and an old man with a newspaper tucked under one arm. They looked at each other and at the child, at the boys sitting cross-legged on the ground, and at me, and nodded sympathetically toward my father.

"It was important to me, then, that I was ready for Josy, so I could pace him to his goal. After that, I knew my life would never be the same, and this opportunity would never come again. I needed one more practice mile.

"Josy had stopped jogging and was off to the side, stretching. But I toed the starting line, crouched and ready. Sal squatted at the line, stopwatch in hand. 'Billy,' he said to me, 'you are just building those obstacles yourself. And they are all right here.' He tapped his forehead and chuckled. 'Well, go ahead if that's how you want to live it. But tonight, there are no obstacles out here. No place for them on this track. Tonight, you're running free, and well—you can run faster than any human can.'

"He grinned at me and then looked at his watch, ticking the seconds away, counting down, in almost a whisper, 'Three... two...one... go!'

I set off racing around the first curve of the track with legs flying more than running. I saw Josy leave the track, done with his cool-down for the night, but I closed my eyes and pictured myself running next to him, striding side by side perfectly synchronized. The next turn came and went and we were heading toward the end of the first lap in what seemed like an impossibly fast time. Panic flooded me and I could see that thought pass through my mind like a message on a moving marquise."

My daddy stretched his hand wide, dragging invisible words into the air in front of us. We stared at the empty piece of sky left behind, waiting for the words to appear.

He read it to us. "Impossibly fast time...impossibly fast time... I could see it enter from the left side of my mind as it played in front of my eyes, and it searched for a place to settle in the right-brain hemisphere, somewhere that it could live and keep me locked out of trying anything 'impossible'. Finishing the second lap, my legs strong but burning, my lungs heaving, but controlled, I fought against those words on the trailing marquise message -- 'impossibly fast time'. Starting the third lap, Sal held up his fist, thumb up, making me wonder if I could hang on to this pace, this impossible pace. A battle grew within me beyond the physical struggle I was fighting. I wanted— I needed— to run with Josy next week. I needed to stay right by his side, and not fall back or step off. I needed this but my mind was furiously warning me to let go, because this was an 'impossibly fast time'. As this battle raged within my soul, I suddenly heard a new voice drowning out that warning, deep and demanding from across the track that I 'just breathe'. My lungs filled easily with my next inhalation while a mighty hand suddenly plucked those rolling words from the forefront of my mind, crushing them in its huge fist and flinging them violently over my shoulder, to tumble in a wreck on the track behind me."

I looked behind me, too, but there was nothing but a crowd of long legs and baseball mitts.

"And having escaped those words, I was suddenly free to move as fast as I wanted, as fast as I could, and that night I believed I could run as fast as Josy." We both smiled at this.

"There were no crowds or coaches or stopwatches keeping track of us. 'Just breathe' hissed the voice, and I still don't know who was saying it. But I knew when I headed into the final straightaway of my fourth and final lap that I had been running faster than I ever had. I could feel it and I know Sal could, too. I saw him glance at the watch in his hand, but I doubt it told him anything new. And so I pushed those last one hundred and ten yards, legs stretched further and arms driving harder than I had ever done before, crossing the line, as the image of Josy faded behind me.

"Through the sweat and the spit splattered on my chin and gasping wide-open mouth, I lifted four fingers into the air and formed a silent question to Sal: four minutes?

"Sorry Billy. You're gonna have to get something else to worry about now. You just ran 3:59:58! Think you're ready to pace Josy next week?"

This is where those nearby listeners started to smile patronizingly at my father, and waving him off, began to drift back to their own lives, as I'm sure they did in the hospital several years ago.

"You don't have to believe me," he called after them, "but I know it's true." Looking back at me he continued. "Runners know their pace and their limits and I knew mine had just been torn apart."

No matter who was listening, he was always talking to me, and I didn't doubt a word he said.

"It was definitely under four minutes. No one was there to witness it or to prove it or to measure it. But that doesn't matter, because we knew it.

And once a man knows something-- knows that it is true because he has experienced it himself-- then it becomes easier to un-believe all the other impossibilities that he has fed himself. The things that might change his life from a repetition of years and habits to one of purpose. That kind of change. When Sal and I jogged back to the empty streets and turned our own ways to head home, I was not the same man who had entered the track that night. A wall had fallen and my confidence had soared. For a little while anyway.

"Because the next day while you were fighting your way into this world, making your momma and I race to the hospital instead of to Boston, Mr. Bannister was making all the headlines with his physiological break-through in running. I didn't know that at the time, of course. I was focused on something else."

Smiling, he pointed at me. "But you fought inside your momma for hours and hours, tangled up and facing the wrong way, until finally just a few minutes after midnight, on May 7th, you were yanked into this world, limp and lifeless. We were all worried that you wouldn't pull through. The doctors hurried around and whisked you away while your momma and I cried and prayed and hugged each other. Just hours earlier I had been so sure about my own power, and now I was absolutely powerless. So I took your momma's hand and I just kept saying to her the one thing that was stuck in my mind: 'Just breathe, just breathe' over and over and over. I don't know if I was saying it to her, to you, or to myself.

"But in the corner where the doctors were huddled around and the nurses were huddled around them, with you in the middle, I am absolutely certain you heard me."

He looked at me then, for my own confirmation, which I always, enthusiastically, provide.

"And finally, after making me sweat and shake and worry, you finally-- finally!-- gave your own long, loud wail. The whole room cheered, and the doctor put you in your momma's arms, saying to me, 'Lucky lady there. We thought it was going to be impossible to bring her back.' But looking at you, Gracie, with those big blue-black eyes staring at me, I knew it wasn't luck; it wasn't anything mystical either. Just you, showing everybody what it means to beat the impossible."

And then I threw my arms around his neck and leaped onto his back as he half hugged, half tackled me. As I got older, and the story would reach its end, I'd snuggle into his strong warm hug, and just like that day in the park, I'd feel like the whole world was smiling around us.

# 3  JAPLO

The refugee camp is as crowded as the park, but tension, fear, and hunger are prevalent, and there is no singing.

I cannot let go of Yeni, for I do not know how I will find her if we are separated.  A seven-year-old child does not understand, so she squirms every time I grab hold of her, or when I tie my scarf to her wrist.  But she does not complain. She tries to obey.  It is only her innocence that forgets now and then, and I will be suddenly tugged away from my sitting, my stirring, or whatever tasks my blindness will allow me.

I do not know how many days  we have been here.  It seems like years, but of course it is not.  It is the memory of my life before violence that makes it feel so long ago.  My home, my husband, my children.  It is less painful if I just imagine it as a dream from long ago, if I can let it drift into meaninglessness.

Some nights I have dreams that feel more real than this nightmare I have fallen into.  I believe I am back in our home, sitting at the table with Tam and Kai and Saa and Yeni.  I can feel Tam's hand in mine.  I can smell his breath and the odor of his body after a long day at work.  It is strong and pungent, and I know he would want to get up from the table to wash. But without his smell I am afraid he would be gone completely. So in my mind I hold onto him with all my might.  I hold him next to me while we watch our children around the table.  At first there are three toddlers, smearing pieces of potato and squash into their mouths and along their cheeks. Tam and I smile at each other.  He kisses me and I kiss him back, feeling my desire for him build.  Beside these little ones sit four-year-old Yeni, five-year-old Saa and Kai, chattering and dreaming of imaginary adventures and games.  At the end of the table my lovely fifteen-year-old

Kai brushes bread crumbs from her lips as she pours out the many questions of adolescence in which Tam, my wise and gentle Tam, so readily engages. Saa, the Saa I last knew, sits between his sisters, as he twists and turns to shoot paper bags and plastic bottles into the air. Yeni is the only one who refuses to sit. She climbs over the table to me, tugs at my dress and pulls at my hands until somehow she grows into a giant little girl. She tugs so hard that I am pulled away from the rest of them, the babies, the children, the teenagers that had just begun to live. Tam smiles at me and waves. Kai waves and adjusts the braid of her hair. Saa waves, bouncing an empty plastic pop bottle off the top of his head. Yeni pulls me farther away, and while I do not want to let go of her, I yell at her to go back. We must go back! Da is waiting. We must go back!

I know I am awake only because I can no longer see anything. I hear Yeni crying as the large hands of a woman gently shake me out of my dream.

"Now, now, there. Shhh, it's alright now. Yeni is right here. She's not going anywhere. Shhh."

My cheeks are wet and the blanket beneath me is twisted around my arms. I unravel myself and reach out. "Yeni?"

"Ma?" She is slow to return to me, so I know I must have frightened her.

I vow to keep this terror away from her. I vow to fill both of our minds with the memories of love and family, the ones that will make us smile and yes, sometimes sad. But these memories must fill our minds and our hearts so that there is no more room for the nightmares.

Talks of peace continue, but so do the distant explosions of gunfire. Every day, a line of women and children file past me as they, too, look for safety in this camp. Kara tells me there are nearly thirty thousand people here. We have very little food. Sometimes a bag of rice or bulgur is brought in and we cook it in plenty of water so that we can scoop out tiny cups full of starchy soup to the children first, and then what is left, we share amongst ourselves.

When Yeni crawls into my lap I can feel the sharp edges of bone pressing into me. I can wrap nearly my whole hand around her thigh, and I pray for more food every day. We all do.

The speaker is turned on during the dinner hour, maybe to distract us from our empty plates, and we listen to the progress that is being made, or the threats that are being made, or the pleas or demands or speculations that are being made by people in fancy clothing, sipping coffee and complaining about the lack of butter with their croissants.

I can only believe that those people do not know how bad it is. They cannot know the horrors that we thirty thousand here have witnessed and endured. They cannot know! If they did, they would certainly stop it.

Or are people really that evil?

A man's voice interrupts the reporting, cutting loudly into our collective prayers.

"Attention! Attention! The UN has scheduled another transport from Liberia. Those who have family living abroad will have first consideration to evacuate. Please see a camp marshal to put your name on the list."

And then back to the reporting. It was almost too fast to hear, too loud to listen to, and the women are asking, "What did he say? Something about a list?"

But I heard him. That is all I do now. I listen to everything. I hear everything. I pull on the scarf that ties me to Yeni.

I do not want anyone to follow me, so I whisper to her, "Take me to a camp marshal."

I don't know how he might be identified as a camp marshal, but Yeni just starts walking again. A sense of urgency pushes at my heart, but I walk carefully behind Yeni. A few women hurry past me, sometimes getting tangled in Yeni's leash, but I keep calm, keep moving, keep following her zig-zagging lead.

She stops suddenly. "He is right there, but there is a line."

"How do you know he's a camp marshal?" I ask her.

"He has a clipboard. No one else has a clipboard," she reasons.

I pull her in front of me. Bending to her ear I whisper, "Don't let anyone get in front of us." I embarrass myself with my selfishness.

The message has been repeated and now more and more women are pushing to get in line. I push my elbows out wide and move closer to the line in front of me, inching our way to the list.

"Name." His command is quick and impatient.

"Japlo Umunna and Donyen Umunna."

He seems to hesitate. Perhaps I misheard the announcement after all.

"Is it just you two?"

I keep my chin from quivering and say boldly, "Yes, it just the two of us. My husband, Tambo, is... is not with us."

"I see. You have family outside of Liberia?"

"Yes."

"Who? Where?"

"My husband's brother. Jahn Umunna. United States. Chicago."

He writes our names down, and puts a piece of paper in my hand. "Don't lose this. You will need it to get on the plane."

"When? When do we leave?" I ask.

"We don't know. Just listen, and be ready to go when they arrive. It could be tonight. It could be next month. We won't know until they are here."

His voice becomes gentle, and he leans close to me, adding softly, "I knew your husband. He helped my brother when he was injured at the factory. The company wanted to deny him medical coverage, but Tam made sure he was taken care of. We never got to thank him. Of course, this was years ago. Before all of...this," he says. "He was a good man, a peaceful man." He puts his hand on my arm. "Is he..?"

I shake my head before he can finish. "No," I say with a knot building in my throat. "He did not make it out."

He lets his hand rest a second more before sending us on our way. I am so very ...sorry. Madam, blessed be your journey."

"Next!" he calls out, turning away from me again. I hope he does not see me as I cry.

Yeni and I squeeze back through the mob, but I am afraid to go too far away, in case they call for us soon. I do not know what the paper says, but I must guard it with my life. It is the only way I can save Yeni. Even if I myself cannot escape this place, I will get her on that plane at any cost.

We move far enough away to avoid trampling feet and then squat down to wait. Behind me, the voice of an old woman warns, "Don't get your hopes up. I have seen the promise of UN planes many times. It is always a mad rush to get your name on a list. Hope. Anticipation. Trust. Then disappointment as time goes by. And then you forget about it until the next announcement comes, and you rush again to put your name on the list."

I hold Yeni close to me. "That may be," I answer her, "but this time it will be different. This time it will come."

Something wakes me before I can think clearly enough to know what it is. But somehow my body knows, and I am sitting up, waking Yeni, telling her, "It is time to go."

My conscious mind catches up to my sleeping mind and I remember the soft monotonous drone over the speaker that announced the UN plane's arrival. Announced it once. If you heard it you might still think it was part of your dream because it is followed by silence.

But I heard it and having been waiting for this announcement for the past three weeks, I am ready.

Yeni is still rubbing sleep from her eyes. I push her harshly, much too severe, yet I must be so severe today.

"Yeni!" I hiss at her. "Move! Go to the plane! Now, Yeni!"

She stumbles forward, and I cannot be certain that she knows which direction to go, but I most certainly do not know, so I pray and I pray for God to lead her, to lead us, in the right direction, fast enough, safely enough, to get on the plane.

I feel other bodies quickly moving past us, but in the same direction, so I am relieved slightly.

We have left the security of the fence, the mass of people, and the wind tells me we are in the open, a feeling that I now associate with danger. Yeni stops and a queue of whispered voices precedes us. Suddenly, the hum of a motor chokes to life and a blast of warm engine-air blows onto us.

"Hurry. Hurry up. Move along, then." A man is marching beside our line, a touch of controlled panic in his British voice. Radio static intermittently updates him on flight plans and departure status. A series of gunshots in the distance increase the panic in all of us.

I am still clutching the piece of paper the camp marshal had given me. I do not know what it says, but I pray that it will allow me entrance to this plane. I hold it out in front of me, tightly gripped between my fingers so it will not be blown away or torn from my hands.

I can feel the coolness of the plane's open doorway just feet from me. Yeni is tied to me at the waist. Someone takes hold of the paper in my hand, tugging so that I will let go. But I only loosen my grip so that a little more of it can be read, afraid to part with it completely.

A new round of gunfire sounds a warning much closer to us.

The British man, on the edge of panic to begin with, calls an end to the boarding.

He shouts through a megaphone now. "Danger! Please return to the camp now! You are in immediate danger! We cannot take any more people at this time! I repeat, please return to the camp immediately!"

My ticket is still caught between my hands and this last step to freedom. But I am afraid that if I let go, we will be pushed back, and I will have lost our ticket forever.

Cries of fear and the begging of mothers, like me, echo all around us.

"Ma'am, you are going to have to let go of this if you want to get on the plane."

A young woman's voice firmly cajoles me into letting go, and as I do, Yeni pulls me up a ramp and through the small doorway to the plane.

We are shoved into two seats as the plane shifts to a rolling taxi, then full throttle speeding down a short roadway. I cannot see them, but I can hear the anger of the rebels as they shoot at our plane lifting over their heads, heaving this huge metal body away from the land, away from our country, away from our home.

Forever.

# 4  GRACIE

When my father graduated from Harvard in 1954 he was offered a job in Chicago as a Human Resources associate for the Chicagoland Private Schools Network. He recruited, interviewed, hired and trained anyone from custodians and coaches to teachers and principals. Dad was a people-person, so it was easy for him to find the right man for the right job and to weed out the lazy or deceitful. He was busy, but his time was flexible, so he spent as much time with us kids as he did at work. At least, it seemed that way to me. And every day, no matter what the weather was like, he'd slip into his track shoes and slip out the door for his run around the neighborhood.

It was a difficult move for my mother, who had lived on the East Coast her whole life, but she soon grew to love the lively neighborhoods and cultural richness of this city. My parents rented a small flat in Riverside before buying a tri-level brownstone in Old Irving Park right before my sister was born. Two sisters, my little brother, and I all grew up on one of the few tree-lined dead-end streets in a city of skyscrapers and factories. Just a few blocks in either direction the trucks rumbled in and out of big potholes, and police cars wailed and screeched. But our street was quiet and smooth, protected by a labyrinth of one-way streets and a slow curve around the corner. We had the benefit of a long, wide stretch of road on which to ride bikes and challenge the neighbor kids to running races. When I was seven and eight years old, all I knew was that it was fun. By the time I turned eleven I also knew that I was fast.

Sixth grade was all about the thrill of the chase. The bets were set at school, usually due to the prodding of some tough-acting boys, who challenged me to a race. Sometimes it was one-on-one. Other times an entire gang of kids would offer up a dare. It didn't matter to me. I just liked to run, and if I had someone to chase or someone to chase me, it made it that much more fun.

Sixth graders are a funny group. While they are keenly aware of the differences between boys and girls, the one truth they ignore is that girls have a huge advantage in size and strength at that age, which also leads to an enormous amount of confidence. I was a skinny fast girl, running against chubby short boys. It was no miracle that I could out run them. But stereotypes settle hard into the belief systems of little kids, so in our minds, it was truly remarkable that a girl could out run all the boys. And when the boys lost -- which they almost always did-- they were teased mercilessly, especially by whomever was the last kid to be outrun by a girl.

To my parents, we were just a bunch of kids playing outside after school. They did not know about the challenges, the dares, the races, the victories, or the teasing that followed.

Not until my sister told them.

"Everyone is making fun of Gracie," Kelly reported one evening at dinner. "Nobody likes her."

My mother lowered her fork and looked at me, then at my father. "Gracie?"

"That's not true," I protested. "They're just jealous."

My mother burrowed her eyebrows. "Jealous? Why? What are you doing?"

"She runs!" Kelly shouted, as if that accusation alone would have me sent from the table.

I shoved a piece of bread in my mouth. "They can't run as fast as me, that's all."

My father stopped chewing and looked at me. "Who can't?"

"No one," said Kelly. "None of the fifth graders or the sixth graders or the seventh graders. Not all the eighth graders have tried, but I bet they can't beat her either. They are all lazy anyway." Kelly was trying to embarrass me, but I could see she was a little bit proud of me too. I smiled at her and kicked her under the table. She kicked me back.

My mother looked concerned. "Are you racing against the boys?" she asked.

"Yes," I answered proudly.

"Oh, honey, you shouldn't be running against the boys. That's not good for their self-esteem to be beat by a girl like that. Isn't that right, Billy?"

My father was looking at me, but he was a million miles away. He was seeing a long stretch of track, a flurry of spikes, and a flash of legs and arms. He was trying to find a face amongst all that and wondering if maybe it might not just be mine.

That weekend, instead of running outside to meet up with my friends, I went with my father to the high school a few blocks away. I stood against the chain link fence as my father walked onto the dirt circle that wrapped around a football field. Scattered along this circle were long-legged, bare-chested teenage boys. They ran in pairs or in large groups, some quick and short, others slow and steady.

One of the coaches greeted my dad excitedly, shaking his hand and pulling him around to meet the other coaches and a few lingering parents. After the pleasantries were over, my father directed his attention on me, pointing at me, and then to the track, and then to himself. The other coaches chuckled and shook their heads, but my father became more serious, agitated even, until I could hear them say finally, "Yeah? Have her prove it!"

The men grinned at each other, and turned back to the boys stretching out on the grassy infield.

Before they could stop him, my father gestured me out onto the track.

"Stretch it out and warm up, kiddo." I had no clue what he meant by that, so I untied my sweatshirt from around my waist and pulled it on. My father was done paying attention to me so when he told me to get on the starting line, I just did as he told, alongside the rest of the kids. In my bell-bottoms and a sweatshirt I poised myself for the countdown. "Three—two—one — " I could not hear anyone shout "Go" due to the loud blast by my side. Instinctively, I started running.

In just a few steps the group of skinny boys was in front of me and pulling away fast. I had never run against someone so old or so fast and it infuriated me to be left behind. I pumped my arms wildly, literally trying to fly around the track. My legs spun fast with a long stride and a full kick. My head was up and back, my chest leading, the way little kids run. I just saw a blur of colors as I ran past a border of people lining the track. Halfway around one lap and my lungs were burning, but the boys were pulling farther away. Tears pierced the corners of my eyes, but I squeezed them away, running blind toward the place I had started. As I crossed the line, the group of boys was already leaning against each other, heaving and spitting, their ribcages inflating, their legs wobbly. They pointed at me as I ran right past them. I could feel the shame building in me and I wanted to run straight off the track and home. My father stood off to the side, staring at me, and a new wave of humiliation flooded me as I realized he had wanted to show off this daughter of his, who said she could run fast. How horribly I had disappointed him!

Instead of slowing down and moving off of the track as the boys had done, I simply stopped running and tried to catch my breath while sobs rumbled out. Half-choking then, I suddenly had a swarm of bodies collapse around me as a second, and then third group of boys finished their lap behind me. My father motioned for me to come over to him, so still blurry and out of breath, I stepped around the others and curled into his comforting dad-hug.

One of his colleagues leaped over to us. "You weren't kidding, Billy! Wow, that girl can run! But here? With them?" He pointed to the group of boys I had followed.

"No, no, Sal. Not with them. Just around them. I'll help you coach, for free, and I'll just bring her along, give her her own workouts, maybe a pacer once in a while. Come on, Sal. Who else can she train with? I don't think there's a school in all of Chicago that'll let a girl run with them. She needs this."

He put his hand on Sal's shoulder and lowered his voice. "Dammit Sal, I need this. How about it?"

And that is how I joined the Immaculate Heart High School track team.


For two years I tagged along with my dad to their practices. I learned what a split was, a hand-off, an eighth inch spike, an interval repeat, and shin splints. I learned pacing and how to kick at the end. I ran clockwise on Mondays and Wednesdays, counter-clockwise on Tuesdays and Thursdays and tagged behind all of them on Fridays as we jogged across Kedzie to the North Branch Trail.

I loved Fridays because that was the day that I ran with my father. Sometimes it was just the two of us; sometimes other kids joined us. On occasion the other coaches ran with my father, and while I was not part of that run, I could jog behind them listening to them discuss running strategies and theories and recent race results. My father seemed to float as he ran, his feet barely brushing the earth. Sal had been a sprinter in his high school and college days and it showed in the way his feet landed beneath him, as if each step became its own starting block, pushing himself forward. They debated proper form, proper warm-ups, proper nutrition, proper pace. It seemed they couldn't agree on anything, but both had been standout athletes, so obviously whatever each of them was doing, it had worked.

One Friday afternoon in late April, I was jogging easily behind the coaches, who ran easily behind the boys' team, who were also taking it easy.

"Did ya hear what happened in Boston?" Sal asked my dad.

"Boston? No... Heck, I haven't been back there in... gosh ... ten years?"

"Fourteen, Daddy," I reminded him.

"Oh, that's right." He smiled over his shoulder at me. "Boston! Now, there you've got some real hills! Maybe it's time to go back for a visit. I kinda miss those hills."

I smiled back.

"Well, you might want to look up a few guys while you're there.

Remember Arnie? From our track days? Not on the team-- not even a student, I don't think. You know, the guy who'd just show up after work, run, and then head back home?"

"Arnie, yeah, I heard Harvard made him stop and so he just went to some of the other Universities instead. Man, he was tough!"

"Well I don't know how true that is, but I did see his name in the paper last week. After the Boston Marathon."

"Neat! Did he win?" My father chuckled, but sounded excited too. When he gets excited, he runs lighter, and quicker, and he started doing that now.

I couldn't help myself. I had to interrupt them. "Daddy, did you ever win the Boston Marathon? I mean, before I was born?"

Sal let out a sound that was half grunt, half laughter. My dad shook his head and his pace eased back a little bit.

"Gracie, I know your dad is fast, but running a marathon takes a lot more than quick legs. And winning a marathon takes a nearly impossible combination of endurance, speed, discipline, and downright luck." He patted my dad on the back. "No offense there, Billy."

"None taken." He patted him in return, grinning, and pushing him slightly away from him to break Sal's stride.

"No, honey, I never ran Boston, but I've stood along the course and watched it a few times. Like Sal said, it takes a special training and talent to run a marathon. Those guys run miles and miles to prepare for this. And only the best of them enter. No, I don't have the time or the endurance for that." Turning back to Sal, "So what's the big news? Arnie ran it? Won it? Dropped out of it? What?"

"Oh he ran it all right. I figure he's run that thing ten or fifteen times by now. Never won though, but tough runner nonetheless. No, that's not why he's in the news. It's who he ran with that gave him his notoriety!"

"His notoriety, eh? Who was it?"

"A woman."

The soft tread of their feet, one synchronized sound after another, filled a silent tension into which I ran, pushing me back slightly. As a thirteen-year-old girl I was, after all, the closest thing to a woman out here on the trail. I suddenly felt like I had done something wrong.

"And?" my father asked.

"And women don't run Boston."

"Oh, that's not true. I've seen several women run it."

Sal shook his head again. "No, you've seen women jump in or tag along. You've never seen a woman enter the Boston Marathon and run that thing with a number pinned to her. Never. But somehow he got a woman registered. And to the starting line. And all the way from Hopkinton to Copley Square. With only one minor problem along the way."

He laughed softly. "I guess a few miles in, the director of the whole race, and a bunch of reporters and photographers were driving along, making sure everything is going fine, when they see this gal with a name and number pinned to her chest, running alongside a bunch of guys. Well, the director, he goes nuts! Jumps off the truck, charges after this lady, and starts shoving her off the course."

My father has slowed his pace, and his feet seem to drag a little. I have to keep myself from running past him, so I tuck in close behind him. I can watch Sal's animated gestures, his reenactments, more closely.

"So, you know, she's just a girl, really, maybe twenty-one or twenty-two years old, so she can't fight back. Bet she was about to rip the numbers off and step out. Wouldn't have blamed her, either. But Arnie yanks the guy off of her and yells at him. So, he had been coaching the gal for the past few years -- years! -- so he wants her to run this thing.

"And then another guy, maybe her brother, or boyfriend -- somebody like that-- who is also running with her, throws a massive shoulder block into the guy and sends him flying. The best part? The photographers are all right there, watching, clicking away, reporting it move by move."

The quiet returned. The pace returned. My breath stayed shallow.

After a minute, my dad, looking straight ahead asked, "So, she ran the whole thing, huh? No problems the rest of the way?"

"Nope, other than her pictures all over the paper, and the comments written in by some mean SOBs." My dad scowled at Sal and nodded his head in my direction.

"Oh come on, Billy. If you're going to keep this girl running, you and she both better get ready for an awful lot of shit getting thrown her way. A few choice curse words are just the tip of the iceberg." Sal turned around and ran backwards, facing me. "You do want to keep running, don't ya, Gracie? I mean, it'd be a shame to let all that work and talent get pushed to the sidelines."

I had never thought about wanting to run. I just ran. I had assumed I would always run. I knew I had limitations of speed and strength, but I also believed those were merely functions of my own training, that given more practice, more time, more effort, I could be as fast a runner as anyone else. Only now did I realize that being female was its own limitation, one that I could do nothing about.

My eyes held the question as I looked to my dad for an answer. Not do I, but can I?

Our run along the trail of dirt and gravel had returned to the cement sidewalks along Ainslie, one block away from school. My father and Sal looked at each other to start their typical last stride -- a race kick that causes them both to nearly collapse at the end. This time my father also looked back at me, tapped his forehead, and sped away. I chased him, keeping my feet kicking high behind me and his feet just inches from my own. As we crossed the unofficial finish line, my father, gasping for air and on wobbly legs, grabbed me by the shoulders to hold on. Catching his breath, he wheezed, "Well. It looks like... you want to keep running...Very nice... Then that's what we'll do!"

# 5  ANNA

Chicago is a beautiful city in the summer, a vibrant place of skyscrapers and parks and beaches.  The Loop bustles with an energy that comes from commerce, art, sports, and leisure.   Cubs and White Sox fans saunter robustly, half-cocky, but also half ashamed, devoted to a fickle sport and a nostalgic dream. Funky art students spill out of the coffee shops and diners to smoke their cigarettes, laughing louder than they need to, scowling more than they should and staring condescendingly at the black suits and high heels  clipping past them.  Those who are here for leisure gather along the main walkways toward Millennium Park, strolling amoeba-like to enjoy the sweet stench of caramel corn, the bluesy street music, and the patchwork of people along the way. These tourists, both local and foreign, give no value to time-- their own or others. They linger, they converse, they contemplate, they backtrack, and they consume, all in a suspended bubble of non-time.

Winters in Chicago, on the other hand, consume us. The gloom of gray skies, biting wind, and filthy slush pushes us into narrow snakes of movement, crowded with parkas and wool scarves. Although the streets are absent of tourists, they are loaded with slow moving buses, snowplows, and spinning tires. Summer or winter, all this pedestrian and vehicular traffic is above all else the most frustrating cause of blood pressure spikes and mini strokes among those who come to the Loop to work. The Mercantile Mart, the Board of Trade, the lawyers, consultants, designers, investors, controllers, and government, government, government--they create and maintain the great engine of commerce that makes Chicago the powerhouse it is, regardless of economic dips and downfalls. Their business is business and their blood is equal parts money and time. A river of concertgoers and a snow-phobic path of cars are nothing more than time thieves to the perpetually behind-schedule Loopers like me who are forced to do the unthinkable: wait.

I look over my shoulder twice as I edge my dark green Impala into the pedestrian crossing at Washington and Dearborn. The red hand is blinking furiously, warning the walkers to stop, but they keep coming, daring me, really. I never back down from a dare so I inch farther into the flowing crowd until I am completely enveloped. Most people simply step around me, but one young guy shouts, "Get the fuck out of the way!" and another one kicks the back end of my car. When the light finally changes I am stuck, blocking the left turn lane onto Washington, which means more road rage directed toward me. Finally I can pull ahead, which gives me the perfect opportunity to punch my left hand out the open window and into the air, middle finger saluting everyone in my wake.

"Oh, fuck off!" I roar into the fumes and frustration behind me.

I scan both sides of the road for a parking spot, although odds are totally against me. The meter will rob me of nearly eight dollars for the two hours I might be inside, but that was better than twenty-eight dollars at the parking garage. The bigger problem is finding a spot in the first place. The black slush of early March is packed against curbs and melting into gray puddles, limiting parking spaces even more. I circle around the block, then increase the perimeter to two blocks, then three, then back to Dearborn again. Twenty minutes pass of slow circling, swerving from left to right. I see a middle age man hurry towards a car and I slam on the brakes, hoping he will leave the spot open for me. He pauses, then crosses the street instead. I shake my head at him, but he just shrugs. What does he care?

Finally, a space appears just beyond a hot dog diner on Wells, so I pull into it front first at a thirty-degree angle. The back end of my car is still jutting out into the bike lane, and I am not sure if the car behind me can get out of its parking spot at all. I try backing up and inching forward, but it just seems to get worse, so I turn off the engine, buy a one hour parking pass, and cross my fingers that I'll be out before the driver of the car behind me gets back. Checking my watch, I see that my meeting is scheduled to start in two minutes. With three blocks to walk, it is unlikely I'll be there on time. Well, they sure can't start without me, can they?

I have dressed in my power outfit for this meeting and although I think I look incredibly powerful it is unfortunately also slowing me down. My dear deceased grandmother always said to me, "Anna, be proud of your curves. They show that you are sexy and powerful."

My mother, on the other hand, suggested that my curves showed that I was in fact overweight, and she also suggested that I try to limit the size of my curves. So sometimes I would skip a meal or two, or order a salad instead of the Italian Beef Sandwich that I really wanted in order to bring my curves down a notch. But days like today made me love my curves and this power outfit made the most of them. Besides, my mother's not here any more either.

A fitted white short-sleeved blouse accentuates my breasts but I still look serious, not slutty. A high-waist black skirt that is just a little too tight across my butt falls just below my knees and appears both conservative and feminine. But the red shoes turn the whole thing into an exclamation point, drawing everyone's attention down my legs to the thick high heels in fire engine red, thin red leather ankle straps, and pointy red toes.

I love these shoes! I don't care that I am already towering over most women and several men. I am five foot ten inches and with these shoes on I am over six feet tall. These shoes make people stop talking just long enough for me to give them a quick and direct proposal, which, according to my statistics, three out of ten times results in a sale.

But today, "Damn these shoes!" I sputter as I am trying to race down the sidewalk. I don't really mean it, but they are slowing me down as I pick my way amongst puddles and sewer grates, and the onslaught of pedestrians always, always, always in the way.

Finally I swing through the revolving door of a towering office building and head straight for the elevator. When the doors open, and those descending have exited, I follow the line of people in front of me, squeezing through the doors as they slide shut behind me.

"I think there are too many people in here," a voice chirps from the back of the box. A ripple of movement swells against me, pinning me to the closed doors.

"No, we all fit just fine," I answer, knowing that comment was meant for me. I try desperately to claim some personal space. Elevators are so uncomfortable to begin with -- where to look, which way to stand, what to say. But in this situation everyone is grinding into the butt of the person in front of them, with no room for "personal space". I am facing the doors, ready to disembark, when I suddenly feel a hand pushing into the space between my legs.

I give a sharp grunt of disapproval and twist away from the fingers. It's too crowded to move or to turn around, but the hell if this pervert is going to intimidate me by waving his alpha dick at me. I know a threatened man when I see one -- or in this case, feel one. When the first stop rings, and the doors open, I step out to allow room for the others to exit, eager for more breathing room. I turn around, ready to snap off the head of this pervert.

"Who was groping me?" I demand. I scan the possible offenders. First, I am blown away by the most beautiful pair of dark, deep blue-green eyes I have ever seen. And these eyes are set into a tanned chiseled face with dimpled cheeks and framed by a dark military crew cut. Certainly wasn't him. Next is a teenager, affected by a variety of pubescent changes in half-doses. Hair sprouts from his chin, and his nose is way too large for his face. But maybe it just looks that way due to the acne or to the way his eyes were squinted nearly shut. He's a definite maybe. To his left is a fat balding man, in a suit that is too tight and a shirt that he probably slept in. Equally gross and therefore equally guilty. Behind them I just see ponytails and baseball caps and a whole lot of legs. "Well?" I demand.

Eyes shift side to side. I am looking for a sign, something subtle that will give away the guilty scumbag.

"One of you was groping me, and if it happens again, if I feel so much as a hangnail on my leg I will break off every fucking one of your fucking fingers! Got it?"

As the last words stab into the group in front of me, a movement of legs draws my eyes down.

"Oh, no," I let out my rage in an embarrassed sigh. "I didn't realize..."

With a stuffed pink pig in one hand, a small boy pokes his other hand out between the sea of legs. He is four or five years old, if I have to guess. His face, peeking at me between jackets and dresses, morphs into a terrified still life as he pulls his hands in toward his chest, curling his fingers in to protect them. Once his lungs have filled to capacity, a frightened wail shudders out of his small body.

"Oh shit," I mutter.

I let the elevator doors close. I can hear his crying fade as they continue up without me.

And I still have twelve more floors to go.

I walk into the conference room and push past the group of Trump wanna-bes huddled by the door. I am late for my own presentation but I decide to use reverse psychology and blame someone else instead.

I look directly at the young man standing next to the overhead screen and ask, "Are you done with your sales pitch yet? I have an important meeting to get to after this so I'd like to get started right away."

The room falls silent and the young man looks from me to the gentleman sitting beside him whom I recognize as Carl Montgomery, the CEO of MediaMates Inc. He shrugs at the geek standing next to him and then nods to me, which I accept as an invitation to get started.

"Thank you, Mr. Montgomery. Anna Rigaldo. Nice to meet you."

I shake his hand with the strength of any man, but let my grasp linger just a second longer than necessary. I can see he is pleased.

The long sleek conference table begins to fill with people I do not know or care to know, but I smile at all of them anyway, then dive into my presentation.

"Thank you all for taking the time to meet with me today."

"You're late."

I don't know who said it but I ignore the statement. However, I can feel my hands start to tingle which means my blood pressure is on the rise.

"As you know, the huge growth in social media over the past two years has impacted nearly every subgroup of business, art, community, government, and education that exists. The ability to market to growing numbers of consumers, especially for small, local, or independent organizations, is nearly leveling the playing field. While marketing dollars are still paramount to an organizations success, the use of social media is quickly becoming a fast and inexpensive hook to snag college students, gourmet diners, gym rats, mall shoppers, and even voters. It has become a race among marketing agencies to reach the most followers the fastest, and honestly, tweets and fans and bings all seem to be working. For now.

"But let's look ahead. What are you doing for your clients to not just help them catch their customers, or even to reel them in, but to create customer loyalty through market specificity? I'm willing to bet you are doing nothing. And that path leads straight to a brick wall, Mr. Montgomery. What I'd like to do is help you create a plan for long-term market ventures through social media specificity -- which I call SMS-- and take you through that brick wall. I want to help MediaMates become the leader in SMS by being at the forefront of innovation and information analysis. Are you ready for your business to explode?"

I slam both hands down on the table in front of me and lean down to stare into the eyes of Carl Montgomery. He is straight-faced, giving me no hint as to his thoughts on my proposal. I narrow my eyes and let a small smile soften my hard glare.

He clears his throat and looks at his watch. Shit! The watch is such an easy crutch.

"Miss Rig-ididi-aldo. You have some interesting ideas. Very interesting. However I think we do an excellent job of helping our clients maximize their marketing budget through both time-tested and innovative marketing strategies. If we feel that we could bring benefit to our clients through your-- what is it? S&M? -- proposal we will be sure to contact you."

He stands up and walks toward the door.

"Carl, I am fairly certain that --"

He turns to me. "Very nice outfit. Love the shoes."

I watch him walk away, a short man with thick curly gray hair, his hands fishing in his pocket for his phone or PDA.

"His name is Mr. Montgomery," quips the geeky brown-nose standing behind me. "Don't call him Carl. He hates that."

"Oh like I give a shit!" I grab my briefcase and leave.

I can see the lights from a block away. I pray it's not my car, but sure enough, there it is, hanging from the tow truck's hook and chain. I walk as fast as I can, trying to run, but that is impossible due to the shoes and skirt and slush of course. I try calling to the driver.

"Wait! Wait! I'm right here! I can move my car!"

He releases the button that is controlling the chain, pulling my front wheels off the ground and dragging the back of my car onto a ramp.

"Sorry. Too late. Once we get the call we gotta tow it in."

My hand snaps forward to press the reverse button.

"Hey! Stop it!"  He reaches out and I instinctively slap his hand.

Oh my god. What did I do? He picks up his CB radio and speaks into it.

"Truck 4-2-7. We need police support."

The officer is sitting in the front of his car, calling in my driver's license info. I am in the back, trapped, but at least not handcuffed. I knew enough to get ahold of myself before the police arrived so that I was as calm as possible.  When the tow truck driver relayed his version of the story, I sounded like a crazy psycho woman, which I clearly am not.

"Officer," I said calmly when it was my turn to speak, "obviously I was not happy to see that my car was being towed, but I was not irate or irrational or violent at any time. I simply asked the driver to release my car so I could leave. Perhaps he does not usually have contact with the person whose car he is towing, but I can guarantee that my reaction was quite subdued compared to how most others would react."  I tried to convey an understanding nod to Mr. Policeman but he did not return it in any way. Instead he took my license and seated me in the back of his car, so here I am.  Finally the officer opens the back door and leans down to talk to me, handing me my license and registration.  My car has since disappeared, so I am left transportation-less.

"Here you go, ma'am."

I am stunned by the financial exorbitance of this minor infraction.

I now have a $600 ticket for illegal parking, obstructing a bike lane, and interfering with the duty of a public servant--which is probably not even a law and won't stand a chance in court.  In addition I will need to pay $175 to have my car released from the pound, and I'll need to pay at least another $30 for a taxi to get me there.  Thinking about the $140 currently in my checking account, I start to shake, my jaw clenching tight.  I step one foot out of the car, and it feels as if the world is spinning around me.  I refuse to pay these stupid tickets! I reach out to help pull myself to standing but my hand feels as if it is swimming through the air, clutching at nothing.  I can hear the officer saying something, but he is so quiet and so far away that I just ignore him.  Instead I blink slowly, trying to lift my head, which has suddenly become very heavy.  My throat feels tight  and a hot knife of light stabs through my temples before complete darkness envelops me.

I become aware of the pain along the left side of my face first. My left arm seems to grab this pain and pull it down into my shoulder, along my elbow and onto my wrist. One of my legs is twisted behind me and I can feel an embarrassing breeze, indicating my skirt is gaping for the whole world to see. The officer leans over me, repeating "Ma'am, ma'am, ma'am" until I finally respond. "What? What happened?"

I try to sit, but it hurts to put any weight on my left arm to push myself up. And Officer Friendly does not even attempt to help. Once he sees that I am awake, he turns back toward his radio. The wail of an ambulance pulls up behind the police car.

"What happened?" I repeat my question, this time with the expectation of a response. Nothing. All I know is I have a shit-load of fines, an injured arm, and an empty bank account.

The paramedics want to strap me onto a cot and haul me to the hospital.

"I do not need to go to the hospital," I protest. They check my pupils and inspect my wrist. They don't think it is broken, but I really should have it looked at by a doctor.

"If I had money for a doctor, trust me, I would go, but I cannot even afford this ambulance, so I don't know why you are here. It's all his fault anyway," and I point to the officer.

Maybe I shouldn't have said that, because he starts to take out his thick pad of tickets again.

One of the paramedics takes my pulse and widens her eyes in surprise.

"Do you have any chest pain?" she asks. "Shortness of breath? Pain down your left arm?"

Oh my god, I am having a heart attack! I knew it!

I feel my throat tighten as I nod to her. My left arm begins throbbing. How did I not notice this before?

She calls out to the others. "We have a potential myocardial infarction. Immediate transport. I need an IV, stat!"

The next thing I know I am shuffled into the ambulance, a mask is hooked across my face and a needle is jabbed into my arm. Sticky pads and wires are pushed onto my chest, my head, my neck, my feet.

So this is how I am going to die. I close my eyes and let myself be pulled toward whatever light I am supposed to see. Instead, I suddenly remember that Pop is waiting for the car.

"Oh shit!" I cry out, although I doubt anyone understands me through this oxygen mask.

"I need to get home. I need to call my Pop. He's waiting for me, for the car, and he doesn't know where I am and…" I try sitting up. I need to get ahold of Pop before anything happens. The paramedic shushes me like I'm a child. She stares at the bouncing green lines that run across a small screen at my feet. I press my lips together to keep quiet, but I keep my fingers tapping so she won't forget that I have something important to do.

The doors of the ambulance are flung open. I am wheeled out and handed off to two nurses in the emergency room by the paramedic that sat with me during the ride. "Here you go, Anna. These people will take good care of you, okay?"

I hear her whisper to the nurse, "Spas-tic!"

The tests all show that my heart is in excellent condition, but my nerves are not. I am still propped up in one of the beds in the emergency room, but they will be releasing me soon to make room for people who are actually having heart attacks, and not just freaking out about having one.

"Knock knock!" A high-pitched voice calls outside my curtain. I do not know if it is for me, so I just say, "What?"

A tall, willowy woman floats into my room. Completely noiseless, smooth, graceful, she enters as if part of the wind.

"Anna?" Of course she knows who I am. Who the heck is she? I just stare at her impatiently. She is probably in her forties, but she looks like a hippie to me.

"Hi Anna. I'm Hera Strauss, an intern here at Loyola Medical. How are you feeling?"

She smiles at me, but I am in no mood to smile back.

"Well, since you ask, I am pretty pissed that I was tricked into coming here by being told that I was having a heart attack. I can't believe how incompetent these people are. I am not going to pay for this!" I fold my arms across my chest and dare her to argue with me.

"I don't blame you," she says. "if you are brought to the hospital under false pretenses you should be compensated in some way."

Oh! I like this woman. She totally gets what I am talking about. Finally, I catch a break!

"Maybe you'd like to talk sometime." She hands me a card, a business card. It is light blue with an image of a wave or wind or smoke on it.

"I'm here on Wednesdays and Fridays, but I have a private office closer to the Loop if you want to visit me there."

I'm confused. How will talking with her in her office help me get the compensation I need? "Shouldn't we be talking with customer service or something? Is there a complaint form I can fill out?"

"Oh, I don't think so, honey. What is it you'd like to complain about?" Her sweet smile becomes a sarcastic, patronizing sneer. I read her card, the small print, and burst out laughing.

"You're a Life Coach? Seriously? What the hell is a Life Coach? Someone who yells at you when you fuck up your life? That sounds great. Just the thing I need." I roll my eyes at her, but she keeps smiling.

"No, Anna, a Life Coach simply helps you figure out how you want to run your life. We don't judge." She waves a hand lightly as if rolling judgment right off of her palm.

"I see. Are you saying I need help running my life? Are you kidding? Not only do I run my own life, but I've had to spend the last six years running everybody else's in my family too. Is that what you mean by helping me run my life? Or do you mean you want to help me figure out why my dear old mom took off to run her own life? Are you the one who helped her with that? Is that why, every day, I get to remind my dad to wash his underwear and pay the electric bill? Or maybe you want to work on fixing my dad? Is that it?"

Hera just keeps smiling and I want to slap that grin off her face. It is quiet. Hera won't stop smiling, and I refuse to stop scowling at her. The curtain swings opens and breaks the tension for a moment.

A nurse comes in, followed by the police officer who wrote all those tickets. I am embarrassed and a little nervous, but he, too, seems nervous, which now makes me feel bad.

"Ma'am, I just want to make sure you are alright. Make sure you got the help you need. Are you okay?" He seems overly concerned to me, but I appreciate the change in his attitude toward me.

"Yes, I'll be fine," I answer just a bit coldly. "Once I get out of here --" I glare at Hera.

The nurse jumps into the conversation.

"Ah, yes, I am sure you are ready to go. Has Hera explained the terms of discharge?" Hera has not done anything but smile at me, so I shake my head no.

"Well, Officer Kirkpatrick has recommended an alternative consequence to the numerous tickets and fines you incurred. He has agreed to drop all charges on your court date, provided you meet with a licensed social worker to help you."

"To help me do what?" I am starting to sweat again. Who the hell is this guy to decide what kind of help I need?

The nurse continues, "It appears that your symptoms and possibly your panic attack were both due to high levels of stress. And the stress seems to be, in most cases, self-induced."

"You are saying I do this to myself? To myself! Are you fucking cracked? I --"

"You!" interrupts Officer Kirkpatrick, "You, are a danger to society with your loud mouth and impulsive reactions and oblivious attitude! Do you give a shit about anyone except yourself?"

I am shocked by the sound and intensity of his voice. He seemed so passive and detached. Where did this guy come from?

Hera puts a hand on my shoulder. "So you see dear, it might be a good idea to come talk to me after all, don't you think?"

I have no choice. I am a prisoner of a multi-faceted attack. Just what I need.

I have Hera's card in my hand as I walk out to the front lobby. I collect my tickets and personal belongings, and grab the first cab that drives by. My car will have to wait.

"Loomis and Taylor. And don't take the Dan Ryan -- it's a mess this time of day. Just go west on Van Buren to Halsted, then..."

The driver has pulled onto the exit ramp for the Dan Ryan expressway. What's the use?

I open the door quietly when I get home. But I needn't have bothered, since my father is just waking up. He works the third shift, five pm to two am at the bakery, so he takes an hour-long nap every day before he leaves. I can see him sitting on the edge of his bed, shoulders hunched over, a old sleeveless undershirt stretched across his beach-ball belly. His legs, dangling from his boxer shorts, seem so skinny, like they belong to some other man. When he hears the door click shut he lifts his head, like he's surprised to see me.

"Hi Pop," I try to sound cool and unperturbed. "Did I wake you?" I wrap a big hug around him and kiss the top of his head. His graying hair is sticking out on the left side of his head, flat against him on the right side. I use my fingers to try to put the pieces smoothly into place.

"No, no, not at all, Anna-banana. Just talking myself into standing up, that's all. How was your day, sweetie?"

I don't want to tell him, but he sees my arm bandaged up and worry floods his eyes and the burrows of his brow. Before he can ask, I say, "My day was great until I fell trying to keep my car from getting towed. Just scraped my arm a bit. But I'm fine. Unfortunately, the car got towed anyway. But I'll get it tomorrow, okay Pop?"

His concern seems to lessen and he nods his head. "Okay, as long as you're alright. Don't worry, I will take the bus. No problem. But your arm? It's not broken?"

"No, Pop, I was just about to take this bandage off anyway."

And sufficiently reassured, he heads into the bathroom to get dressed for work while I go to the kitchen, my stomach growling. I freeze as soon as I walk through the swinging half-door.

It is obvious that Pop has been cooking something, which apparently exploded in bright red bursts over most of the yellow linoleum counters and a large section of the floor. There are three large pans on the stove, two of them encrusted with the burnt remnants of whatever exploded covering the bottom, dry and hard now. Scraps of tomatoes and onions fill the sink, and the packaging from ground beef floats in a red, watery pool on the counter. My foot sticks to the floor more than once as I cross the kitchen.

"I cooked you some dinner, Anna!" Pop calls from his bedroom. "I made your Nanna's gravy and a big batch of rigatoni noodles. There are meatballs, too. *Mangiare!*"

"So I see," I say half-heartedly. This is going to take me all night to clean.

Pop is standing in the doorway to the kitchen, in his white baker's pants and t-shirt.

He looks at me apologetically. "I was gonna clean those. Don't worry about them. I'll wash them when I get home."

I groan impatiently. "No, I'll do it. I just don't know why it is so hard to clean up as you are cooking. I mean, look at this -- how much easier could it be?" I squirt some soap into the pots and fill them with water to let them soak. He has turned away and is grabbing his wallet and coffee thermos as he leaves through the back door.

He calls back to me over his shoulder, "Okay, Anna. Thanks sweetie! See you later!"

I hunch over the pots and begin scrubbing as hard as I can, holding the pots with my left arm, my hand dangling useless. I make the water as hot as I can bear, and then just a little hotter, so that my right hand turns red and numb. The scouring pad leaves little splinters of metal under my fingernails. As I scrub, I recount the day's multitude of injustices. I just don't understand how someone like me, who is trying her hardest to get ahead, like me, is always thrown the worst luck. Nobody else has shit happen to them over and over and over again like I do. It's hard enough being the one to take care of Pop -- he's been a mess ever since Mom left. I don't blame him either. She moved out on a Saturday and was moved in with Pop's long-time buddy by Wednesday the next week. I don't know if they had a thing going before that or not, but it damn near killed Pop either way. I haven't talked to her since then. She would call every day at first, but I hung up on her or just wouldn't answer the phone. She must have finally gotten the message. I know she's in the city somewhere, but I hate her and I hope to god I never run into her. Now it's just me and Pop.

You'd think Ollie could help his own father, but no, he's too busy with his career, and with his girlfriend. It's always been this way. Even though I am two years older than Ollie, he's the one who has gotten the lucky breaks and opportunities. I got one whole year of college in before the divorce, then moved home to be with Pop and help Ollie finish high school. Little did I know that Ollie would go on to finish college and then move to L.A. while I just continued to run this hell-hole of a house.

I look for a clean dishtowel, but they all seem to have tomato sauce splattered on them. I get a hand towel from the bathroom and begin drying the dishes.

At least Pop still goes to work, but he is barely making enough to cover the taxes on this place, so I work every stinking job I can find. But I have a plan-- lots of plans- that I just know can make us rich. Rich as shit. I am just trying to catch one little break. One tiny break that will let my plan take wings, but people like old-fart Mr. Montgomery and flighty Hera Strauss keep getting in my way.

Hera's office is in a loft on south Michigan Avenue in a quieter part of the city. It is less crowded here than in the Loop, and the bus speeds down Roosevelt Road faster than I anticipated, so I am fifteen minutes early for my appointment. I duck into a coffee shop to get a double espresso, afraid I might otherwise fall asleep in my meeting with this Life Coach. My neck bristles like a dog when I think about this -- the condescending manner of her "help", not to mention the offensive attitude of the officer. But, on the other hand, I am happy that I will be spared over eight hundred dollars that I cannot pay -- so long as I show up to Hera's six times between now and my court date in four weeks.

I am not motivated to do anything but get in and get out ASAP!

I breathe in the earthy scent of dark roast and feel the steam drift upward around my cheeks and across my nose. I take another breath as I walk back outside, ready to cross the street to Lofts on Michigan. As my foot steps onto the sidewalk, a parade of colorful long sleeve t-shirts and spidery legs jostle and sprint past me.

"Hey! Watch it! " I shout after them.

I am pushed back in to the store by my own unwillingness to be that close to a group of runners. My coffee splashes and splatters as I try to keep my cup level and full. I am only somewhat successful.

"Excuse us," quips a small voice. A straggler, left in the dust. These people are obnoxious.

I hurry across the street to Round One of Hera versus Anna. I down my coffee and feel my defenses rise.

When I enter Hera's office, a tripped out sixties vibe greets me, rather than the therapeutic sterility I was expecting. A rust-colored shag carpet covers the floor and a rainbow of stiff looking chairs circle the room. Motivational posters hang on the walls, encouraging visitors to Dare to Dream and Take Charge and Be the Change.

Hera welcomes me, waves to a chair, and then disappears into a back room. I scan the layout of the room, but I cannot tell where she will be sitting. I prefer to stand until the other person sits so that I do not put myself into a position of passive subjugation. The chairs are not close to each other, but they all face inward, to the center of the room.

While I am waiting, the door suddenly slams open and loud voices bellow their way in, three men just a second behind, and each plops into one of the chairs.

Who are these guys? And why are they here, now?

I am about to tell them that they are in the wrong room when Hera returns with a tray loaded with cups, cookies, and a teapot.

"Oh, good, you've met!" She puts the tray down on a large round table. It looks more like a drum to me, with a piece of olive green leather stretched across the top and sewed haphazardly to a tie-dye blanket stretched across the bottom. But it holds the tray and contents, so a table it is.

One of the men grabs a handful of cookies and sits back into his chair. He needs a shave and probably a shower, based on the smell heading my way. With his eyes on Hera, shoving a cookie into his mouth, he nods in my direction.

"What's she doing here?"

I step up to his chair, feeling tall and powerful, and looking straight down at the fringe of stringy hair circling his head, I say, "No, what are you doing here? This is my appointment time!" I look at Hera. "This still counts, you know. Just because you can't keep your own schedule organized doesn't mean I have to pay for it!"

Hera smiles and waves that hand of hers again. "I thought you were going to sit down, Anna."

I glare into her eyes, but she does not alter her smile, nor look away, so finally I just sit in the turquoise chair farthest from Mr. Smelly. Two chairs over, a line-backer sized man in his early thirties is squeezed into a purple chair, and next to him, a very short Asian man, his hair covering his eyes, sits on the edge of a yellow armchair. Although his is by far the most comfortable chair in the room, he refuses to sit back into the cushions, perched as if it was lined with tacks.

What kind of fucked up group did she drag me into?

As we glare angrily at each other, Hera pours tea for everyone and I am surprised to see these guys all take a cup. Probably some weird LSD-laced herbal tea. I sniff at mine, but it just smells like flowers and mint. I refuse to drink any, holding the cup in my lap instead.

Hera walks around the chairs, speaking softly, privately to each of the men. They listen without looking at her, nodding slightly, gazing at the floor or the cup in their hands. And finally, she bends close and speaks to me.

"Hello, Anna," she whispers. "I'm so glad you are here. I know that you have had many upsetting events happen in the past, but I want you to feel at ease here. There are no demands on you in this room. No expectations. Okay?"

I have no response. I have no reason to respond. Furthermore, and for the first time in a long time, I have no irritation prompting me to respond. So I nod and lift the cup of tea to my lips, drink a sweet sip, and simply relax.

It seems that all of us are here because of traffic-related incidents, and particularly anger or stress-related traffic incidents.

The small Asian man, Dan, tells me that he recently slapped a school bus driver who was stopping traffic to let the kids from the bus cross the street. Dan yelled to move and let the kids wait. The bus driver leaned down to Dan's open car window to yell at him to be patient, and Dan wound up and smacked her across the face. Oh, yeah, the bus driver was a sixty-five-year-old grandma.

The smelly man, Steve, was responsible for causing a two hour traffic delay on the Kennedy Expressway when he pulled his truck across three lanes of traffic to run down the Honda that cut him off merging from Washington Street. He wedged the Honda between his truck and the wall along the median, obstructing rush hour traffic and receiving numerous verbal attacks and a few thrown punches as a result.

Ron, the linebacker guy, sits so calm and quiet, I can't imagine that he is here for the same reason. He mumbles quietly that he has been driving to the grocery store and back without too many problems. Hera pats his hand and says, "One step at a time. Don't forget."

They are looking at me now, waiting. I feel an angry frown creep onto my face and Hera quickly reminds me that there are no expectations here. "Do only what you are comfortable doing. Say only what you are comfortable saying." I take a deep breath, prepared to say "pass", but instead I begin to talk about the tow truck, the hospital visit, and my Pop.

"So, sure, I guess I got pretty upset with the tow truck… and the police… and the paramedics. But see, I just need to take care of me and Pop, and I guess I get a little too protective at times. Just trying to be a good daughter!" I smile and shrug. I'm sure they can all sympathize.

But Dan does not. He leans even farther forward in his chair and hisses at me.

"If I was the car you blocked in, I wouldn't have just had your car towed. I would have busted every window and flattened every tire and waited for you to return and busted your kneecaps on top of it! Selfish bitch!"

I feel the blood fill my cheeks and pound against my temples, as I search for a sharp response. But Ron interrupts. "So, what you are saying, Anna, is that you, your life, your problems, and your needs are the only thing that matter. What if the person whose car you blocked was trying to get home to his Pop? Or her sick baby? Or his dying wife? Did you ever think about that?"

They stare at me and I stare back, but the silence stays thick and unbroken.

The truth is, no, I have never thought about that. I have had enough to worry about with my own life. I am not going to worry about other people's lives on top of that.

"Maybe," says Steve finally, "maybe you should spend more time around people who don't piss you off so much. See if you can find any of those!"

The men all chuckle, like they are in on a secret joke, and their anger seems to evaporate instantly.

Without answering, I put down my cup, check my watch, and announce that it is time for me to go. As I hurry out the door Hera calls to me, "See you on Friday, Anna! And thanks for sharing."

I fling open the door onto Michigan Avenue and just barely miss crashing it into a little kid on his bike. "Lousy parents, nowhere around, of course!" I mumble to myself.

I hurry up the street, waving wildly as my bus pulls away from the stop at the end of the block. I can't believe it didn't wait. He had to have seen me! I continue to walk, but a woman and her small Pekinese wind back and forth in front of me. I am about to tell the woman to do a better job controlling her dog when she looks up at me and I can see that she has been crying. She realizes I am behind her and scoops up the little dog, hugging it close to her and burying a new flood of tears in its silky coat.

I move away quietly and soon I am next to the wide-open spaces of Grant Park. The park is a dull gray-green, but there are plenty of people strolling, biking, sitting, or running through here. It is warmer today than it has been the last few days, so I sit down on one of the stone benches lining the inner walks.

A familiar group rises over the bridge and bounces toward the sidewalk. Their arms and legs move methodically, but they shift up and back, turning their heads from one side to another as they either listen or speak to each other. Some of them seem deep into serious discussions; others laugh and joke and punctuate their talk with open hands and emphatic gesticulations.

What was it that bothered me so much when I saw them earlier? Or the kid on his bike, or the sad girl with her dog? Why am I so irritated with all of them? I cannot remember what any of them did that was so terrible. Only that they exist, and their existence interferes with my own.

Another routine day ends in the same routine evening. I finally scraped up some cash so I took the bus to pick up our car this morning, and had two more meetings that resulted in a polite and abrupt walk to the office door. "Sounds like a great idea! We'll call if we need your help!"

Slam.

Made it to my retail job just in time to spend six hours climbing up and down a ladder restocking inventory that no one should want. Plastic Ferris wheels, cheap, painted trinkets, and thin "Chicago!" t-shirts are stacked from floor to ceiling, just waiting for tourists to make their big purchases. My arm is better, and no longer wrapped, but it still aches, and I don't mind letting my co-workers know. They could care less.

Picked up a pizza on the way home, and some more bleach to wash Pop's bakery uniform as soon as I walk in the door. Wednesdays are Pop's weekend, so we finish off the pizza as the sky grows dark. I take the garbage out, folding the pizza box as much as I can before pressing it all into the one big bin in our alley.

From outside I see the flicker of soft lights in the living room and the kitchen light beaming clean and bright on the freshly scrubbed counters. When I walk back inside I lean against the doorway into the living room. Routine day. Routine evening. Except for the thoughts swimming through my head.

"Pop? Are you happy?"

He is sitting in front of the TV, remote in hand, pointed at the screen, but the chatter of in-home shopping keeps blaring, so he must not want to change the channel. He doesn't seem to want to change much, lately.

He reacts as if my voice was on delay, suddenly perking up and turning to me with a huge smile.

"Anna, you know I'm happy! How could a Poppa be unhappy with a daughter like you -- working so hard, taking care of the house, the bills, the errands." He points his remote around the room, as if all of those things are just a click away from being performed. "You're my sunshine, princess!"

Part of me wants to give him a big hug; another part of me wants to throw a shoe at him.

"Yeah, Pop, but what about the rest of your life? Your friends? Your social life? Don't you want to have more fun?" Even though I say it as if it's a good thing, Pop recoils from the idea, drooping back into his chair, resting the remote on his belly.

"Hmmm. Friends -- who are they?" he bites back at me. "You think you have friends and they stab you in the back. They steal your family right out from under your nose. They destroy your life and then walk away."

His cheeks and nose turn pink and he pulls himself deep into his round torso, like a turtle hiding in its shell.

"I'm sorry Pop. I know it still hurts. But Pop, you gotta have friends, right? What's life gonna be, without friends?"

He points from me to him and back again. "You and I -- we don't need friends, Anna. We got each other, and that's better than friends. That's blood. Nothing stronger than blood, princess. *Ti amo.*"

He turns up the volume on the TV, as if he is actually interested in purchasing the extra-strength vacuum being featured. I doubt he even knows what it's for.

When I get to Hera's office on Friday, Ron is already there. He is sprawled out in one of the chairs, his legs straight out in front of him, his elbows resting on the sides of the chair and his head hung back, staring at the ceiling.

I don't see Hera, but clinking sounds coming from the back room indicate she is here and preparing snacks again.

Before I can announce myself, she calls out gently, "And Ron, think about what Julie would want you to do. Do you think she would want you to spend your days trapped inside your house? Or do you think she'd want you --" Hera stops when she enters the room and sees me standing there. She changes the subject swiftly and without batting an eye. She offers me banana bread and hot chocolate, and returns to her flighty rambling talk, but I notice her observe Ron from the corner of her eye, and relax a little when he pulls himself up straight in his chair as the other two men arrive.

Steve brings a carton of donut holes to share since this is his last time here -- as ordered by the court anyway. He gives Hera a wink.

Dan pops one after another into his mouth, barely stopping to chew.

"Didn't think we'd see you again," he mutters, directing his comment to me. Donut crumbs shower the space around him and powdered sugar clings to his lips and fingers.

Steve shoves Dan's hand out of the box and grabs a couple for himself. "Yeah. Figured you'd just pay the six hundred bucks and keep sharing your bucket of sunshine self with the rest of the world." He grins at me, either to underscore his meanness or to ease it. I grin back.

"Nope, I'm not paying it. Sorry, but you underestimate my ability to put up with a couple of loud-mouth jerks for a few weeks." I keep grinning, too.

"Alright, then, let's get started!" Hera sits next to me and indicates that our group session has officially begun. "Today I'd like to do some problem-solving. We will always have stressful events occur in our lives, and maybe even some real tragedies, but it's important that we know how to keep ourselves afloat through those problems. Not get sucked in to them."

Good description -- getting sucked in. Sinking, swallowed, stuck. Isn't that where my life is right now?

"So rather than fixating on the problem, the annoyance, the pain-- let's look at a completely opposite activity or thought or behavior that might give us a break from the problem-- at least in our mind. For example, when I am upset with my daughter, instead of complaining or yelling at her, I go into my room for a little yoga time. I might start my yoga feeling angry, but when I finish, I am clearheaded and can decide how to address my problem. I might not even think of it as a problem at all anymore."

Well, I'm not surprised that Hera does yoga. But I didn't know she had a daughter. I wonder about her, how weird it would be to have Hera as your mom. Then again, I haven't seen my own mother in over five years. Bitterness rises into my heart, but I quickly bury it.

"I sew stuff," says Dan. "When I am pissed off at a customer or one of my lame brain employees, I go in the back room of the cleaners and pull out whatever needs to be hemmed or altered or resized and start sewing. It's so mindless and repetitive. And it's hard to do while angry. Jab yourself with a sharp needle once, and you figure out you better calm down!"

Hera smiles at Dan. "Thank you, Dan. I should try that. God knows I have plenty of ripped clothing!"

The room chuckles and I wonder if I am the only one who is missing something.

Ron kicks his feet out and rubs his hands across his belly.

"I eat!" We laugh at that and I'm pretty sure we can all relate. There's something about tearing into a hamburger that seems to relax my jaw and eventually my mind.

"It's the cooking that calms me though," Ron continues. "Measuring, chopping, mixing, simmering...and it all smells so good, tastes so good! It even feels good. Like Dan said-- you have to pay attention when you are chopping walnuts or slicing onions. If you don't --" he holds his hand up, middle finger folded down -- "ouch!"

"How about you, Anna?" Ron asks. "How do you blow off steam?"

"I guess I've never thought about blowing off steam before. Basically I just blow up."

I shrug like I don't care. I don't know if I care or not. Maybe I over-react a bit, but I don't think it's a problem. At least not for me.

"How do your friends feel about that?" Hera poses the question so innocently. But it stabs me.

"I don't really hang out with many friends. I'm too busy. I don't have time to go out and have fun or meet people either. I'm either working or taking care of my Pop's house or something. So I don't really have too many friends," I repeat myself.

I swear I can hear their empty eyes blinking as they just stare at me. Steve nods slowly. "Uh huh. That's why you don't have friends."

I am about to reach across the room to pull his stringy hair when Hera makes a suggestion.

"Well, let's think of something you can do that will help you blow off steam as Ron says, and will also help you meet people. Sound good?"

I want to be cynical, but the three goofs in front of me are grinning and nodding so hard they look like the three stooges and I can't help but laugh.

"Sounds great," I say, "but I'm not doing any yoga!" I twist my arms into a weird pretzel shape.

"Not necessary, Anna. You just want to do something that feels good, and gives you a chance to appreciate a community of people having fun. You do remember what it means to have fun, don't you?" She smiles, and although she acts like she is kidding, I think she knows the truth.

"How about bowling?" suggests Steve. "Some buddies of mine have a league team. I could hook you up, put you on one of their teams. If you're any good, that is."

"Any good? Yeah, I'm pretty damn good. I can probably kick everyone's ass. Sign me up."

Hera holds up her hand. "Anna, do you think this is something you will have fun doing? And is bowling a little too...competitive, perhaps?"

She's right of course. I can't see me making a lot of new friends by kicking their asses or getting mad if they mess up.

Dan offers up his idea next. "My wife walks with a few of her lady friends a few mornings each week. They just walk and gossip for an hour or so. Leaves me to get some peace and quiet once in a while. I never thought about how it might be a way for her to get away from--" he stops abruptly.

I try to picture myself strolling along beside Dan's tiny Asian wife as she talks about her life, Dan's life, their life together. I become bored just thinking about it. But I do like the idea of talking with some friends, maybe even getting some good ideas by networking with other people. I'm not sure I have the patience to walk that long, however.

Ron leans forward in his chair, almost talking to the floor. "Maybe you should go for a run."

I remember the group that pushed past me earlier this week, and the easy way they seemed to chatter with each other, and the swiftness of their stride. I try to picture myself running alongside those quiet, swift people. I can see it — I really can.

Perhaps no one else can, however, because everyone is staring at Ron as if he just suggested I jump off a bridge. I think Hera has stopped breathing. The hell with them.

"I actually think that's a great idea, Ron. I see a lot of running groups around Chicago. They look fun. So, no matter what the rest of you think, I'm gonna give it a shot."

Ron tilts his head to look up at me, raising one eyebrow, and gives me a quick nod.

Hera looks like she's going to explode, her grin is so big. Her hands are clasped in front of her and I can tell she is trying very hard to control her relief. I suppose this means she won't have to keep seeing me if I can just prove I am dealing with stress better.

After a few more motivational quips from Hera it is time to go. As I get up to leave, she puts her hand gently on my arm. "Remember, it's not a competition. Just smile and have fun, okay, Anna? Report back next Tuesday."

"Sure, Hera."

Two days down; four more to go.

I can see them just a few hundred meters away. I am trying to tie my shoe and fumbling to find a discreet place for my car key, but the group is already drawing together. They are so diverse to begin with, comprised of men and women of all ages, all sizes, all personalities and levels of athleticism. Standing, stretching, chatting, jostling so randomly it seems. And then, on some unheard, unseen signal, the noise level drops, and they fall into a suspended stillness, perched on their toes, leaning all in the same direction, and no more than a half of a breath goes by until finally, instantly, the run begins.

As the group disappears from the trailhead amongst the trees, I try sprinting to catch up with them. By the time I reach the trailhead they have fallen into small little cliques. Speeding down the lakefront path, I reach the last group and suddenly grind to a slow wobble. Oh great! The walk-run-walkers. I scowl, irritated by this impasse. They make up in size what they lack in speed, and by that I mean they walk-run four across, creating a blockade for anyone who would like to move faster than a snail. It's not that I mind what pace they run or walk or whatever. I just get annoyed that they take up the whole entire running path, without blinking an eye. I take a deep breath and remind myself to smile like Hera said to do, to appreciate the community of runners out on this lovely evening, even if they are blocking the whole lovely path.

"On your left!"

I announce my approach with the universal call to move the hell over.

In unison, they turn to look over their shoulder, then back around, squeezing together just enough to let an ant crawl past them.

Fine.

I take another deep breath, glare daggers into their backs, and swing around them, off the path. Three strong steps and then I land ankle deep in a puddle of rocky sludge, twisting my foot awkwardly and painfully.

"Oh blast it! What the hell?" I am working hard to control my language along with my temper, but it is difficult when I am in this much pain. I hop one-legged, shaking out my drenched and muddy shoe that has now gained an additional two pounds, then plop down on the grassy edge.

"Oh dear!" exclaims a portly middle-aged woman, the one closest to me.

Her male counterpart, a young guy with a baseball cap pulled over his eyes, chuckles, and says to the other two women, "I guess it's a good thing we are slow and steady, huh girls?"

"Oh, Mick, you crack me up!" Two more ladies in their early twenties at best, giggle like little girls and hang all over their funny friend, Mick.

I feel my anger, confined to this pressure-cooker of control, boiling to the surface, looking for an escape.

"Need some help? How about I lend you a hand?" Mick reaches down to me beaming that oh-so-pleasant grin.

They all laugh sympathetically.

"Help?" I explode. "It's a little late for that, don't you think? How about you help everyone on this fucking running path by not being a pack of fucking path hogs! That's what you are, a selfish bunch of fucking path hogs!"

I instantly regret the viciousness of my verbal attack, but I don't know how to back down, so I continue my rant as I hop toward my car. I can only keep my balance for a few hops though, and I eventually topple over, catching myself with my injured foot, causing me to collapse onto the ground again, screaming.

A strong hand wraps around my arm and yanks me into the air. I am flung across Mick's back, fireman style, which means my ass is in the air and I am straddling this guy's shoulder.

"Put me down!"

He marches easily across the parking lot to my car, as if he is carrying a small child instead of a large woman. He heaves me off of his back and onto the hood of my car.

"See, we all need help sometimes."

He winks at me and then turns around. He gallops away, a long-legged sprinter. He glides so smoothly and quickly that he appears to be moving in slow-motion, but he is back to his group in just a few seconds, joining the women who have resumed their run-walk already. He looks over his shoulder and gives me a thumbs-up.

"Well, fuck it," I mutter, and slide back into the car, turning the key in the ignition, and gunning the engine for a second before I pull out of the parking lot and back onto Lake Shore Drive.

I am late for my third meeting with Hera and the Road Rage Boys. Steve has graduated, so it's just Dan and Ron sitting on either side of Hera when I walk in. Dan has one more week with us. He has been coming here for the past six weeks, in addition to a fine that he paid. He said this was to help him avoid losing his entire business. I hope it is helping. I can't imagine what he'd be like if he couldn't find some time to get away from all the idiots that come into his store. If he couldn't find a corner to just hem and stitch.

"Actually," he continues, "I am even more worried about Yoshi. What she would do if I -- if it ever happened again."

Once again, Hera nods, Ron nods, and I am clueless.

"Who is Yoshi, and what did she do, and more importantly, why do you even give a shit?" I hate having to ask for an explanation. It should be clear to everyone that since I am the new one here, I am in the dark on all their crazy friends and events in their lives.

Hera answers. "Yoshi is Dan's wife. It's up to Dan if he wants to share any more."

Dan slumps forward in his chair, holding his head between his hands, his long black bangs creating a screen to hide behind.

I tap my foot, waiting. He shouldn't bring it up if he doesn't want to talk about it. It's just rude to start talking about something in front of someone else.

"I hit her..." he mumbles. "The receipts were missing and she was the last one to see them and she is always losing stuff. She doesn't understand how important those are. I didn't mean to hit her, but she's always losing stuff. Always..."

His back gets rigid and I can feel it myself as his shoulders tighten and creep higher toward his ears. He leans forward, and then clutching the seat of the chair he begins to rock back and forth, just slightly at first and then more forcefully as he continues his accusations of Yoshi's continual forgetfulness and the immense irritation it leads to.

The rocking is starting to drive me crazy. I fight the urge to shove him against the back of his chair.

Instead, Hera slaps her hands against her own thighs and abruptly stands up, a firm frown in her eyes.

"Let's go," Hera says and grabs the back of his shirt. "You too," she motions to Ron and me. Without a word we get up and follow them down the stairs and out onto Michigan Avenue.

"I'm not going to let you build up so much hate against a woman you obviously adore. She's probably out walking, sorting things out," Hera says. "So let's sort stuff out here, okay Dan?" She drops behind him, and then behind me, as Dan leads our fucked-up little group towards the park.

Unlike me, Dan barely lifts his feet, his fists are shoved into his pants pockets, and his head hangs low. Whenever my feet hit the ground, no matter where I am, my body fills with an urgency that pushes me to hurry, to get in front, to move ahead. I have to hold myself back, keep from powering down the street, since I have no idea how far Hera intends to take us. I inhale slowly, force myself to ignore the jittery nagging crawling like spiders up and down my leg muscles, and look around the city once again. It's warm and the sun is dipping lower now, so a silver shimmer bounces off the lake to the east.

I take this opportunity to announce my progress so far. I call out to the pair strolling behind me.

"Oh, Hera, you wanted me to report back about my run? Well, I didn't run, and I lost my temper, and I swore at some fat people, and, well... I guess I do need to blow off steam... like you all said." I look over my shoulder at Hera, but she's talking to Ron. Dan pats me on the back lightly and moves into a slow jog. "I guess we all do."

He and I run slow like that for a couple blocks. Quiet at first, and then he starts telling me about his first date with Yoshi, nearly forty years ago, how nervous he was as a sixteen year old, how cute and shy she was. He tells me about his parents still living in China, who sent him to America to earn money for their family when he was thirteen years old. How Yoshi taught him to do American business. How beautiful she looked as an eighteen-year-old bride. How they never had children and how every once in a while Yoshi cries about that.

We've both lost track of time. His eyes are soft and dreamy when we jog past Hera's office, and we have to double back a few steps. Ron and Hera are just packing up to go home, too, when we walk in.

"There you are," Ron greets us, unworried.

"Better?" Hera asks. I'm not sure who she is asking, but both Dan and I answer, "Much!"

This time I am early. Not first, but I have plenty of time to get my shoes on in the car, watch the group gather, and try to figure out who's in charge. I pray it's not the guy who hauled my ass off the path last time. I see a short skinny woman with a clipboard, handing out signs with a time written on each of them. People are checking in with her as they arrive so I lock my door (keys in pocket? Check) and jog over to her, hoping she will not question my self-appointed status as one of the group.

She looks up, way up, when I approach her. I tower over her, and ordinarily this makes me feel powerful, but today I just feel conspicuous.

"You're new," she states.

"Yes, I am, kind of. I tried to run with you guys last week, but I ran into some problems."

Behind me a deceptively soft voice interjects with a stinging, "You mean, path-hog problems?"

I know it's one of those fat ladies, but I don't turn around. I don't even acknowledge that I heard her. I just stare at the tiny woman in front of me.

"Uh huh. I see. You're Hera's friend, right? She said you'd be coming back. That you needed help finding the right group. Is that right?"

My jaw drops open. What the hell is Hera doing talking to her? This is not okay! I am going to rip her apart next week! She should mind her own fucking business for once!

"Maybe you can run with me today and we'll figure things out. Okay?"

She smiles briefly and then turns away to greet some more runners. I want to leave, to go straight to Hera's and let off some steam by ripping her head off. A stream of runners floats past me and their sudden energy pulls at my anger, pulls me along after them, so instead of leaving, I am ready to chase after them. I hop in place a little, eager to move my body, keeping the anger from settling too deep into my muscles or my mind.

Once all of the groups have taken off, even the run-walkers, Hera's friend nudges me onto the path, but in the opposite direction.

"We have to meet up with my running partner," she says, and we start running, not jogging, but running, away from the others. I stick with her because even though she didn't do it on purpose, I am relieved to be away from all those other people I pissed off. It's hard to make friends when your first impression on people is being a foul-mouthed name-calling baby.

I want to do better with this lady, who probably knows all my shit already anyway, despite any codes of confidentiality.

"So.... You know.... Hera...right?" This is much faster then my jog with Dan, so I can barely spit out more than two words at a time.

"Yes, I do," she answers.

I wait, but that is all she will give me. Okay, lady, two can play this game.

"Well, she never talks ... about you…"

"I wouldn't think so. Confidentiality would prohibit that." She easily responds in complete sentences. Multi-syllabic words and everything.

"Well," I answer, slowing a bit so that I can finish my thoughts completely. "She obviously breached... all sorts of... confidentiality.... by talking to you... about me."

She looks startled all of a sudden. "Oh, are you one of her patients? I just thought you were looking for a running group."

My face warms slowly to an embarrassed burning that spreads down my neck and into my armpits. I can't tell if she is fucking with me or not, but either way, I wish I would just keep my mouth shut.

I want to ask her what she knows about me. I want to ask her if she was one of her patients. And if so, why? She doesn't seem like the angry type, but I've only known her for a few minutes and everybody has something mean and vicious inside them. Right? I want to know if she has ever met Dan, and what she thinks of Hera's crazy decorating choices and the creepy way she is just so chill about everything. But I force myself to shut the hell up for once.

I feel like I swallowed a bee hive, all these questions, demands, refutations, and accusations just bubbling up inside me, stinging me on the inside, until I am running faster and faster, way faster than I can possibly keep up, and sure enough, in just a minute or two I grind to a stop, heaving over a garbage can, my lunch from earlier making a second appearance.

But the bees have left, and now it is just a queasy calm that is lingering in my stomach.

She did not run with me. She kept to her pace and now that I am doubled over she slows to a stationary jog.

"Better?" she asks. I nod. People keep asking me that.

"Good. Our running buddy is up there by the fountain. She's waiting for us."

And she puts her hand gently on my back. There is no pressure, or pity, or pleading. But I am instantly connected, so I wipe the puke from my chin, pull my legs back into a jog, and follow this fast, steady lady to the dark woman leaning against the fountain, waiting, not watching us, but waiting for us to arrive.

# 6  GRACIE

In 1969, after three years of practicing and listening and cheering, I finally got a chance to compete for myself. There were a handful of Chicago area high schools that now had a girls' intramural track team, but even in those cases there were only a few girls on the team. However, as in my case, those girls were there because they loved running, they were fast, and because someone believed in them. At Immaculate Heart we had seven girls who joined intramural track, mostly due to my constant pressure to find female competition. We had fun, but I was the only one who was consistent. The other girls had boyfriends, or jobs, or little brothers to babysit or homework to finish, and none of them had a coach for their dad.

Eventually there arose an interest, by coaches or parents or maybe somebody from the IHSA, in letting us girls compete in front of a crowd. A ladies exhibition heat for several events was planned for the May 17, 1969 Northern Illinois High School Regional Track Meet. There would be no state meet for us. This was our one and only formal competition. As a sixteen- year- old junior, I was the youngest girl to enter the meet and the only one from our school. This was pretty insignificant though, since there were only fourteen of us who were eligible to begin with.

We were limited to the 440 or lower as agreed upon by the schools' athletic department rules at the time, a reflection of the AAU competitive rules. Because there were so few of us, we ran it all -- the 50-yard dash, the 110, the 220, 440, the 25 yard hurdles, and the 440 relay, provided there were 4 girls on one team, which there weren't. Although we were not allowed to race anything longer than a quarter mile due to the belief that greater distances were detrimental to our reproductive organs and frail temperament, for some reason the physical demands of racing up to six events was completely ignored. This was considered quite groundbreaking due to the overwhelming condescension towards women in sports at the time.

Of course, I was nearly oblivious to all of this. By this time my father had taken over the Varsity distance team and coached them, while Sal was the head Coach for the sprinters. It was a paid position, but not enough on which to support a family. But in the winter of early 1969 a small Division 1 private college in the suburbs offered him a full time coaching position. Already well known for several state meets and a steady flow of local talent, St. Hebert College was planning to build a nationally competitive team, and who better to coach them but Billy Carlson. While my dad had yet to accept the position, he and Sal were already planning dual practices for the high school and college students. If he took the job, which was a greater possibility each day, this would be his last year as Immaculate Heart's head coach, and his last regional high school meet. I wanted to race well, make him proud.

So I practiced my start, my kick, and even my victory lap, never losing a bit of confidence. My dad timed me, and although I would be racing once around the track at most, he had me run time trials of two, three and even four times around -- a full mile! After each lap he would call out the time, urge me to relax my shoulders, or lift my knees, or pick up the pace. I had trained myself to respond to his direction, so no matter how I felt at the time, I always did what he said. And no matter what my time was, my dad always gave me a big hug when I finished. He was never excited or disappointed. A big hug, and we were either on to the next workout or packing up to go home.

My body had grown long and lean over the previous two years, so that even at five feet two inches, I was all legs and arms, with defined smooth muscles along my calves, hamstrings, and triceps. I tried hard to run just like the boys on the team. I had learned to keep my hips stable and my arms relaxed. However, even though my teammates encouraged me, it was always clear that as a girl, I just didn't have what it takes to be a super star like they hoped to be.

On race day, I sat with thirteen other girls on a long bench at the end of the track, just a few yards from the concession stand, our view of the track blocked by the constant stream of fans. All of us wore a boy's track singlet over our own shirt. My singlet was bright red, and I wore a white t-shirt under it, along with my black gym shorts. I had real racing flats but they were made for a boy so they were wide around my ankles. I tied the laces as tight as possible but my feet still felt like they were swimming. My hair was in a braid, as were most of the other girls'. We talked about school, boys, our families, food, music -- anything but running -- as we waited for our events to be called.

"First call for the ladies 100 yard dash!" The announcement was pronounced slowly and deliberately to give the crowd time to understand the significant difference of this event. This was the first of my three events, so I stood up and shook out my legs, then jogged over to the start line. The varsity men were running their first of four heats, so I still had time to get loose.

Three other girls joined me in the staging area. A short red-head named Caroline from Rockford; Greta, a tall, skinny Scandinavian girl with long legs; and Helen, a stocky Polish girl from Chicago's south side.

Behind me, the JV milers were stretching, preparing to run after us girls.

I jogged in place, nodding my head from side to side. From the corner of my eye I watched a couple of the milers from St. Bert's become hypnotized by my swinging blond braid, until, with a sharp blast, the whistle announced that it was time for us ladies to line up.

The four of us had trained similarly, learned the same rules and rationales of girls in sports. There were no starting blocks, so we just crouched lightly with toes touching the white chalky line in the dirt, our elbows bent, hands clenched, arms frozen and poised. We were not allowed to push off from a sprinters crouch, the kind of start that has fingers on the dirt, butts shooting into the air before the launch from the line. That type of start was considered too unladylike for us.

So at the gun, we all took off in a very awkward and inefficient race for the finish line at the end of the straightaway. Despite that, we all had a drive and determination to fight hard for the win, so the finish came fast -- Helen, Greta, me chasing each other down the track in under 14 seconds, and then Caroline, a few seconds behind us. Helen won; I finished on her heels; and Greta took third by a stride. Catching my breath, I hugged the other girls, congratulated Helen, and we started back to our seats. The crowd had barely looked up from their hotdogs. But we weren't running for them anyway.

As I jogged off the course a tiny familiar voice reached across the field. "Gra-a-a--i--ce-e-e-e!" From the other set of stands my mother and little brother, Eddie, were calling and cheering, a lone duo of encouragement. Eddie stood on the bench next to my mother, one hand on the top of her head, the other waving and waving as he jumped up and down, bouncing the line of spectators next to him. For a three-year-old kid, he sure was loud! I waved back, content that at least my biggest fans were watching.

The announcer continued to call out the events, the results, the current records and any which were broken during this meet. So far there was only one -- in shot put. The boys' mile was next, and my dad took a keen interest in this event. He had told me the story of his sub-four mile over and over already, and just a couple years ago Jim Ryun had been the first high schooler to do the same.

He stood close to the start line on the field, his arms crossed in front of his chest, a light bounce in his stance. As the boys lined up for a waterfall start, the IH runners looked at my dad, waved a quick sign of the cross on their shoulders and chest, and then glanced heavenward for extra support, almost as an afterthought.

I leaned against the fence outside the track, facing my dad. He gave me a wink and a thumbs up, then focused on the race as the gun went off.

These varsity boys made running look so easy. They were long and skinny, and just one of their strides was equal to almost two of mine. Their hips didn't bobble about and their long chests held huge balloons for lungs, enabling them to practically gulp oxygen by the gallon. I admired their athletic talent, but more than that, I envied their freedom to run. Sure, I could run for miles and miles in practice or on early Saturday mornings. But in competition I was limited to a tiny little once-around circle to apply all the running that was just bursting inside me. I wanted to feel my legs carrying me four laps, eight laps, even twenty laps around this circle. Heck, one lap was barely enough to get started. I wanted to race off this circle and onto the trails along the Chicago River, or leading into the prairies out west of here. My feet pawed at the earth with impatience.

With each lap my dad would mumble split times to each of our guys and they'd either pick up the pace, scale it back, or try their best to hold steady. Our runners were fast, but not winner-fast. Our guys were tough, but not winner-tough. And today, even the winner wasn't all that tough, finishing in 4:17, and then falling on his back, arms outstretched, until his coach came over and threw a cup of water on him.

After patting each of our guys on the back, my dad crossed the track to come stand by me.

"Think maybe he'll be at the state meet?" I teased.

"Who?" Dad asked.

"The next Jim Ryun or Josy Barthel."

My dad grinned and rubbed my head. "Maybe. We'll see." He leaned against the chain link fence that separated us from the boys.

"Actually, Gracie, I was hoping it might be you," he said, warmly.

I laughed.

Finally the ladies' 440 was called and all fourteen of us headed to the start line. There are only 8 lanes on a track, so there would now be two heats for us, too, with eight runners racing first, and then six of us racing next. From watching the boys events I knew that the winners would be whoever had the fastest time, regardless of which heat it was. Waiting for the times to be compared and the top three runners to be determined and announced had slowed the pace of the meet, but had also heightened the runners' anxiety. I raced in the second heat, so I got to watch my competition from a relaxed vantage point. It's tough being in the first heat because you are not just racing the girls around you, but the girls that might be faster than them in the second heat. It's a guessing game, and it forces the lead runners to push even harder. Which meant I would have to be ready to respond.

When the gun fired for the first heat, the girls jerked off their starting lines and pulled around each other. The staggered start makes the race hard to judge until the last 150 yards. Initially, the girl in the most outside lane appears to be in the lead due to her forward placement at the start. But the wider turns eventually bring her back in line with the lane one runner and everyone in between as they head into the last stretch. This is where runners fight to pull ahead or keep a lead, or realize they've misjudged their own pace. This is where, just as you need it most, the spring and power in your legs freeze up, and you pray that your legs won't quit before you reach the finish. Sometimes they do; sometimes they don't.

Today, the first heat proved to be tougher than any of us anticipated. Despite the staggered start, three of the eight girls came into the final stretch at nearly the same time, elbows pumping, and painful grimaces contorting their faces. Side by side they ran, each girl reaching farther in her stride. I was trying to estimate the time, measuring it against what I knew I could do, and nervousness started inching its way into the pit of my stomach. But with less than thirty yards to go, in a heartbreak of a finish, two of the girls  froze up, their legs refusing to cooperate with the rest of their body. What had just been a long and fluid stride suddenly choked up into a rigid march, the girls flailing and stumbling toward the finish line. The rest of the girls easily sped past them, despite their slower pace. The race finished with several seconds between the first--Helen--and third--Caroline. The crowd had stopped talking, stopped eating, to watch this human mess as the two last girls flung themselves across the finish line in slow, robotic lunges and then crumbled to the ground. Medical assistants rushed onto the track, gingerly lifting the girls in their arms.

A large man in a sweatshirt bellowed from the stands, and pushed his way to the fence surrounding the track. The girls were already being carried off the track, but the man grabbed one of them and plopped her back onto the ground, sprawling in front of me. She lay on her back, supporting herself on her elbows, glaring at this man. He was not angry, but he was not sympathetic either. The girl was thin, but muscular, both legs and arms. Her two brown braids made her look young, but her face and hips indicated that she was probably in her late teens. Her face was flushed and sweaty, but her breathing had calmed.

"Dad!" she scowled at him.

"Get up," her father ordered in a deep, soft voice. "Running is hard. Racing is harder. No matter how fast or slow you are moving, you carry yourself off this track. Got it?"

She squinted her eyes at him and pressed her lips together hard, looking like she wanted to spit at him. But then she pushed herself up to standing and walked over to Helen to congratulate her. The crowd, shaken from its initial shock at the girls' collapse, and then compounded by the rough treatment, started a slow rumble of surprise. As the rest of us walked out onto the track to take our place, the crowd's applause, cheers, and challenges grew loud and attentive.

They were hooked, and now I had an audience.

This made me both excited and nervous. I was used to working hard but unnoticed by everyone but a few sideline observers. Positioned in lane three, I felt far behind a thin dark girl in lane six and safely ahead of Greta in lane one. But it was lane four that concerned me the most. I felt certain I could finish the 440 in under sixty-five seconds -- I'd done it before-- but I was less confident that I could outrun lane four. Jane Highwater was the only girl from the central valley of Illinois and she had made headlines for her raw power, calm demeanor, and most significantly, her Native heritage. Rumors flew about her tribal chants and pre-run voodoo. None of it was true, of course. But photographers took pictures of her, dressed in moccasins and beaded shirts, running along the banks of the Illinois River with her long black braid swinging across her back to completely solidify the stereotype. Today she looked like the rest of us, but confident, too.

Toeing the line, shoulders square to the track, arms loose, legs tensed, we waited for the gunshot, telling us to start.

Then from down the track, from the boys waiting for the relays, a ripple of applause began, and it grew and it grew until the entire stadium was on its feet, shouting, clapping, whistling. The gun was lifted into the air, and one heartbeat later a puff of smoke, followed quickly by a loud blast, shot through the air and we were off.

Around me, the air was silent and solid. I pushed through the space, a tunnel of speed surrounding me, but feeling myself take a long first step in slow motion. Adrenaline poured into my legs and arms, and in a blink I was pulling around the first curve, legs turning over, over, over. Panicked by my slow start, I pumped my arms harder, and looked over my shoulder. Too difficult to tell who was in the lead, who would pull away. So without closing my eyes, I stopped looking at anything around me and let the sound become my guide. And there it was, Eddie's high-pitched squeal and then in its wake, my mother's voice, urging me to "Push, Gracie! Keep going, Gracie!"

One hundred and fifty yards into the race and my breathing caught up to my legs, both of them suddenly overwhelmed by the initial surge of confidence and adrenaline. Just a few steps earlier I had been fleet-footed and self-assured. Now my lungs were burning, trying to inhale deeper as they tighten and close. I could feel my legs slow down to allow my breathing to return. As miserable as I felt, however, I tried to believe that the rest of the girls must be in just as much pain, having just as much doubt as me. The winner would be the one who could fight through that pain and doubt the most.

At the halfway mark, we curved into the far end of the track, the gap between us closing in some cases, opening further in others. I watched lane six, then lane five, give way to their own doubts as their form grew sloppy and slow, so I passed them easily. Glancing over my left shoulder, I could see Greta in lane one just a few steps away, but lane two was a safe distance back. The long black braid of lane four still led me on through this one hundred yard curve, and I wanted desperately to catch it.

Make it to the straightaway, I told myself. Just go! Go! Go!

Leaning into the final turn, the strong call of my dad's familiar direction pulled me toward him. Echoing him, Sal shouted in his sharp East Coast accent, "Come on there, Gracie! Pull those elbows back! All the way through!"

The braid ahead of me, Greta's long skinny legs inching closer. I drove my arms up and back as hard as I could, begging my legs to follow, feeling the muscles tying themselves together, threatening to seize up completely. I stared at the end of the track, like a target, and counted silently with each step, one, two, three, four... and on until, barely a breath away, before eleven even finished its count, the braid disappeared, the skinny legs disappeared, and I was in the lead.

In an instant, I flew across the finish line, and let my legs slow down gradually, so I wouldn't collapse by coming to a complete stop. My thighs were cramping and my calves tightened up into hard-as-walnut knots. It hurt, but I kept moving, jogging, heel-walking, to release some of this pain. I didn't even look to see where the rest of the girls were until I jogged back to the line. I had crossed the finish first, that was certain, but I did not know where I fit in to the other eight girls who had already raced. Did my win place me in the top three overall?

Jane and Greta were leaning on each other, still catching their breath, but they congratulated me when I jogged up to them.

"Wow," Jane exclaimed quietly, her breath shaky. "I've never run so hard in my life! At least, not against another girl."

The crowd was standing and cheering. Sal burst onto the field with my dad right behind him. He pointed to the crowd, and then to me.

"That's for you, Gracie! You! Amazing race!" Sal never seemed so excited about a race before.

My dad was shaking hands with the other girls, especially Jane and Greta, talking to them, a huge smile lighting his face.

The boys' 880 started lining up, so the girls headed back to the bench, the crowd resettling into their seats once again.

My father grabbed my arm. "Whoa! Hold on! Girls, get back here!" He motioned to Jane and Greta to return. We stood in the middle of the track, the runners lined up behind us, but clearly confused by the obstacle blocking their start. One of the officials hurried over to us, waving his arms.

"No, no, no. Girls off the track," he ordered.

"What about their results? You had two heats. You have to give them their final results, don't you? Who won?" My father kept his grip on my arm, and reached out to Jane and Greta as well, who had now turned back again to return to the stands, and stood frozen, uncertain, on the track.

A stocky man in a red windbreaker and a red baseball cap jogged over to us. He held out his hand to my dad. "Pete Logan. Race Director IHSA. What's the problem, coach?"

My dad shook Pete's hand, allowing me to step away a bit. "Hi Pete. Billy Carlson. We're waiting for the girls' final results before moving on to the next race. Okay ?"

The boys fidgeted behind us, bouncing, stretching, bending. "Come on, get off the track," a voice mumbled, sending a ripple of complaint through the line and into the stands.

"Listen, Billy, let's step off to the side here so the boys can start their race and we can talk. No reason to disrupt the flow here."

"Right, let's not disrupt the flow. Let's finish the ladies 440 by announcing the results before you start the next race. Isn't that how it works?"

The two men faced each other in silence. A blanket of tension seemed to swell up from the track as Pete, the boys on the starting line, the coaches on the side, the fans in the bleachers stared and waited for us to leave the track. I inched farther away, praying that my dad would follow me, that all eyes would return to the runners. But my dad didn't budge.

"Billy, um, we don't have exact times for the girls. This is just an exhibition race. It doesn't matter who won. But if it was my guess, I'd say this little blondie beat them all. Okay?" He put his arm around me and squeezed my shoulders too hard. "What's your name?" he asked me.

"Gracie. Gracie Carlson."

Pete looked at my dad and let go of my shoulders as he realized our connection.

"Okay, I get it," he said. "You got your dad looking out for ya." Then to the crowd he shouted, "The winner of the ladies 440! Graaaaacie Caaaaarlson!"

He lifted my arm into the air, like I was a champion. The crowd didn't utter a sound. Jane shoved past me, and Greta hissed into my ear, "Must be nice having your daddy as your coach."

"Can we run now?" mumbled one of the boys on the starting line.

"That's not what I meant," said my dad, his jaw clenched. I pulled him off of the track as Pete turned and jogged back to the judges' table. "It's okay, Daddy. Like he said, it doesn't matter who won. It's just great that I get to run, to compete." And then I lowered my voice, embarrassment climbing up my neck and into my cheeks, and quietly pleaded, "Please, Daddy."

He looked away from me, leaning onto the fence surrounding the track as he watched the start of the boys' half-mile, the intensity of the coaches and officials along the track, the surge of energy from the crowd. He watched the officials, crouched at the finish line, stopwatch in hand, thumb poised and ready to click, measuring to the nearest tenth of a second each runner's time. He looked at the girls sitting on their bench, away from the crowd, away from the team, away from their coaches, away from the track even.

He didn't say anything more at the time, but he didn't have the same excitement about the remaining two events. He watched without timing, without cheering, without coaching.

Two hours later, as our bus unloaded the team in our school parking lot, Dad walked Sal to his car while I climbed into the front seat of our station wagon. Opening the window to let the cool spring air in, I heard him apologize. "Sal, you've been great. The boys have been great. And you'll keep being great. I just have to do something-- something more-- for Gracie, sure, but it's more than that."

"Billy, man, I will be the first one to support you and Gracie -- absolutely! You know I want her racing! She's got more raw talent and tough determination than any of the guys on the team. If I could mix that with Bernie's kick or Mikey's power, holy cow, we'd have a chance at a state title, for sure! So I'll do whatever I can to get her racing more, get the conference to have more girls' races. Why do you need to take her off the team?"

"Sal, that's just it. She's not on a team -- there is no girls' team. Why would there be, if there's no real competition for them?" He shook his head and leaned against Sal's car.

"You and I got good because we raced against good runners. Really good runners! Sure, Gracie is good. For a girl. What about Jane? And that chubby little girl from the south side -- she totally surprised me! Or the others who get to run around only when the boys are doing something else, or when the track isn't being used by the guys? Who is training them? Who is going to help them get better? Who even cares if they get better?"

"It's not fair, Billy, I know. I'm not saying it is. But don't leave!"

Leave? What was Sal talking about? I leaned out the window, looking right over Sal's shoulder and into my dad's bright blue eyes, panicked. He kept his gaze calm and steady.

"I don't know, Sal. If I keep coaching the boys, move up to college level, well, sure that'll be great. For me. But we both know that means Gracie will have fewer and fewer places to run, to train, to race. I'll be working afternoons, evenings, weekends with guys who have half the talent, half the drive. Where does that leave Gracie? It's not like she can just tag along, you know?" He shook his head. "That's not what I want for her. And if it means that I have to be the one to get these girls together, to make a team for them, then that's what I'll do. Keep my job in HR and get a girls' team together in the evenings. I'll figure something out."

"Billy, I really respect you. You've got a heart of gold all right, but think! You're on the brink of a great career! You can't walk away from that," he lowered his voice, so I could barely hear him say, "for a team that doesn't ...even...exist."

We all face choices in life -- some of them simple, some of them significant. Where to sit, whom to talk to, what to believe, whom to trust. These choices shape our lives and unfold our future. And while few of our choices slam the door closed on our own opportunities, we may not always realize the impact those same decisions have on other people, even people we have never met.

Dad stood with his hands on his hips, head bowed, looking straight into the ground at his feet. Chilly, or maybe too scared to hear anymore, I closed the window as Dad turned back to Sal, giving him a short response, a grin spreading across Sal's face. He didn't look at me as he got into the car and turned the key. He didn't say anything as we pulled out of the school parking lot and turned onto Lawrence Avenue. We rode home with only the night noises creeping into the car for the short drive. He was weighing his choice, and the impact of that choice. Judging the difference between supporting a family and supporting a dream. I was just trying to figure out what dream.

# 7 ANNA

It is my last required day with Hera. Tomorrow is my court date and I am hoping my punctuality and positive attitude will convince Officer What's-His-Name to drop all the fines I have stacked against me. Hera will play a big part in his decision, so I stand outside Hera's office for a few extra minutes to get super calm and to paste a huge smile on my face.

It's mid-May now and spring is starting to make a consistent appearance finally. Of course, Chicago weather is never predictable, so even though today is sunny and warm, we all know there could be three feet of snow tomorrow.

I close my eyes as I let my breath relax into me. The absence of visual distractions lets my mind relax in some ways, while in other ways it perks up even more. I don't have all those people and faces and bikes and cars bombarding me, so the part of my mind that is always busy looking, criticizing, evaluating who and what I see is taking a little nap. But the lazy part of my brain -- the part that listens to kids laughing and bike wheels clicking by -- well, that part never pays attention and now, standing here with my eyes closed, those quiet little sounds seem like a thunderstorm. The warm breeze brushes my cheeks, and footsteps shuffle and stomp at varying paces. Before he even speaks, I can feel Ron is standing next to me, feel his darkness and chill and pain that he drags behind him everywhere. I open my eyes as he squints down at me. "You okay ?"

I nod, but he is opening the door already, heaving his strong, sad body up the three flights of stairs to Hera's office.

"Why do you keep coming here, Ron?" I blurt out. "You have to be the most chilled out person I know. Besides Hera, I mean."

He glances back over his shoulder at me, but there is no emotion behind those dark eyes of his.

"Of course, she's a lot more cheerful than you," I continue, hoping to get at least a smile out of the big lug. "Dude, you act like you're at a funeral half the time!"

He stops so quickly I run right into him. Hera is standing in the doorway, a big lipsticked smile on her face, but it drains away quickly when she hears my attempt at humor.

She shakes her head slightly, but I don't need her to tell me I said something wrong. Every muscle along Ron's neck and arms has contracted, making his veins bulge and a rim of sweat collect at his shirt line.

I really want to be sensitive, but this is just too much. I push past him instead. "We all have problems, Ron. Time to let this one go, don't ya think?"

Before I can sit down, Ron has grabbed me by the arm and swung me around toward him, his big sweaty face only inches from my own.

"Who the hell are you, to tell me to let go? You have no clue what you are talking about!" he spits at me. "You've been here, what-- four, five weeks? And you are suddenly an expert on letting go? Ha!"

I am not really afraid of Ron, although this is definitely a side of him he's kept hidden. But he is pissing me off by grabbing me like this and shouting in my face. I can feel my own temper creeping up my back, but before I can say anything, Hera interrupts.

"Ron. She's right. Let go of her."

Ron, still squeezing my arm in his big hand, looks at Hera with eyes filling fast. His face twists into a grimace, and as he pushes me away, he sputters, "I'm trying. But I just don't know how."

"Well, that's a good start," I say, rubbing my arm where the pressure of his hand still pulses.

As if snapping out of a dream, Ron is suddenly apologetic and concerned. "I'm sorry. Did I hurt you? I am so sorry! Oh, shit, what did I do?"

"Ron, don't worry about it. You don't realize how tough I am. But seriously, that came out of nowhere. I don't mean to pry, but what is going on with you?"

Hera puts her arm on Ron's shoulder as he slumps into one of her big cushy chairs. "Maybe it's time to talk about it, Ron. It's been almost two years. Think you are ready for that now?"

Ron nods his head.

We spend the next forty-five minutes talking about Ron, his wife, the fight they had the morning that she died. The way he was ready to throw their marriage away when it was suddenly ripped from his life. The accident that threw her across three lanes of traffic. The way he refused to answer the phone, knowing it was her, just to make her cry a little longer, when in fact she was clinging to her last breath. The hole that was left in his heart since then. The way he shut himself off from the world ever since.

"This is the only time I get out," Ron said. "Everywhere I go I'm reminded of her. We traveled nearly every street of Chicago together. It's impossible to go anywhere without seeing Julie's face, or hearing her footsteps, or remembering her laugh. I hate it. I absolutely hate it."

Hera rounds out the picture. "Julie was a runner here in Chicago -- a competitive runner. So Ron would bike with her and her mom as they'd run in different parts of the city. "

"Except that one day," growls Ron. His fingers curl into a fist.

"Oh, so you think she died simply because you weren't there, don't you?" I ask, finally putting it all together. "Wow, that's a lot of pressure to put on yourself."

Hera is nodding her head, quiet, watching Ron as he lets that settle into his mind.

"That's what Hera's been saying."

"Well, there are a million things we might have been able to change in our life," I say, "but it's impossible to know what, or if the changes would have mattered anyway. Ron, you can only go forward."

And as foreign as it is for me, I reach over to Ron and put my hand on his, and give him the most sympathetic smile I can.

This time when his eyes meet mine, I feel a bolt go through me and deep into my heart. I am locked in his gaze. An eternity goes by before I take another breath.

Hera clears her throat loudly, which breaks whatever spell Ron had cast over me. I pull my hand back to my own lap, and try to cool the flush that has swept over my cheeks.

Suddenly, her hands fly into the air as Hera exclaims, "Anna! It's your last day! We got so distracted, we need to finish up and-- and -- give you a farewell and --"

This time I interrupt her.

"Thanks Hera, but I think I should keep coming, too. I mean, I haven't even told you about my running group yet."

I look at Ron, to see how he reacts. Maybe this is too close to home for him. But then again, it was his idea. He smiles and nods. "Yeah, I'd like to hear more about the people you yell at on the running path." I am pretty sure I see a smile pushing its way into a corner of his lips.

I have been joining the running group for nearly five months now. But I keep to the back, tagging along behind different groups each time. Hera suggested I practice developing empathy by running in another person's shoes for a change. So I do. Well, not in their shoes, but in the path and flow of their shoes. So I have followed the run-walk group, and listened to their struggles and lack of faith in themselves and the encouragement they give to each other and the pride in their finishes. I have run breathlessly behind the swift-footed racing groups whose light little bodies allow them to practically float on air. Their movements are measured and counted and met without complaint. I have tagged along groups of easy-jogging friends -- whether they were friends before running is not clear, but the after-run parties and sharing of pictures and  dating woes grow bonds of friendship stronger than I have ever known.

But most of the time I run with just two women -- Gracie, the lady who organizes this thing, and her unlikely running partner, Japlo. I say unlikely because she is blind. At least mostly blind. She said she can see some shadows and movements through one eye, but in general, the woman cannot see a foot in front of her. So how she keeps moving straight ahead, even with Gracie's help, is a mystery to me. She is from Africa. I am not sure where, but I know that there was a terrible war going on in her country and she lost most of her family along with her eyesight. But she and her daughter made it out alive about five years ago and they came to Chicago, the home of her husband's brother. Her daughter is part of a refugee assistance group called Go Forward, which connects her to educational and social activities in the city. One of those activities is this running group. And that is how Japlo started running with Gracie.

I like running with them because between the two of them, they have so many stories to tell. All I have to do is listen and keep moving.

Until today, because I have just come up with a great idea — a fantastic idea!

"Come on!" I plead, running in step behind Gracie and Japlo.

The two women do not slow their pace, but I can see their hesitancy in the slight shake of their heads.

Gracie speaks first. "Anna, our store has always been a contributor to local charity runs, but putting one together ourselves? That's a lot of work and I honestly don't think I can do it."

"Well, I didn't say you'd have to do it alone. In fact, Gracie, I mean that I will do it. I'll get sponsors, I'll get the volunteers, and the equipment. I'll run it all. You just need to put together a course and leave the rest to me. What do you say?"

We are back at the water fountain. We take turns sipping the cool water, regaining our breath. Farther down the path, a small brown girl, on the brink of adolescence, waves to us as she hurries toward her mother. Her smile is wide, and when you know the horrors she's lived through you wonder how she can smile at all.

"Ma! Hi! It's me, Yeni!" Japlo smiles toward the voice, and Gracie, too, smiles.

I wonder if all mothers recognize their daughter's voice. I don't think my own mother would know it was me if I was screaming right into her ear.

Gracie and I watch the mother and daughter hug, each of us having our own flashback I suppose.

As the girl leads her mother away, toward the bus stop at the corner of Sheridan and Diversey, Gracie grabs my hand.

"Okay," she says. "Let's do it."

I have a plan growing in my mind, and a to-do list growing in my notebook at home. This is nothing new. But for the first time, there is meaning to it all. And it has nothing to do with me.

I slam the folders down on the smooth mahogany table, creating a sharp smack that is just loud enough to shoot a little adrenaline into this semi-circle of gray curls or balding heads popping up in surprise.

I love it.

These are the Board members of one of Chicago's oldest family corporations, and every detail about them is precise and professional. Five men in dark blue or black suits lean back in their thickly padded chairs. In front of them they have a notepad and slim black pen, steaming coffee on the left, Blackberry on the right. The three women are wearing conservative navy blue or gray A-line skirt suits, with one colorful accessory each.

This Board clings to its purse strings tightly, and is not typically known for its philanthropy.

I am here to change all that.

"Thank you for meeting with me today," I start, looking each one of them in the eye. I am in my power outfit again, although the skirt isn't quite as tight, and I feel relaxed and organized.

"Please, open your folders." I wait while they hesitate to follow my direction, which I knew they would do. But I am silent until they have all opened their folders and they have all looked into the big brown eyes of the girl in the first photo.

"Her name is Katrine. She is fourteen years old and until last October she lived in Rwanda. She has been raped and tortured and she watched her father's brutal execution, but somehow, somehow, she has made it here, to this city, to our city, and look... she smiles at you."

Some of them want to turn to the next page; others, I can see are trying to envision this beautiful, skinny girl experiencing these horrors, trying to decide if I am just feeding them bullshit.

I am not feeding them bullshit. I wish I was.

"On the next page, is Yeni, from Liberia. She was only seven years old when she watched her mother and sister as they were viciously raped, witnessed the abduction of her brother, and somehow, somehow, miraculously saved her blind mother, leading her, eventually to this city...to our city... and look, she smiles at you."

"These girls are smiling despite the tragedy they have lived through, for one simple reason. They trust you. They trust me. They trust that this city, this new home of theirs, is going to care for them, is going to help them heal and learn and above all, they trust that you will help them to live."

I pause, and watch their eyes. Eyes droop or roll or tear or squint or soften to communicate the message of the heart, regardless of the words being spoken.

These eyes are sad, of course, but they are disinterested as well. They dart from the picture, to the text below each one, to the folder in their hands, to the steam rising up from their coffee just off to the side. It is not their daughter or grand-daughter who was chased from her home, her safety, her family. So it is difficult for them to feel more than a little sympathetic, which borders on pity, which is the cousin of condescension.

"I am here today to invite you to join with Run the World, one of Chicago's oldest and best-loved running stores, to host a charity half-marathon race, the objective being to raise a portion of the funds needed by Go Forward to help these refugee teens become positive, healthy, contributing members of our American culture. To help them with social, educational, physical, and therapeutic assistance that one who has gone through so much, might need."

One of the women, who looks to be in her early fifties, cuts to the point. "You are asking for money?" She stares at me accusingly.

"Excuse me," I say softly, then step out of the board room, and beckon to my running partners, waiting by the doors.

This is the first time I have seen them in anything other than running clothes, so I am still surprised when Gracie stands up and turns to the woman sitting beside her. Gracie's tiny body exudes power from the strength of her poise and her breath. A fitted long sleeved forest-green dress hugs the small but firm curves of muscle along her arms, back, and thighs. The woman next to her lifts her hand until she feels Gracie's fingers, then follows the curve of Gracie's arm up to her shoulder as she stands up. Her dark brown skin is rich against the loose white dress and white headscarf she is wearing. Brown-black ringlets spill over the scarf and down her back. A necklace of green and purple beads is wrapped close to her neck, and a pair of purple-hued sunglasses are perched on her nose, blocking the light for eyes that do not see. With her hand gently touching Gracie's shoulder, the two women enter the board room as I hold the door open.

Gracie walks up to the edge of the table, takes the woman's hand and presses it into the palm of the Board Member who asked if this was about money. Lucky choice.

"Hello," smiles the woman in white. "My name is Japlo. I think you have seen the picture of my daughter, yes?"

*****

71

We are skipping our run today because it is time to celebrate, and that means food and wine and dancing in some of Rush Street's loudest clubs as far as I'm concerned. We have been granted a generous gift from our new benefactor, supporting the race and the organization that has brought the three of us together.

Gracie laughs a little as we settle around an outdoor patio. "I think I'm a little too old for the nightclubs, Anna, but I would sure love a glass of wine. Japlo, how about you?" Her hand is still lightly touching Gracie's arm, shifting in response to her movements, like a loosely stitched marionette. Japlo smiles and shakes her head. "No, no wine for me. No alcohol. In my family we do not drink."

"Never?" I ask.

"Never."

"No one?"

"No one."

"That's crazy! Why?" Gracie elbows me, but I have already scolded myself for my blunt blabbing.

Japlo just smiles. "It's not so crazy. First of all, it is not something we brought into our house in Liberia. We lived in the country, away from stores and bars, so it was easy." Her voice dips lower and shakes a bit. "And then, of course, it was the weapon of the rebels. It is the way they poisoned our boys. Turned them into monsters."

Her voice remains soft, but her jaw becomes rigid, and her eyes hidden, blink rapidly chasing away whatever terror was creeping into her memory.

Dammit. "I'm sorry," I mumble, knowing it's too late to erase whatever image I stirred awake. I pull a chunk of bread from the basket and dip it in a platter of olive oil and grated parmesan. Maybe if I fill my mouth I will stop making an ass of myself with my words.

"You don't have to be sorry. It is what happened and it was very painful. I cannot change that. But I can decide to let pain destroy me, or I can destroy the pain. I choose to destroy the pain, with the help of all of you."

Gracie pats her hand lightly.

"That is why I will be running with you." Japlo beams as she makes this announcement.

I catch my words this time before they rush out of me, but Gracie knows what I am thinking.

"I will lead Japlo during the race. I have seen guides for blind runners in many races, and Japlo and I have been running together this way for several months. Even in the crowds, she is very good at following the slightest shift in movement."

Japlo's smile grows wider.

"You can run with us too," she says, "but I know you like to go fast, and I will be slow, certainly. Perhaps you could run with someone else? Someone who also needs a guide, but who is much faster than I?"

"Who?" I ask.

"My daughter, Yeni, would like to run. She says that she wants to run with friends again; that the women we were with in Liberia were our friends, and she misses them."

Japlo shakes her head slightly. "See, she remembers that pain as running with friends. She is right, of course. Friends lift you up through the painful moments in your life. She says that she wants to run with friends." Japlo smiles as she repeats herself.

"I will be happy to run with Yeni," I answer. "Everyone needs friends, right?"

Gracie lifts her glass of water in a toast. "To my friends!"

As we clink glasses together, a loud ringing elevates our cheer. Japlo reaches for her purse. "Oh, that's Yeni now! I will tell her she has a partner!"

She pulls out her phone and answers, "Yeni, love, hello! I have great news for you!"

She places her phone on the table and directs Gracie. "Can you put it on speaker phone?"

As the sound is amplified to all of us, we can hear Yeni's insistent "Ma! Ma! Ma!"

She sounds like a typical impatient teenager. But Japlo's face grows serious suddenly. "What's wrong, baby? Are you okay?" Japlo bumps the table as her mom-instincts take over. And now I can hear the choke in Yeni's voice, the one that sounds like tears being kept under control.

"Ma! Uncle Jahn is here with a letter. From Da." Japlo falls back into her seat. "Oh, Ma! He's alive! He's alive and he is on his way here!"

Japlo might not be able to see out those dark brown eyes of hers, but she is looking at something in the back of her mind that causes a crashing of pain and love to pour down her cheeks. Gracie has wrapped her arms around her, and she too, is crying the quiet kind of tears that prove that our greatest joys and deepest despairs are never ours to bear alone.

"Anna, I'm going to take Japlo home, okay?" Gracie is already pulling her sweater on and packing up Japlo's purse. She digs through her own wallet for money.

"Of course!" I answer, waving her credit card away from me. "I've got all this. How much can a few glasses of water and a loaf of bread cost?"

They are a few steps away already before Japlo stops and turns back to me.

"Will you come with us? Please? I would like my friends with me now, especially."

Her hand reaches blindly out to me.

So I reach back, and we all pile into the closest cab that will take us to Japlo's tiny apartment, to meet her brother-in-law, Jahn, to hear again that Tambo, her husband whom she had feared dead for so many years, has in fact been searching for her, in their homeland, the war-torn, blood-soaked and battered land of Liberia. And he will be on a plane by the end of the week, headed for Chicago.

Jahn looks deep into Japlo's unseeing eyes. He holds her hands in his.

"Japlo, there's one more thing. He is not coming alone. After the peace talks, once the Rebels lost their leader, the packs of young soldiers turned into gangs of hateful and angry young men. He found Saa with one of these gangs. He has Saa with him --"

Her hands fly to her cheeks, and tears flow again. "My son? My son! He has rescued Saa?"

Yeni and Gracie join her tears and hugs and laughter.

But Jahn is hard and serious. There is no joy in him, and that seems weird to me.

"Japlo -- he is not the same boy he was years ago. You should know that. He has done some pretty terrible things --"

Japlo shoots through his warning with a fierceness I have never seen.

"I know the things he has done. I lived them myself. Not from Saa, but from the sons of many other women. I know the poison that filled them and the cruelty that invaded their minds.

"Do you think I love him less because of that? No!" She slams her hands down into her lap. "Does it break my heart more? Yes. And this is what a mother does. She holds the broken pieces of her heart, and the broken hearts of her children, and she keeps those broken pieces, so that when it is time, they may be put back together."

Her hand is now a fist, and I can see the pieces of her heart, and Yeni's and Saa's, along with little bits of my own, held in that tiny dark fist of hers.

Then opening her fist, she slaps that hand, hard, against her own chest.

"Well, Jahn, it is our time now."

I believe her.

# 8  EVA

"Tell me what you are thinking. "

I could only shake my head and shrug and give as soft a smile as possible. Benjamin was trying so hard to be patient and understanding, but I have never known how to answer that request.

"Nothing. Really."

He puts his hands on his knees and looks at the floor, sighing deeply. I am a petulant child of thirty-one years. Instead of climbing out of bed I pull the sheets over my head and let the sound of my own breath drown out the buzz of his complaints.

I am not living up to the life I had inadvertently promised to give him. I was supposed to be smart and dashing, cute and entertaining, motherly and neat. I am none of those things. I can act like that, but I am not and never will be any of those things.

"Let's go," he says, pulling at the edge of the sheet. "It's almost nine. They'll be here soon. And I need to leave for my interview."

"They" are his sister and brother-in-law. Michelle is only eleven months older than Ben, but has achieved twice as much as he has, according to their mother. And this is always said with a slow wag of her head and a sad look in my direction.

I get up, so that I can help Michelle plan her next great achievement. But once Ben closes the door, I fall back onto the pillows for one more snooze.

Michelle will be turning thirty-five next March, so she is working even more diligently to complete her to-do list. Apparently turning thirty-five is some sort of finish line or a check-point. So far she has successfully attained a law degree from Harvard, a husband from MIT, a beach house along the lakefront, and a partnership in one of Chicago's largest firms.

She has also traveled around the world twice, once solo, the second time in love. That was when she returned with a ring on her finger and a complete schedule of engagement parties, showers, receptions, and of course, a rough draft of the Big Day itself. At the time I was nursing our youngest child, Maddie, Jake was still being potty trained at three years old, and seven-year-old Katie was learning to read. I felt like one of the seven dwarves – sleepy, achy, or leaky – at any given time. It was tough to get into the whole drama of the wedding itself, since I remembered mine as a quick call to the local VFW hall, and a discreetly altered dress being the highlight of the nuptial planning.

Michelle has tried to be my friend for the past thirteen years. She has called me with every exciting piece of news she had to share. Her promotions, her vacations, her romance and her life celebrations were all exciting news, and I am lucky that she wanted to share that news with me.

"Oh Eva, isn't it great?" She'd always close with the same request for agreement.

"Yeah, it sure is." I wanted to be happy for her. I really did. And I can be a very agreeable person when called upon to do so.

So it's not surprising that I agreed that a birthday party-adventure outing would also be "great". And it would also be great if I could help her plan the exciting event and it would also be so great if I could make sure everyone came to the spectacular event.

Everyone.

Last summer, Michelle sat at her kitchen table, a bowl of oranges deliberately placed and balancing the otherwise neutral scheme of colors around her. Her sprawling suburban colonial feels like a monolith to me, with its high ceilings, wide doorways, and space -- lots of wide-open space, enough to get lost if you wanted, I suppose. Wooden cabinets and floor, granite counter top and sink, copper utensils. Nothing superfluous or misplaced. The bowl of oranges seems larger than it is, like a ball of fire contained, controlled, subdued. Michelle had tapped her pencil lightly against the pad of paper in front of her. Her initials are scrolled on each page, top left, MJM. She had a list of items to accomplish, a date by which each should be started and another for its date of completion. Of course, PDAs and online calendars were created for just this task. Michelle will certainly use these tools, but she always begins with a pad of paper and a pencil. This is a good thing because I, on the other hand, do not have the same kinds of hi-tech organizers she has, so I will be given the piece of paper after Michelle has transferred it all.

We tried to decide what type of adventure outing to book. Hmmm...that's a tricky one.

Should we go somewhere warm and exotic, perhaps engage in scuba diving and cave exploration? Or should we stay local and try a ski excursion? Perhaps a desert camping and horseback riding trip to the southwest?

I might as well have been planning a trip to the tooth fairy. Our family vacations are more along the line of camping and mosquito repellent. Unfamiliar climates and exotic environments has never been a choice in my life, so I have very little feedback to give. Aside from financial concerns, which would remain cloaked in subtleties and evasive word-play.

"I think everyone will want to go somewhere warm in March, don't you?" she asks. Everyone has become a code name. It's like the Bill Cosby routine where as a child he thinks his name is Goddammit because that is all his father ever calls him. So we are planning this party for Everyone. This way neither of us has to say what we actually want or don't want.

"Well, do you think Everyone can afford to go to the tropics for ten days? That's a pretty long time for Everyone to be gone."

I pretended that Everyone does not include my family. I also pretended to ignore the fact that length of time gone equates to money spent in the form of an increasing credit balance. A balance that is spinning out of control recently.

"Besides," I continue, "I don't know if the kids can miss that much school."

"Oh, ten days is nothing! It'll be a great learning experience for the kids and you're lucky -- you don't have to worry about taking off from work or anything like that."

No, of course not. My work goes with me everywhere I go, twenty-four hours a day. I am so lucky. Too bad the pay sucks.

But to Michelle I nodded my head vigorously, confirming the flexibility I have in being a full time stay-at-home mom.

"And, if we book through Tom's company we can get a great discount for everyone. That way we can travel together the whole time, too! Isn't that great?"

You know what I said.

Then it was fall, and all three of the kids were in school. Last year, Maddie had been in morning kindergarten, but those few hours didn't really give me much time to do anything, so I'd either just go home and nap a little, or stay at school and nap in my car. I don't know why I am so tired all the time, but I am, and it seems to annoy people, especially Michelle.

But now, I will be free of all motherly duties from eight in the morning until four o'clock in the afternoon, and Michelle is dying to know what I will do with all that free time.

I've been wondering the same thing.

The phone rings and when I answer I try to shake the sleep from my voice, but she can hear it anyway. Or maybe she has just come to expect it.

"Eva, it's after ten o'clock! What's wrong?"

"Nothing, just tired," I answer, not even trying to deny that I was sleeping anymore.

"Well, it's a good thing I couldn't come over, after all. Did you even remember? Oh, never mind that now! Just listen. Now that Maddie is in school all day, it's time for you to get out here in the real world. And I have a great opportunity for you!"

"Mm-hmm," I mumble.

"Our office is looking to hire someone to help out during the day. I told them you could do it! It'll be great, won't it?"

I shoot up to sitting, panic pounding its way into my chest. I imagine myself in a pinstripe pantsuit, my hair in a bun, and an intimidating lift to my eyebrow.

"You said what? Michelle, I don't know a thing about law!"

She snorts. "Oh, Eva, I know that! It's not a law position. It's in the cafe on the first floor. You would just need to pump some coffee and wrap a few bagels. Very low pressure. I'm sure you can handle it."

I slump back into my pillow. "That is just what I need," I droll sarcastically.

Michelle sighs impatiently. "Well then, what are you going to do? You have to do something with your time. Don't take this the wrong way, but you don't want to make Benjamin carry the whole load for you guys forever, do you?"

I can feel the exhaustion creeping back into me as she finishes her well-intentioned assault. For a few seconds our breathing is the only sound over the phone line.

"Well, I guess you'll figure it out. I just don't know what I'd do if I had all that time to myself!" she exclaimed. "So, let's reschedule the birthday meeting, ok? Ok."

She hangs up, having answered for me, and I slide back under the blankets.

At night, Benjamin helps Katie with her homework while I get Jake and Maddie bathed and ready for bed. Maddie screams as I brush out the tangles in her hair. I leave her sobbing and only half-detangled to check on Jake. His pajama bottoms are in a heap on the floor and his pajama shirt is twisted over his face, his arms swinging wildly as he tries to pull it over his still-damp skin. He is growing long and skinny, but his tummy is round and boyish. I reach for the neck of the shirt, to guide his head through.

"I'll help you," I say. Surprised, he screeches that he is naked, mom! and demands that I leave the room immediately.

I stop in Katie's doorway and see Benjamin snoring on her bed as she finishes her homework, sitting cross-legged on the floor. She is so intent that she doesn't notice me at all.

I resist the urge to wake Ben, to remind him that we are supposed to be doing this together. Instead I return to Maddie, her tears, and the curls she hates so much. Eventually she and Jake are tucked in and drifting to sleep, so I, too, retreat to my own bed.

Katie must have finally finished her homework around midnight, because that is when Benjamin stumbles into our bed. Barely awake, he pulls me close to him, spooning himself around me. I am starting to drift back to sleep when I feel him grow hard against my legs. His hand shifts down from my waist until the familiar prodding and searching of fingers prepares me for his entry. As he rolls on top of me he whispers, "Is this okay?" I'm not sure what he means by that. Is he asking my permission, or if my diaphragm is in place, or for an evaluation of his foreplay? In any case, I am lying when I say, "Oh, yes."

We have joked about our sex life frequently, just like most parents of young children do. We have learned to be quick and quiet. We have stared innocently into the faces of our sleepy toddlers as they ask for a glass of water while "Daddy is rubbing Mommy's back". I guess, as with anything, the longer you do something the easier it is to keep doing. And so sex, when we have it, is a momentary delay in my sleep schedule and an effortless release of Benjamin's stress.

Quick, quiet, a burst of sweat over Benjamin's back and a trickle of semen down my leg. In five minutes we have moved to opposite sides of the wet spot on the bed.

So now it is March 5th and I am as deep into my winter depression as I can get, and buried under mountains of flannel and fake goose down comforters. As the years have gone by my winter depression, clinically referred to as SAD -- not that I have ever been clinically diagnosed-- has expanded to include bits of autumn and quite a few weeks of spring as well. I may have additional reason to be SAD, but I prefer not to think about it. Ben has packed our suitcases and he is shouting to Maddie and Jake reminders of underwear, deodorant and swimsuits.

Katie does not need reminders. She is packed and perched on the couch in the living room, ready to go. That girl has been early since the day she was born. Prematurely, of course. Even then she stared right at me with a plan in her eyes. I think that that is what scared me most at the time. Not my age, my lack of experience, lack of support, lack of money. No. It was this child, this newborn, who fell into my eyes with such high expectations of me, of what should be, and I felt that she had a better understanding of our new life than I did. It is still that way.

When I became a mother I was too young to know the depth of love that is yanked from your heart and implanted into every move that your infant child makes. I also did not know that the umbilical cord is simply a symbol of this emotional yoke and is certainly not just clipped, sealed, and dried. No, the cutting of the cord is like pruning a bush that simply creates multiple off-shoots, rooting itself into the child's emotional, physical, spiritual, educational, social, financial dramas for the rest of her life.

I kick the covers off and stare out the window. It is cold, dim, and dismal, although it's already nine o'clock. I am going on a vacation to Ixtapa, the land of sun and surf and margaritas and all I want to do is crawl back into bed. It sounds crazy, but there is so much more to this vacation than that. This is not like one of the Griswold's vacations, where we will play tourist and hug warmly when we meet people we think are our relatives.

This is a vacation of triumph and there is no room on that podium for me.

Maddie pounces on the bed, and I pull the covers back over my head, pretending to play, hoping she'll believe it too. No such luck. She stares at me.

"Mommy, when you gonna get up, huh? Get up! Get up!"

"Oh, I'm up, I'm up," I announce. I drag her off the bed and onto my back, piggy-back style, and we gallop into the bathroom. She laughs and pulls on my hair to direct me around the room. She is seven years old, still young enough to have fun bouncing around like this, but she is getting big, too, so I lower her to the floor and tell her to wait for me in the kitchen.

She gives me a giant hug around my tummy and starts to skip out the door. Instead, her foot slips and in no time she has flipped into the air and onto her back. And then I feel the blood--not her blood, but mine-- running down my legs as I cramp up into a ball beside her. She is starting to cry, more from surprise than pain, but when she sees the bright red puddle growing bigger, she screams hysterically. "Daddy! Mommy! Daddy! What happened? Huh? Huh? Daddy!"

Benjamin pokes his head in to the bathroom, and when he sees the mess-- the horrible mess-- he starts to panic.

"Oh my god! Eva? Maddie? What happened?" He searches Maddie for the source of all that blood, but it is mine, and it takes him a minute to figure out that no one is injured. Technically.

He wants to call an ambulance, but I ask him not to. Maddie is sobbing in Benjamin's arms, staring at the red floor.

"My god, Eva, this is not normal, is it?" Although we have been together for fifteen years, and I have had three babies and numerous menstrual periods, and he knows damn well this is not normal, he has no choice but to believe me when I say, "Well, it's not abnormal. I'll be okay."

As the pain unclenches its grip, I begin to move to the shower, throwing a dark towel over the stain on the floor.

Is this normal? I don't know. I know I am supposed to have some heavy bleeding. Some cramping. I figure that is supposed to be normal.

But then again, I have never had an abortion before.

I let the water become hotter as it pours down my back, drawing beads of sweat from my skin and rinsing the smell of death off of me. But the blood is still a dark river swirling toward the shower drain and I stare at it, waiting for it to lighten and eventually fade. It doesn't.

The bathroom door suddenly swings open, smashing into the wall and Michelle flings the shower curtain to the side as she gasps, seeing the blood pouring from my crotch. Benjamin stands behind her, quiet. He looks small and helpless, as if he is trying to fade into the background. He shrugs his shoulders at me, a sort of apology, I guess. I can't blame him — at least not for asking for her help. I feel thrown into the fire, naked.

"Eva! What's wrong?" Michelle gasps. "This is not normal! Are you all right?" She is staring at my legs, so it is hard to answer her. I want to turn off the water and wrap up in a towel but the bleeding won't stop. I reach for the faucet as my uterus clenches tighter and tighter into a knot. Michelle is shouting commands, but I can't understand any of it. Waves of nausea and pain shove their way into my whole body. I am trying to remember what the doctor had said, how much bleeding I might have, but the pain stabs into me and I contract into a ball on the shower floor and squeeze my eyes shut.

When I open them again Michelle is wrapping a towel around my body as Benjamin leads a team of paramedics into the bathroom. Despite my protests, they strap me onto a cot, rolling me out the door of my house with an IV in my arm and bags of both clear liquid and dark red blood resting on my chest. The paramedic has wrapped a blood pressure sleeve around my arm and he is pumping away every few minutes. I can hear Jake crying in the living room as Benjamin calls over and over to him that Mommy is okay, she just fell down. His eyes meet mine when he says that, and I turn away. Maddie is clinging to Katie, her face buried in Katie's long curly hair. And Katie just stands in the doorway, staring impassively through me. I am certain that she knows. Michelle pulls the girls back into the house, and I think she shakes her head at me, one of those tiny little reminders that I messed up. Again.

Benjamin leans over me as I am folded into the ambulance, covering me with his hesitant hugs and kisses.

"You'll be okay, sweetie," he whispers to me. "I'm going to follow you in the car. I'll be right behind you. You'll be okay," he reassures me again.

The ambulance doors close and I am left alone with the Paramedic who picks up a clipboard with his plastic-glove hands and starts writing. Occasionally he checks his watch or my heart rate or the levels of fluid, then jots down his findings. When he finally talks to me I am nearly asleep.

"Ma'am," he says, "what was the date of your last menstrual cycle?"

The ambulance has turned off the siren and pulled into the hospital parking lot.

"December thirteenth." I have counted back from that day so many times it is carved into my mind.

"That's over ten weeks. Is that typical for you?"

The driver puts the vehicle in park and I can hear him talking on a CB radio, announcing our arrival.

I shake my head, but that just makes me dizzy. I lean over to the side, afraid I am going to throw up. The ambulance doors are flung open and I see Benjamin just steps away, painfully worried, reaching toward me.

The paramedic asks, "Is it possible you were pregnant?"

And without thinking I tell him the truth.

"Yes. Yes, I was. But not anymore."

Benjamin freezes, his eyebrows pull toward each other as he tries to understand the meaning of what I just said. I want to explain, but there is no good explanation.

I am taken in to the emergency room and I become aware of other people in the midst of their own physical and emotional crises. Between screams, sobs, and angry outbursts, the ER staff leaps from one curtain to another. I can hear a woman next to me loudly complaining about her heart attack. I don't know how she could be so loud and forceful if she was having a heart attack, but I figure her chances of recovery are excellent.

My bleeding has subsided a little, but it is apparent I need help to stop it completely. A young short blond woman with round metal frame glasses sits at my feet and carefully slides a speculum inside me to get a closer look at the damage. Dr. Theim is a resident in her third year and she is being assisted by one of the gynecologists on staff here at Loyola. Benjamin sits with me during the whole procedure, his arms folded across his chest. His words of comfort have stopped and he directs his questions to the doctor, not me.

"What happened to her? How far along is she?"

Dr. Theim looks at me, then at my chart, then back to me, which confuses Benjamin even more. He begins again.

"How long has she been pregnant? Is she going to," he lowers his voice, away from me, "—is she going to lose it? I mean, lose the baby?"

She looks at me silently before giving a slight nod.

"I need to finish this procedure, Mr. Flanagan. Once I do, you and your wife can talk about it and I will be happy to explain Eva's -- Mrs. Flanagan's -- prognosis."

"If that's what you'd like," she adds, looking at me.

Benjamin rubs his hands against his thighs impatiently. I stare at the ceiling as Dr. Theim pokes and scrapes and wipes. I try to remind myself why I did this, why I am here. It is so hard to see Ben this confused, struggling to understand. But how can he ever understand? This wasn't his body or his decision. How can he understand the chasm that lies between the joy of motherhood and the sinking time-trap that it creates? That it is possible to love your child infinitely and yet panic at the prospect of doing it all over again?  How can he know that my decision was as much protective as it was selfish?

"Okay, Eva, looks like we got the bleeding under control.  The, um, procedure was text-book perfect, but you most likely exerted yourself too abruptly.  It can take as long as four weeks to feel completely back to normal after something like this.  You'll be a little weak for a day or two, and you should certainly take it easy, but you should move around a little too.  Maybe a nice walk, to keep the blood from pooling up or causing any clots.  And no lifting anything more than a couple pounds for at least a week. No piggie-back rides for the kids!" She grins at us uncomfortably.

Ben's eyes penetrate me accusingly at the word *procedure* and I can see how removed he feels from this whole conversation.

I look away from him as Dr. Theim pats my shoulder. "Do you want me to send someone in who you can talk to about... your feelings?"

"Maybe she could start by talking to me," Benjamin snarls.

I glare at him, but answer Dr. Theim. "I'm fine. Just tired is all."

"Well, all right then.  Just remember what I said, and you'll be good as new in no time."

She squeezes my hand  on her way out the door.

Benjamin, shocked, stares at me before hurling his confusion at me. "Eva, what's going on? I'm-- I'm lost!  Did I miss something?  Did you forget to tell me something?  Like the fact that you were pregnant!" He spits the words at me.

I can feel him standing close to me, but a giant wall pushes us apart.

He presses his hands into his eyes and takes a deep breath. Painfully he whispers, "Please, give me something.  What happened? What did you do?"

I am crying now, a steady stream of silent tears. I want to tell him, but my words, like so many others in my life, twist themselves together into a choking knot in my throat.  Instead a slow-burning resentment settles in to my heart.  I say nothing but turn away from him, my only means of communication, and he understands that well enough. It is too easy for him to guess the truth, given my bleeding, my crying, my shame. But he refuses to say it as well. He drags his fingers through his hair and tilts his face toward the ceiling, as if he is listening to a silent conversation from above.

Finally, distantly, he speaks.

"I don't understand this, Eva. I don't understand you. What is it that you need from me, that I am not doing? What do you need me to say, that I am not saying? Goddammit, Eva! You don't talk to me; you don't touch me! I feel like I'm forcing myself on you when we do have sex, and then-- and then-- well-- this!" His voice is controlled in volume but raging in its directness. "How could you not tell me? Why won't you talk to me? Why? Why?"

I pull deeper into my self-created shell until the things I see around me are like a TV scene-- cold, but familiar. My eyes burn, but I have stopped crying and my body feels rigid and heavy, like I am a sinking weight. I am sinking. And it feels like a deep, long journey down into a miserable frigid existence.

His breath shakes the silence from the room, and he waits for my response in the same exasperated manner that he has waited for me to get my shit together for the past ten years. And as minutes crawl forward, in silence, his waiting turns to resignation.

A tiny bell chimes from his pocket. He glances at his cell phone and then placidly interjects what should be an easy question to answer.

"Michelle said she can take the kids to the airport. They will leave in an hour. What should I tell her?"

I don't know what he should tell her. A good mother would not send her children away without her. A good mother would not keep her children trapped in Chicago, either. Of course, a good mother wouldn't be here in the first place. I don't know what I should tell him.

My response is little more than a shrug.

Dr. Theim pokes her head into the room and sensing the dull tension, asks if she can answer any questions.

Benjamin turns away from me. "I'm waiting for Eva to do that," he says. With his back to me, he continues, "I am sending the kids with Michelle. I'll take a later flight. I think-- I think it would be better, Eva, if you stayed home." He adds, unconvincingly, "To rest."

His jaw tightens, then to Dr. Theim he mumbles, "I'll be getting some coffee. Let me know when she's ready to go."

There are different types of silence. Sometimes silence is calm and peaceful, rocking you to sleep with its rhythmic breath. Sometimes it is electrified by anticipation, the waiting, hoping, wondering. And sometimes, like today, it screams at you in a way that never stops, more than any screaming baby could. That kind of silence holds the pain and anger and resentment of years in a bubble of space around you, so that even if you move, the screaming silence moves with you.

The drive home from the hospital is consumed by denials and avoidance. Benjamin drops me off at home, where I crawl back into bed, as he goes to the grocery store and the pharmacy to get the pain killers and antibiotics I was prescribed. We have little food in the house, since we were planning to be gone for ten days, so he buys fruit and salads and frozen pizza and orange juice to keep me fed for a few days. All the while, we pretend these are the doctor's orders, as he tells Michelle and the kids who are waiting at the airport. Creating a new script for this forced and imaginary life of mine. He arranges my medications, my cell phone, the house keys, and a list of contact numbers on the table beside my bed. He says he will call when he gets to Mexico.

This is his way of making sure I am taken care of while he leaves me.

"I'll call you from the airport," he says, letting his fingers brush across the top of my head when he says good-bye. He pauses, "Eva? What the hell made you decide to..to...? Eva?"

But I pretend to be asleep. The taxi's headlights gleam through the bedroom window.

"Never mind," he mutters, clicking the door closed.

I hear him greet the driver and then shut the car door. The headlights turn away, fade down the street and are gone.

In one sweep of my arm, I send the medicine, phone, keys crashing to the floor.

How does someone make a decision like this? I'm sure it's different for every woman, every couple, but I blame Thanksgiving.

I had a turkey defrosting in the kitchen sink. It was soaking in tepid water, although Michelle says that is how people get salmonella. I assured her it was only soaking for an hour to give it a head start. The next day Benjamin's parents, Michelle, and her husband Thomas would be joining us for Thanksgiving dinner. They were all pitching in — Michelle bringing a salad and Benjamin's mom baking a pumpkin pie. The rest was up to me.

The T.V. was blaring a constant barrage of commercials laced with holiday music and clips of happy children, proud parents, and piles of presents. Katie has learned to separate our family from those on the T.V., but Jake and Maddie are still suckers for every hundred dollar toy they see.

"Mom, I want that!"

"Mom, tell Santa to bring me that!"

"Mom, do you think I've been good enough to get that?"

It's that last question that gets me the most. How do I tell my perfectly wonderful children that no, they have not been good enough for that, whatever it may be? So don't ask and don't expect it. Because Santa doesn't get these things for free.

I lay down on the couch to rest while the turkey soaked and the kids drooled over remote control airplanes and American Girl dolls. I closed my eyes, but continued to see a swirl of pleading faces and scornful scowls of disappointment. I felt something pressing on my chest and tried to push it away but when I opened my eyes, there was nothing there. The pressure was from my own ribs, like a giant stone rolling over me, crushing my heart and squeezing the air out of my lungs. For some reason I felt hidden and safe.

And then Maddie pounced on me, and the stone is gone, replaced by her little hands slapping against my chest, her knees digging into my stomach.

"Daddy's home! Daddy's home!" she squealed, then climbed off of me and into Ben's arms.

"Hey, you're home early," I said, pulling myself up to sitting. "Early Thanksgiving holiday?"

Ben just shook his head and pointed to the kitchen. I followed him.

"What's wrong? Are you sick?"

"Market-Co closed their doors today. Called us in to the conference room, all fifty of us smashed in there, and said, 'Thanks for working for us but we are closing up shop and filing for bankruptcy this afternoon. Grab your stuff and go.' No discussion, no good-bye. It was like the place was on fire and everyone just wanted to get out of there."

My stomach dropped. The turkey seemed to grow larger and larger in the sink, as I pictured it stuffed with money that we already didn't have. Pale and shaking, Ben pulled his wallet out of his pocket and opened it. He pulled out three twenties and two five dollar bills.

"Here," he said. "use this for any more Christmas gifts you need to get the kids. I don't know if there will be any more."

I wrapped my arms around him. "It'll be okay," I whispered. But Ben pushed me away, numbly.

"Yeah. Just do me a favor, okay? Don't tell my family. Even Michelle. I don't think I could handle any more pity from them, you know what I mean?"

Do I know? Oh, yes, Benjamin dear, I know very well what you mean.

That was over a year ago. A family can build up a lot of debt in one year. A family can build up a big pile of lies in that time, too.

The house is empty for the third day, and the silence has become deafening. How many days have I buried my head beneath the blankets to drown out their voices? And today I cannot bury deep enough to make their silence go away.

The bleeding is nearly gone, but I remember the doctor's advice to move around a little. Advice I have so far ignored.

I pull myself out of bed, coaching myself through each movement.

Walking into the bathroom, I see myself in the mirror for the first time since they all left. My hair is tangled and clings to my face in grimy sweat-soaked strands. I carefully unravel wads of hair from around a rubber band that holds sections of a former ponytail. The golden-blond hair of my youth has become dull and grayish. My skin is pale and smooth, sprinkled with freckles, with the tiniest of lines peeking from the corners of my eyes.

It is my eyes that expose the pain nestled deep inside me. My eyes are empty and distant and critical.

I feel like I am looking at a stranger, and I am afraid of her. I turn away from the mirror. I need some air. And a soda.

I peel off the clothes I have been sleeping in these three days and pull on a clean turtleneck, a sweatshirt, a thin pair of leggings, and my gym shoes. I grab a hat and mittens as I walk out the door, letting it close behind me. Too late, I realize that the keys are still on the floor in the bedroom and I am locked out. I don't know what the temperature is, but I can see my breath, and my legs are hit by a wall of cold air. I have seriously under-dressed. I want to get back into my house, into my bed, but despite my repeated jiggling of the doorknob, I am stuck outside. Rather than stand here and freeze, I decide to walk to the police station a few blocks away so that they can help me break in to my own house. I take a few steps, and my feet land like blocks of ice, sending a jolt up my spine and into my jaw. To soften the impact a bit I roll onto my toes, avoiding my heels, and I find that this is much gentler, so I keep moving, almost jogging, this way.

I am pretty sure the last time I ran at all was in high school PE class. And even then, I just remember walking around the track, gossiping about all the cool girls, the slutty girls, the stupid girls, the ugly girls until Miss Reymer blew her whistle at us to start running. We would move into a snail speed jog until we rounded the next curve, and then fall back into our trash-talking stroll.

So today, my body is taken off-guard by this new momentum, and it follows the easy jogging cooperatively. I am getting warmer as I get to the end of the second block, and I take off my mittens. The cold air feels good, so I take off my hat as well, and the cold permeates my hair, my neck, my scalp. I breathe deeply, the cold filling my lungs, too. For a moment, I feel more awake than I have in months.

Cold air has a different sound to it. It carries tiny noises much further than in warm or humid air. It is easy to hear a door click shut, a piece of mail being opened, or a quiet good-bye from down the block. The sound of my feet tip-toe jogging down the street thunderously announces my presence and I am both embarrassed and pleased by this.

I turn the corner onto Clark Street and am hit with a blast of wind that sucks the breath right out of me. I feel like I have been slapped across the face by this bitter cold air and I am defeated. I try to return to a walk. I can see the police station at the next block and I crave its warmth. I lean against a garbage can on the side of the road instead.

I start to whimper. Over and over again, letting a soft whining sigh escape my throat. And then from behind me I hear a quiet but harsh voice.

"What is the matter? What are you stopping for?"

I turn around to see a petite middle-aged woman behind me. She is a runner, without a doubt. She has a wide headband across her ears and short platinum-colored hair. She wears a lightweight green half-zipper top and tight black ankle pants -- the classic outfit of "real" runners. Her cheeks are pink, from the cold air and the warm blood, and she bounces impatiently behind me, instead of galloping on past.

"What do you mean?" I ask her. Then, realizing she thinks I was out running on purpose, I admit, "Oh, I'm not a runner."

She just stares at me, until I feel a need to explain more.

"You don't understand. I can't do any more. It's too cold and I'm not dressed for this weather. It hurts. I'm only going to the police station. Besides," I repeat myself, "I am not even a runner."

"Oh for goodness sake! You just started a half-mile back and you have this many problems already? Stop whining," she scolds. "A little discomfort is good for you anyway."

I am stunned. Discomfort?

"What-- ? How do you know what's good for me, or how many problems I have? You have no idea. None!" I am pissed now. "Who the hell are you? Just keep running, and mind your own business."

I knew runners were a crazy bunch of people.

"Okay sweetheart, but just so you know," and she steps really close, looking deep into my eyes, and waving her finger in my face, "all those problems you have, are just gonna follow you back home. It's probably best to keep them moving, wear them out a little, don't you think?"

And then she taps her wrist, sending a little beep into the crisp air, and bounces away.

The police station is warm and busy and I feel temporarily relaxed until the clerk behind the desk, a bored-looking young man, asks me what I need.

What do I need? What do I need?

"Um, I need-- I accidentally locked myself out of my house. I need to get back in my house."

The clerk hands me some paperwork to fill out. "Got any ID?"

"Not with me. I got locked out -- it's inside my house."

"Anyone we can call to verify?"

"My husband. But he's in Mexico for another week."

"Ok, ma'am. We'll see what we can do." He taps three keys on the phone in front of him. "Sergeant Meade, sir?"

I cannot hear the rest of his conversation, but when he turns back to me he gives me a thumbs up. "Won't be able to actually break in to your house -- too much liability with that -- but maybe we can help you find a way in."

That's good enough for me. The clerk scans me from head to toe and gives a little nod. "Out running, huh? You're one of those die-hard runners, huh?"

I'm surprised by his assumption. "No. Well, not really. I mean I jogged a few blocks to get over here, but I was not out running. I'm not a runner, you know."

"Hmm, you look like one." I tilt my head, puzzled and a little spooked. Did he see my conversation with the crazy lady?

He explains himself. "You know...you have that skinny-strong look about you. You walk like a runner too. Light and on your toes." He laughs a little. "You should try it. Maybe it's your hidden talent!"

His laugh calms me and I laugh a little in reply. "Maybe."

A door opens and a beer-bellied police officer waddles from the back of the station to the desk I am standing at. He has tufts of gray hair curling out from under his officer's cap, and his waddle seems to be partly caused by an arthritic limp. He looks like he should be retired already, bouncing grandkids on his knees or fishing off a pier somewhere.

He smiles at the clerk and then to me. "Is this the little lady who needs some help breaking in to her house? Maybe we should get one of the guys from behind the bars to help her with that!" His jovial greeting receives a chuckle from everyone in the room. Including me.

Getting back in was not as difficult as I thought it would be. In fact, I was surprised to learn just how easy it is to wiggle open our first floor kitchen window. After showing my ID, and promising to buy a window safety lock for all of the first floor windows, and to leave an extra key with a neighbor, I thank Sergeant Meade and close and lock the door behind him as he leaves.

Instinctively, I walk into the bedroom, but before I fall back into bed, I catch a glimpse of myself in the mirror hanging on the back of the door. The sweatshirt is loose on me and I almost disappear in its thickness. My legs are skinny, for sure, but I can also see the rounded shape of my hamstrings and smaller, but defined calf muscles too. I guess years of lifting babies, and then heavier and heavier toddlers, has kept some of my muscles taut and strong. I pull the hat back onto my head and lift my chest high, as if I am running through the gray, wintery streets of Chicago. This is what that crazy lady saw. This is what the police clerk saw, too.

I watch myself in the mirror as I imitate a runner's motions. I remember the freshness of the cold air I breathed in earlier this afternoon and how it first invigorated me, and then how it crushed me.  Or rather, how I let it crush me.

I decide to try it again tomorrow.  With warmer clothes.

# 9  GRACIE

Daylight seems to last forever in June. The last of my junior year final exams was over on a Tuesday, and the next day I awoke to an early sunrise, chirping birds, and the hush of morning pouring through the bedroom window. I shared this room with my sisters who groaned as I crept around the room picking up shorts and t-shirts and sneakers. As much as I tried to be quiet, my stumbling and bumping brought tired and frustrated gasps from the two of them.

Summer mornings are always layers of color and coolness, with the ground layer all shimmery and chilly with last night's dew pinpointed on the blades of grass and crushed stones of cement. Bursts of perfume flow from waves of flowers that either reach up from the stems of hyacinth or bend low from the branches of crabapple trees. Streaks of black asphalt and grey steel create an endless arrow, begging to be followed. A brilliant blue sky wraps around the city and from the east a flicker of sunlight presses its heat into the morning. The first run of summer vacation held an anticipation that was undeniably delicious. I squinted my eyes against its intensity, shook out my legs and dipping my head slightly, fell into the rhythm of the run.

Running alone, in the morning, this morning, was new, however. I guess I always felt that each run was its own creation. The street might be the same, but the weather, the people, the pace, the conversation, the feelings-- yes, especially the feelings -- were never the same. My steps felt hollow without my father's there to pace me. But he had left for work early, and I was too impatient to wait for him to return. I figured I would just run again once he got home. But he had different plans that summer, plans that changed my life for good.

I fell into an easy pace, my breath calm but my eyes vigilant, on the watch for cars pulling in or out of driveways and parking lots. Crossing the street meant waiting for all the left turns to turn, then all the right turns to turn, then all last minute left turns to turn. When I ran with the team, or even with my dad, it seemed there were fewer cars turning.

I was jogging in place, waiting for a space to open up, when a red and white Camaro pulled along side me, stopping at the light. A pretty redhead woman was driving the car and she kept her gaze straight ahead. The passenger rolled his window down and turned his head slowly to look at me. He had thick side burns, a fat mustache, and long tangled dark blond hair, like he had been out in the wind for hours. He stared for a long time at my shoes, then up my legs, then to my chest.

Running alone suddenly felt like a huge mistake. I was ready to sprint back home when he murmured in a slow dreamy voice, "Cool man. Very cool." He nodded his head at my chest again. I looked down. I was wearing my dad's Harvard track team shirt. I'd worn it so many times that the print barely showed on the shirt. It was loose, but it felt good for running, and besides, it was my favorite shirt.

"You mean this?" I pointed to the barely legible "Harvard" on the shirt.

He nodded. "Yep. Just came from Boston ourselves, with fancy new law degrees. We'll be rich and corrupt in no time, right Penny?" He gave a cynical snort.

The woman next to him half-smiled, but shook her head and patted his leg. "You bet, babe."

"But it is very cool to see they are finally getting the message. I'm a supporter of Women's Lib, right, babe?" he turned back to Penny.

"Oh, this is my dad's," I explained. "I don't really know about any message, but my dad was one of the best distance runners Harvard ever had! He got a scholarship and everything!" My pride in my dad swelled.

"Hey, that's real cool, princess. I'm sure he is awesome. How about you? Got any scholarships coming your way? Because Harvard ain't cheap!"

I had never really thought about college or scholarships or running beyond high school. But I didn't want to appear ignorant so I answered as truthfully as I could. "I'm pretty sure I will. I mean I am pretty fast. So, I think so."

Penny looked over at me and chuckled. Her buddy squinted at me over his skinny sunglasses. "I'm sure you are, princess. But you might want to ask your daddy about college. And running. And scholarship money."

The light changed to green and Penny started to pull ahead.

"Why?" I jogged alongside their car. "What do you mean?"

Penny kept the car moving at a slow crawl and spoke clearly and deliberately. "It's different for girls. For women. The scales of justice are completely nonexistent, especially for women in sports. Like me. And you."

A horn blasted behind us, so I moved back on to the sidewalk so they could get back to driving.

"But things are gonna change, right Greg?" Penny grabbed his hand, lifting it in triumph as if they were already on the podium.

"Well, we're trying, Penny." He hung his head out the window and turned back toward me, adding, "You keep trying, too, okay?" as they pulled away.

He flashed a quick peace sign out the window as their car blended with the rest of traffic.

I imagined myself jogging along the Charles River, the majestic rust-colored brick buildings framing the skyline. I could see the hills that my father swears made him stronger than anyone from Chicago, and tried to see myself climbing up and over and around those famous monsters. I pictured myself racing at one of the top schools in the country, against other strong, competitive universities, crushing them all and keeping the Carlson legacy alive. I felt the Harvard 'H' burning itself into my heart, my mind, my dreams.

By the time I returned home, I was, for the first time, a girl -- no, a woman-- with a purpose.

Later that week I learned why my father had left for work so early. He had turned down the job at St. Hebert, and was no longer going to work with the IH boys' team either. Instead, he shifted his office hours to start his day by 7:00 am so that by three he was back at home and tucked away in his bedroom, making phone calls and tapping away on our typewriter. Every once in a while he'd shout out to my mom, or one of us, to sharpen a pencil, or refill his coffee, or to run something down to the post office. Sometimes we'd have visitors, quiet refined men in three-piece suits, or rough, burly guys in flannel shirts and pockets full of pencils. They would gather at the kitchen table while the rest of us were sent off to read, run, or take Eddie to the park.

I wanted to talk to him about Harvard, and my big dream to carry on the family legacy, but he didn't seem to slow down for more than a minute, so I knew it would have to wait.

Finally, one evening as I was sprawled across the couch, half watching the TV and half listening to Helen on the phone, my dad suddenly sprung out of his room in his IH track shirt and shorts, and a new pair of shoes on his feet.

"Come on, Gracie, let's go for a run."

"Gotta go!" I interrupted Helen to hang up, and quickly slipped on my shoes and followed him out the door.

Dad's new shoes were bumpy and funny-shaped, not the smooth leather track shoes that he used to wear. He kind of pranced down the front steps, tapping the soles of his shoes to the wooden stairs and then the cement sidewalks. These shoes were quieter than his old ones, which had always made a soft slapping sound when he ran. As we jogged down the block he stayed quietly focused on something I could not see, and I tried to stay quiet myself, but eventually all the questions I had, and the ones that had grown stronger in the past few days, burst out of me in one ignorant demand.

"I've decided I want to go to Harvard. Like you did. I want to be on the track team too."

Whatever had my father's attention up to this point was immediately put on the back burner.

"Harvard?" he sounded doubtful. "This is the first I've heard you mention college at all, and you want to go to Harvard? Do you know how hard it is to get in there?"

For a moment I felt embarrassed by my dream, but then I remembered something.

"Well, you got in, didn't you?"

My father laughed out loud. "Well, yes, I guess I did."

We were approaching the trail, but instead of dipping down toward the river, my father kept running along the street, turning right and then left every few blocks. I just kept asking about the east coast, about Boston, about the hills and the river and the big old buildings. I asked about running through the streets of Boston and on the tracks of Harvard and Yale.

"Do you think you are ready to run for Harvard?" my dad asked.

"Well I don't really know," I answered. "I think I'm fast, but I'm not in the best shape any more. And I have no idea how fast the other girls on the team are. Or who else will be trying out."

"I've actually been wanting to talk to you about that."

"About trying out for Harvard?"

"Well, not exactly, but along the same idea."

Then, just like when we ran with the team, his pace quickened, his speech quickened, and I could feel his excitement before he said another word.

"You got really good practicing with the boys' team, didn't you?"

I nodded. Of course. I probably wouldn't be running at all any more if it weren't for them.

And Sal. And my dad.

"But you know, there aren't many places that give girls like you that kind of training, that kind of support. College is even worse. Most colleges will at least let women create a club team, or maybe just intramural teams. But as for competition, and training, and coaching, and administration, and uniforms, and equipment...there just isn't any money."

How could there not be any money? I saw for myself the training and equipment that was needed for the guys' teams.

"What does that mean?"

"It means that the reason I could afford to go to Harvard was because I got a scholarship -- the college paid my tuition so I could run on their team. The women don't get that kind of support. And honey, we don't have that kind of money ourselves."

A knot was building in my throat, and the more I tried to swallow it the tighter it became until I could barely breathe. "So, you're saying I won't be able to go to Harvard?"

"I'm saying that the system is unfair."

"Well, then the system has to change," I bit back. I remembered Penny and Greg, and their cynical warning about the scales of justice.

"I know, Gracie. And that's what we're gonna work on."

He eased into a slow jog, then stopped in front of a store that had its door propped open by a large cement block. I followed him as he stepped inside, tiptoeing around extension cords, long planks of wood, and several open toolboxes. Several shelves were lining the walls, and a large bulletin board hung behind a small counter with a cash register and piles of papers on it. Three men were gathered around a ladder in the center of the room, holding a huge post in place. Occasional bursts from a drill interrupted their collaboration as they mounted brackets into the post and the ceiling.

As we approached, however, all work stopped, and they greeted my dad enthusiastically. The man at the top of the ladder called out, "Billy, glad you're here! Got a couple questions for ya."

My dad grinned ear to ear and hustled over, pulling me with him.

"Well, Gracie, what do you think?"

"Of...?"

"Of this. This is my -- no, our -- new store. A running store! With the latest running gear, like these shoes, and shorts and sweats just for runners."

He put his arm around my shoulders.

"Gracie, you want the system to change? Well, this is going to be the way we start making that change. This, Gracie, is where you will train. We are going to sponsor the very first training club for girls -- like you. Girls like Helen and Caroline and younger girls who don't even know they want to run yet, and women who never even tried running."

He pulled me to the back of the store and pointed out into the alley.

"Right there, we are going to build a track -- a small track, but one that everyone can use."

Then he turned to a huge storeroom that was loaded with boxes full of shirts, shorts, and more shoes. Huge posters were leaning against the wall, announcing that Run The World was now Open for Business.

"This is what we are going to sell. And then we are going to train everyone -- not just the kids who are on the track team, but anyone who wants to run."

His pride and excitement suddenly softened.

"Gracie, I may be starting a little too late to get you into Harvard, but I promise you, we *are* going to change the system."

The rest of the summer was spent running to the new store, running around the dirt circle behind the store that would soon become a track, and running to the back storage room for a different pair of shoes for a customer to try on.

My dad expected business to be slow at first, so we were surprised when a steady flow of runners kept showing up at our store. Sometimes they came to buy new shoes or shorts or socks, but most of the time they just wanted to meet other people who ran, too. Schools had running teams, but if you were too slow for the team or too old for school, it was tough to find other people to run with.

My dad set up a corner of the store with a few chairs, a table, and a bulletin board. He'd post advertisements for new products, like shoes with a "waffle" sole. But more often he'd post a running workout that people could do that week. Maybe it would be intervals or tempo or LSD, which always made people laugh, until he explained that it meant *long slow distance*. Eventually, the runners started posting their times for the workouts, and then they'd start a competition.

"I'm gonna run ten four-hundreds tomorrow."

"Ten? That's it? You should do fourteen with me!"

And just as my father hoped, the runners came together and trained. But there was one thing missing.

Women.

A sign at the front of the store had a sign-up list for the Women Run The World team. My name was on the list. So was Helen's. But we didn't see many other women come in to shop, or talk, and certainly not to train. So we were the smallest team in Chicago that summer.

But Helen and I ran together every Tuesday, Thursday and Sunday, following the training that my dad laid out for us. And even though it was just the two of us, it was the best I had ever felt. Training with the boys had made me fast. But training with Helen made me part of a team.

Even if I had applied to Harvard, I wouldn't have gone. I wanted to keep running with my dad, running with Helen, running along the tiny strip of trail by the lake. So once I graduated I entered Chicago's Loyola University where I could study business by day and could practice it at night.

We made some adjustments to our inventory to include t-shirts designed for women and some short shorts that felt awful when I ran in them, but looked great on most women as they went about the rest of their shopping.

Helen and I convinced a group of four more college-age girls to join our running team. We joked about how we were the number one women's running club in Chicago. I even used that phrase on our Women Run the World sign up, which got more jokes than signatures.

Until New York.

That changed everything.

# 10  EVA

The next day, when I hear the sounds of morning rumbling outside my window, it is still dark and cold.  Like a sharp, boney finger, a reminder of my promise to run today is poking at me.  Stupid idea, really.  It's way too cold outside.  I can hear the scrape of a shovel somewhere down the street, and an occasional blast from a siren.  I bury deeper into my bed to escape the unceasing prodding of that one tiny bold statement.

My bed is piled with a thick comforter, lightweight blankets, faux fur blankets, and a homemade quilt pieced together from old fabric.  My blankets are thick and warm, and when I pull them over my head I feel like I am underwater, safe, away from the world out there.  And there is no real reason to come up for air.

Aside from my afternoon police visit yesterday, I have been sleeping for nearly all of the last seventy-two hours.  Before they left, I would sleep once the kids went to school, or while they were watching TV or doing their homework.  I would sleep while Jake read to me and even while I read to Maddie.  I'd sleep as soon as I got home from the café, and I'd crawl into bed as soon as the last good-night kiss was kissed.  I spend my life asleep.  I've come to believe that it's the only possible way to manage it, anyway.

But it seems that for sleep, as for many other things in life, there is a saturation point.  A point which suddenly screams "No more!" and in an instant, at two-thirty in the morning -- four days after they left -- twelve days after my abortion -- I awake and cannot close my eyes again.

I stare at the ceiling.  I flip over and, hanging my head off the side of the bed, I stare at the floor.  The walls.  The clock.  The closet.  The sweatpants on the carpet.  This time when I pull the blankets over my head I cannot breathe.  I kick them off and stare across the room at the picture hanging on the wall.

A framed Cinderella drawing.

It is the only drawing of mine that my mother framed. I remember how proud I felt as my mom and I carefully chose a spot on the back porch wall to hang the Cinderella drawing. I may have been only a four-year-old, but I recognized the importance of artistic placement. I wanted everyone to be able to walk into the porch and look right at that picture. I wanted them to see my name, E-V-A, printed neatly at the bottom. A little higher? A little to the left? my mother wondered. I nodded and pointed and she moved it around in circles until I gave the final okay, and then, beaming, she hammered a tiny gold nail into the wall, a permanent place of honor.

It was a detailed crayon masterpiece of Cinderella, decked out in a pink and silver ballroom gown, surrounded by a curious and admiring audience. She is holding her arms stiffly away from her body because her dress is so billowy. Beside her, reaching out to her, stands her Prince. His hair is Burnt Sienna. I remember how much I loved that color, a perfect auburn. He is admiring her too, but Cinderella is not looking at anyone in the picture. She is staring straight out at you. She has a huge pink smile and large circles for eyes, each with a blue dot in the center and heavily framed with long lashes.

My mother had decided to frame Cinderella because she said I was a natural. I think she meant as an artist, but if that was the case, I never did anything more to prove her right. Just a few years later, cancer ravaged her body, destroyed her spirit, and ultimately stole her from my life. Ironically, Cinderella has been the only connection I have left.

Staring at her today I think she looks frozen and uncomfortable, pleading with me to get her out of there.

Benjamin and I were married before either of us finished college. I had twelve college credits to my name and Ben had forty-five credits. Even if we joined them together we couldn't create a bachelors degree. But babies and hospital bills take precedence over lecture halls and study sessions, so instead of finishing his degree, Ben took a job selling advertising space for small local magazines, and I stayed home to take care of Katie. Our "home" was the basement apartment of his parents' house for five years. I got to see his mother's growing disappointment every evening when Ben came home. "Poor Benji," she'd croon pitifully. "It'll get better soon, I'm sure of it."

Did she mean his job? our home? her home? Or did she mean me?

We were just about to move into our own apartment when I became pregnant with Jake. Ben's insurance covered basic health care, but not maternity care.

Needless to say, our move was delayed until we could pay off the mountain of doctor bills piled up in a box on the floor beside the bed.

And then Michelle got married.

She had bought a 3-flat in the old-rich section of Chicago's Old Town when prices were still under six figures and renovations were just starting to define the neighborhood. Although it had more than enough space for her and Tom, it was not enough to raise their babies to come, so they soon found their North Shore colonial with three sculpted gardens, a huge backyard, and plenty of room for the kids who are still not even conceived.

Instead of selling her place, they offered us the opportunity to rent it from them. We were eager to move out of his parents' house so, with newborn Maddie bringing up the rear, we settled into a place of our own that did not belong to us, that was not chosen by us, and that was, according to Ben "charitably and graciously rented to us for an absolute steal" in a neighborhood in which I, frozen and uncomfortable, do not belong.

I pull myself up to sit on the edge of my bed. Cinderella and I lock eyes but eventually I am the one who has to look away. My body is stiff and sore. I stretch my arms overhead and to the sides and then curve forward, reaching toward my toes. I inhale a nasty waft of my four-day shower-less body. It is time to do something about that.

As I turn on the water in the shower I see the remnants of my last attempt at cleaning myself. Tiny splashes of blood still cling to the sides of the shower wall. I reach under the sink and pull out a spray bottle of bleach. Before I get in I squirt stream after stream onto the brown-red splatter. The bleach melts the blood, and the water and steam combine to wash it away, leaving clean white tile and bleach fumes in which to clean myself.

I pour shampoo into my hands and rub it gently into my tangled hair. I can't really get my fingers through the mess, so I rinse and start over, this time with a hefty amount of conditioner mixed in. The knotted strands of hair start to separate and the grime slowly rinses out, leaving my hair long and smooth. I soap up the rest of my body from head to toe and every crevice in between, letting the water cleanse me.

I step out of the shower and grab a towel. After wrapping it around my head, I face myself in the mirror again, placing my hands over my belly. I know there was a reason I chose an abortion, but I can't remember it now. I only know that I do not regret it. If anything, I am relieved. But I do not know why there is so much hatred in my heart whenever I think about it.

I pull a t-shirt over my bra and step into clean underwear -- finally -- and clean sweat pants. The floors are chilly but I leave my feet bare for now.

Yesterday a burst of thick, wet snowflakes had covered the streets and sidewalks of Old Town. But March temperatures are so fickle and fleeting. Even now, before dawn today, I can smell the change in the air. I open a window and spring pours in.

I make a pot of coffee and as it brews I brush and dry my hair. I turn on a shuffle of *Bon Iver* in the kitchen, one of Benjamin's many playlists. The music feels invasive and foreign in this world of silence. But the silence has been here too long.

I pour a mug of coffee and pull a chair close to the open kitchen window. The chilly-warm breeze brushes across my face, and calm settles into my body. I can hear the splashing of traffic driving through melted slush from the other side of North Pond. Across the street, the houses and two-flats are quiet and dark, but in the distance, tall apartment buildings blink awake as lights are turned on and off. I look around the kitchen, strewn with reminders of them. A+ papers are magneted to the fridge. Benjamin's briefcase leans against the wall next to a basket of winter boots and snow toys. A bin of Jake's Legos spill across the table, half-finished buildings tossed among them. It all looks so normal. There is no evidence of my own failings here.

Katie's purple beach hat and black studded purse are on the counter next to the door to the garage. I think she wanted to take that to Mexico with her. She must have forgotten in all the confusion. The mess. My mess.

And like that, a wave of pain pushes into my heart, my mind, my chest and the momentary calm runs, scared, to try to get away.

From down the street, a soft rhythmic slapping sound moves closer, and I lean into the light to try to see better. And then there she is, a reflective stripe wrapped around each wrist and ankle. I can see her across the street, two houses down, and even in the dark I can tell she glides. When she is directly across from me, she turns toward my window and looks at me. I am startled, but I do not look away. She lifts her hand in a swift hello. I semi-raise mine. And in a few more steps she is gone, a thin stream of energy in her wake.

I don't remember putting my shoes on or walking out the door, but suddenly I am running down the sidewalk, chasing her, chased by them. My keys are in my hand this time, and as I run, my breath becomes strained and my heart beats harder until I need to slow down. But I do not stop.

I cross Stockton Drive and turn onto a muddy path. A group of four silent swift runners moves toward me, shifts to the left as one whole being, and nods in greeting as they pass.

This silent connection grabs me. I run evenly and calmly. The pain cannot keep up however, and so, by the time I circle around North Pond, I am lighter than I was when I left.

I have found my escape.

Tonight the dishes are cleaned and put away. The carpets are vacuumed and the laundry is folded and a big batch of chili bubbles away in the crock-pot. The last time I talked to Benjamin they were getting ready to depart from Houston, their connection city, on their way back to Chicago. This conversation was even more abrupt, more distant, than the brief check-ins he had made over the past ten days. I guess calling from Mexico allowed him to maintain the farce of my rest-period. He had sunshine and paddle boards to distract him. But as the mileage between us grew shorter, the distance only increased. I had offered to pick them up at the airport, but arrangements with a limo had already been made.

So I wait for them to return by doing the one thing that has kept me from drowning this whole week. I layer a t-shirt over a long sleeve shirt, pull on the one pair of cotton stretch shorts I own, and head out the door to run.

Each day I have followed a circular path through Lincoln Park, along the lake, across the bridge, and back home via the gravel path that winds past the zoo. Some days I run the circle once; other days twice; yesterday I ran four loops and even when I returned home, the tightness in my stomach was just starting to relax. I am both excited to share this with Benjamin and afraid of what he will say. Not about the last six days of my running, but about the last six years of our marriage.

Today my legs feel tired and I move slowly. But I am so used to feeling numb, that anything else is a welcome relief. Feeling tired reminds me that I am alive and moving. Feeling sore reminds me that pain doesn't just gnaw at my soul, but can pull its way into calves and thighs and arms and that pain only lasts a day or two. In fact, feeling anything physical at all keeps my mind off of the reason I was left behind in the first place.

Although the days are getting longer, we have not yet sprung forward, so sunset hovers just beyond six o'clock. Their flight will land in the twilight, and I hope that the kids will see the city lights from the plane as it descends toward O'Hare. I wonder if they'll see me, too, this little speck on the ground, and I realize that even if they did, they would not know that it was me. Why would they? I am woven into their minds as a part of the bed, the kitchen, the car. Not the world outside.

I turn south onto the path, the lake to my left, a stream of traffic curving along Lake Shore Drive to my right and the skyline reaching out into the lake ahead of me. The wind is low so the waves are gentle and constant, and I feel my pace synchronize harmoniously with their soft rhythm.

A shadow creeps ahead of me as a runner approaches from behind. I shift slightly to the right to allow for easy passing space, but the shadow doesn't move. I am uncomfortable having someone this close behind me, so I slow my pace to let them ease by. The shadow slows itself, too, which annoys me more than it frightens me. It's too close; I can almost feel it on my shoulders, dragging at me, holding me back.

So I pick up my pace again, lifting my shoulders a little more, kicking my feet a little higher behind me, and deepening my breath as I pull away from this shadow.

Approaching the North Avenue Beach House the shadow disappears and I feel the comfort of solitude once again, a freedom to remove myself from any external pressures to run a certain way. Through the trees and then out onto the half-mile cement path lined with dim yellow street lights. I hear it before I see it. A deep breath behind me and then, sure enough, as I run under the glow of one of these lights, that damn shadow is back.

I feel a rage building in me. I want to scream at it. Oh my god! Get the hell away from me!

Of course there are other people on this path, running, minding their own business, and they don't bother me. But they are not sticking to me like a prickly burr. This one hurts, for some reason, and I need it to stop. So I leap to the side, squat down to retie my shoe, and glare up at the owner of this shadow that won't go away.

It's her.

The perky, nosey, tiny lady who followed me over a week ago and decided my problems were so insignificant without knowing a damn thing about me.

And she stops. Are you kidding?

"Wow! Great pace!" She bobs from foot to foot in front of me. "Hope you don't mind me running with you. But you set a great pace, and I need that sometimes."

She is wearing some kind of long, fingerless gloves that reach up to her elbows, and a bright blue tank top, tight black shorts, and a slim pair of Nike's. Clearly she has underdressed. Poor, stupid woman.

"Come on," she says, tugging at me to straighten up. "Come on, let's go. Get up."

Get up, Get up Get up Get up Getupgetupgetupgetupgetup

She is suddenly hidden in a blur of tears, and for a moment, her tiny runner body reminds me of Maddie, pulling on me, pleading with me. My breath is caught in my throat and it is impossible to move. I blink, the tears fall and my vision clears again. The woman squats down in front of me, and holds my face between her hands. She looks into my eyes, softly, seriously, but does not ask about the tears. Her skin is tight and thin across her cheekbones, but shows the result of years in the sun and the wind, wrinkles that burst like sun rays from her eyes and across her forehead and around her lips.

"Run," she whispers. "Running will help. It always does. It's my turn to set the pace now."

Her hand reaches out to mine, holding it, ready to lift me, but she doesn't pull. I try to take a deep breath, but it is shaky and shallow. Once again, slow, through my nose, and I feel my lungs relax a little. I straighten up and she gives my hand a squeeze for stability, and then drops it to start running again.

My legs fall into the new pattern of reach, step, push off, following this wisp of blue and black. She runs as slow as it takes to keep me just behind her right shoulder. No more words. Just an easy stride, and then with a glance over her shoulder and her left hand signaling, she curves back around, as we retrace our steps back north.

I cling to her like the burr that I found so annoying moments earlier. It is easy to do because although she is in front of me, I know she is matching my pace. I realize my stride has grown longer as we pull away from the Beach House once again. My arm swing is stronger. My breath is quicker. Are we running faster? I am not aware of that happening, but like a melting icicle, drop by drop, step by step, she quickened the pace imperceptibly until suddenly, here we are, running past everyone, being passed by no one. My lungs are starting to burn, but I cannot tell her to slow down, and for some reason my legs won't do it on their own. So I am stuck to her, maybe not like a prickly burr. Maybe more like sticky gum, that doesn't exactly hurt, but is extremely difficult to remove.

She leads me back to Fullerton, dipping below the highway on the pedestrian underpass and up onto the city sidewalks. Night has filled the sky, but the city lights keep us fully illuminated. Our pace slows considerably as we dodge traffic and stoplights.

As we approach my street a long, black limo turns in front of us and we bounce lightly in place waiting for it to clear the crossing. As it does, I see a little face press itself up to the glass. An excited cry bursts out of the opening window.

"Mommy!"

I race after the limo for a half a block, eager to see my babies, who tumble out before the car has even stopped moving. So unsafe -- but I am so happy to see them.

Maddie jumps into my arms, then scrambles down as she reaches back to grab something colorful and sticky out of the car to give to me. Jake is sunburnt and sleepy, so his hug is more of a request to carry him, so I let him crawl into my arms. Katie has waited until the car stops and the driver has opened her door on the other side. She thanks the driver and throwing her backpack over her shoulders, flings her arm around my neck and kisses me on the cheek. Benjamin is paying the driver, so when I look at him he doesn't acknowledge me at all.

Katie mumbles into my ear, "I wish you had been there. Aunt Michelle is such a control freak!" She rolls her eyes. Jake is heavy, so instead of waiting to see if Ben will ever say hello, we turn and walk into the house.

Before I step in, I look up the street, and see my running partner still there. She is standing, watching, but when I nod to her, she lifts her hand to me in farewell and continues away. Maybe I should have said something. Maybe I didn't need to.

The suitcases are stacked in the hallway, bags of colorful t-shirts and beads spill onto the countertops, and the smell of freshly bathed children lingers in the air. Katie's light is still on in her room, so I poke my head in to say good night. Her chin is buried in her chest, eyes closed, but her algebra book is lying open in her lap, fingers curled limply around it. She twitches with an instinctive attempt to stay alert, but she is too deep into sleep to fully respond. I close the book, run my fingertips lightly around her face, tipping her head gently back against her pillow. I switch off the light next to her bed and watch her give in to the softness surrounding her.

Her breath deepens into sleep-breath, meaning she will not budge for hours. So definite in who she is and what she wants -- even sleep. I wonder how I produced such a soul. I guess I didn't, really. Sure, Benjamin and I mixed a little love juice together and produced this body-- or at least the baby version of her body. But who she is, her strength, her focus, her drive, her certainty -- that came from somewhere else. Despite her smooth skin and pre-teen hips and breasts, and limited understanding of math, Katie speaks with the authority and wisdom of an ancient sage. I am both frustrated and humbled by her.

After peeking in on Jake and Maddie, I really have only one more place to go. My bedroom. Our bedroom. I stand outside the door and try to steady my breath. I open the door. He is lying under the blankets, unmoving. I hope he is asleep, but as I step around the bed I can see that his eyes are wide open, staring at the wall.

"Hi." I try to smile a bit, not like I am pretending nothing happened, but like I am happy to see him. I want to be happy to see him.

"Uh huh," he mutters back at me. I feel like I should say something but my heart isn't in it.

I step out of my sweat-stained clothes and pull a t-shirt over my head. I lift the blankets gently, as if I am being careful not to wake him, although I know he is still not asleep. I search the growing pit in my heart, hoping to find a flicker of closeness to share with him. I retreat to the comfort zone of rote apologies and expected admonishments.

"Sorry," I mumble to his back. "I didn't mean to hurt you." Which is true, of course, but is beside the point.

"Uh huh."

"Goodnight," I whisper and turn the opposite direction so that our backs are only inches away from each other.

I can feel my body giving in to sleep, that familiar hiding place, when his voice pushes into my consciousness. "Eva...Eva...Eva...?" Somehow he knows when I am awake enough to listen.

"Eva? We need to talk about it...about the...the... baby."

The baby? There was no baby. I was pregnant. I didn't have a baby. There's a big difference between the two. There has to be.

"It's gone, Ben. That's it. Okay? You don't have to worry about anything anymore."

A wall of fear or denial or pain blocks me from saying any more. But I have sparked a storm in Ben that spins dangerously, desperately, tearing into the frayed threads that manage to keep this marriage together.

"That's it? Are you serious? What is wrong with you?" he demands, sitting up and pulling the blankets off of me. "I don't know what you are thinking, or what you are feeling. I don't even know what you are doing anymore!" His anger mixes with fear in his voice. "I don't feel like I know you anymore," he chokes.

I just turn onto my stomach, search for something to cover myself with, and let him fight his own painful battle of regret. I don't move when he gets up, or when he shuts the door to the bathroom, or runs the water for nearly ten minutes. I close my eyes when he comes out, gets dressed, picks up his phone and his keys.

What is wrong with me?

I can feel him staring at me. I squeeze my eyes closed.

"I know you're awake. You think I don't know, but you forget that I have watched you sleep for fifteen years. You are not fooling me." His voice is raspy and hoarse. "I had hoped that ten days of alone-time would give you a chance to figure your shit out, Eva. That it would be enough solitude that somehow we could be a family again once we got back. I guess not. Maybe you've been trying to get me to leave this whole time and I'm just too thick-headed to figure it out. Maybe this is what you've needed all along."

Is this what I needed? It doesn't feel right, but it's too strong a force to stop.

"I'll be back later. If it even matters to you."

The door clicks shut.

Leave?

I have never thought about Ben leaving, let alone whether it would matter to me. Of course it matters. Why wouldn't it matter?

But now that he said the words, and the door has closed, I feel...free.

I don't know what time it is when I hear the key in the front door. It is impossible to open it quietly, since it is old and swollen from years of use and weather. I can hear Ben shuffle quietly into the kitchen or perhaps into the TV room. All I know is that he doesn't come upstairs. Eventually I drift back to sleep again.

In the morning, a half-empty cup of coffee acts as a paperweight to a note he left behind. *Working late.*

I am still holding the note in my hand as my two youngest race each other down the stairs and into the kitchen. From her room Katie shouts down to them both, "Can you two little rug rats please stop charging around like that? One of these days you're going to hurt someone!"

Benjamin was unemployed for exactly fifteen months. At first, he was optimistic about finding something new, something better, so we collected coupons, visited bargain shops, and let our Visa balance grow. Eventually I had to start working in the cafe in Michelle's law firm after all. I needed to leave before any of the kids were awake, and I spent six hours a day, four days a week, pouring coffee, making lattes and throwing huge muffins into tiny bags for important, busy people who ordered without looking at me. At the end of each week I put the one hundred fifty dollars into our checking account. It was like dropping a spoonful of water into a bucket that was being overturned every day.

"Now you have some of your own spending money!" Michelle exclaimed. "Isn't that fun?" Michelle still did not know about Ben. So she did not know how much fun it is to watch your credit card balance grow, to watch your children complain about peanut butter day after day, and to watch your husband scour the apartment listings for someplace more affordable. She didn't know that Ben was trying to figure out a way to skip her birthday trip the following spring. And even though she did not know, I hated her every time she bought her giant chocolate muffin and asked for an extra shot of flavor in her latte — 'on the house, ok'?

Every few weeks she'd ask me to go shopping with her. She just couldn't wait to see me spend my money on something nice for a change. Finally, when a full year had passed and Christmas was rearing its greedy head once again, I had to tell her.

"You cannot say a word to Ben!" I pleaded. "I'm sure he'll get a new job soon. But right now he's too embarrassed and too stressed out to deal with an explanation to his family as well."

Michelle rested her hand on my shoulder, giving a sad shake of her head, then dug through her purse. She pulled three hundred-dollar bills from her wallet.

"Here. For the kids," she said sympathetically. She continued to shake her head as I stuffed the money into my purse, mumbling that I'd pay her back after the new year.

"Oh boy, you guys," she said. "I don't know what else I can do to help, but if I think of anything I will let you know." She brightened suddenly. "Aren't you glad you took this job after all?"

I told her, Yes, of course. That makes everything so much better.

At first I was just tired. More tired than usual, but how could I even compare? I had spent so much of the last thirteen years exhausted, so being even more tired seemed irrelevant. And now I was waking earlier, working harder, so why wouldn't I be tired?

But after a week of that, the nausea set in. Suddenly the smell of coffee brought the bile streaming up and into my throat. One day, as Michelle was waiting for her espresso to brew, I pulled a pre-made egg sandwich out of the microwave. The sulfurous odor triggered a loud, involuntary retch from my throat that horrified me and disgusted the customers in line. Shocked and embarrassed, Michelle turned away from me, mumbling, "What the hell was that?" as I tried to convince the customer there was nothing wrong with his sandwich.

"I don't know," I mumbled back. "I guess I'm just feeling queasy today."

"Well that was awful. Please don't do that again. I mean, I did vouch for you, and I'd hate for people to think you can't do...this." She waved her hand casually at the mind-numbingly easy role of barista. As she started to walk away, she suddenly turned back, eyes wide and stunned. "Oh my god --- you aren't pregnant are you? God, that is the last thing Benjamin needs!"

"No, no, of course not!" I reassured her. Then, to ease my mind as much as hers, I added with a forced giggle, "We'd need to have sex for that to happen!"

She nodded, relieved and more serious than I expected. "Well, just in case, there's a family planning center down the block -- you know, if you need any "emergency" planning!" And that's when she laughed.

I only vomited at work once, and everyone thought I had caught the flu, so I was sent home immediately. I took the opportunity to pray to god that I was not pregnant. Even the word "pregnant" drained me of all feeling. It would be the last straw on an already broken camel. So I talked myself into a headache, coughing, feeling feverish, and achy muscles to convince myself that I did indeed have the flu. For four days I lay in bed sick, while Benjamin worried and called and emailed about job openings and interview follow-ups, still hiding the truth from his parents, who could have probably helped him the most.

At one point he checked in on me, resting his hand on my forehead. "You don't seem too feverish, but you should keep drinking the fluids. Remember, we don't have any insurance now, so a trip to the doctor is gonna cost us a fortune!"

That might have been the moment I decided to call about an abortion.

A week later I had taken a quick test and the first dose of medication to end the pregnancy.

The next day as I came out of the bathroom, the cramping having started to increase, Benjamin flew through the front door. He grabbed me around the waist and laid a long sloppy kiss on my mouth. "I got it!" he shouted. "I got it! Oh, Eva, we are gonna be okay! Just like you said we would!"

"What are you talking about?"

"Eva, the interview I had yesterday-- they offered me the job! Twice the pay I was making with Market-Co! I told you about it last night, remember?"

That was the night of Vicodin and Ibuprofin so no, I did not remember. He got a job. He got a job.

"Now you can quit working at that stupid coffee shop," he smiled at me. "And our vacation next week is back on!"

The morning sun is hovering just over the lake as I make the turn-around at Oak Street beach. April clings to bits of winter, most remarkably in the wind it hurls at us. I have fallen back into my routine of kids, sleep, kids, sleep, but today I forced myself back out the door and along the lakefront path. Already cold when I left this morning, as I turn I am greeted by a wall of wind out of the north. My cadence slows, but still I am exhausted by the mere effort of keeping upright. As a few morning runners approach me heading south, looking so confident and relaxed, I feel envious until I realize that they, too, will be facing the wind sooner or later as well. That's the way it is when you run from home. Eventually you'll have to turn around and head back, regardless of the wind.

Ben has been coming home from work late every night for the past week, and as soon as the kids are in bed he leaves. I don't know where he goes or what time he comes back home, but every morning his dirty clothes are in the laundry room and yesterday's newspaper is tossed on the floor next to the couch in the TV room. There is no explaining to do, no upsetting the kids. They are used to his absence in the morning, and my withdrawal in the evening. Everything is as normal as we can fake it to be.

As I walk in the door I can hear Katie calling for me from upstairs.

"Mom! Mom! Mom! Where are you, Mothe-e-e-r!"

I grab the scrap of an envelope off the counter, my scribbles as my defense.

"I'm right here!" I call up to her, waving the scrap of paper. "Didn't you see my note? I left it in the kitchen."

She lunges into view at the top of the stairs, wild-eyed. "Where were you?" she blasts at me. "I had no idea you left! I was scared to death!" She places her hand over her heart, for emphasis.

As I get to the top of the stairs I try to hug her, but she backs away.

"Gross! You're all sweaty." She sniffs at me. "And you smell bad."

I try to calm her, reason with her, as if I have any cause to explain my actions to a fourteen-year-old. "Katie, I left a note saying I would be gone for thirty minutes -- that's it! - just thirty minutes while I went running. You know, I have been running pretty regularly for a while now." I smile proudly, but I just get one of her preteen snarls that either means 'I don't get it' or 'you are too weird for words'. In this case, it may mean both.

Jake and Maddie are stumbling about their rooms, still sleepy, but a little wound up, too. They've been home for six days, but it's still tough getting them back into school-mode. I don't know how private schools handle Exotic Learning Experiences, as Michelle calls them, but the public school my children attend expects a continuous stream of test scores and homework completion from its students. So aside from getting back to school, this week is a bombardment of make-up work, make-up tests, and harsh criticism of the woman who caused all this disruption to the scheduled flow of data. That is me, of course, not Michelle.

Jake heard me say "running" and has proceeded to show me how fast he can run. Maddie joins in and in no time I am applying ice to two foreheads and slipping t-shirts over tear-streaked faces.

Katie nibbles her toast, packs her backpack, and watches us.

"Maybe next time, they can run outside with you." She has the valley-girl lilt to her voice that is the mark of every disgusted teenage girl I know.

How the hell did she get to be so old?

"Alright, into the car everyone!" We enter the garage and buckle up. I open the garage door before turning on the car to keep the fumes from affecting Katie's sensitive sniffer. Exhaust, perfume, body odor, fried foods, sewers -- they all drive her to claims of throwing up and headaches. Maybe it's true, but sometimes I think she pours it on a little too thick. I think she enjoys everyone's response more than the fresh air itself.

I drop the kids off at school, still in my sweatshirt and ripped sweatpants. As Katie bounces out of the car she whispers back at me, "Maybe you could go shopping today. You know, for some new running clothes? Something -- normal? So you can actually look like a runner, okay?"

The door slams shut before I can respond.

Well, okay.

I ease back into traffic and begin the drive home, but instead of turning east, I head west toward the rows of shops and stores and boutiques that I never visit.

I pass a high-end women's sports clothing shop. Through the windows I can see colorful skirts and strappy tank tops and athletic bodies and long blond ponytails.

I think it's expensive, but I will take a look anyway. The parking spots are filling up, but I find one not too far down the block. As I open the car door, I am suddenly self-conscious of my clothing. That a comment from my daughter should cause me to feel embarrassed is slightly unnerving. I try to not care, but hurry to the store regardless.

I try to push my way into the store, but it is locked. The floor of the store has women in various stretches and contortions under dim lighting. On the store window a sign reads Morning Yoga in Session  Then another one that gives the store hours. I will have to wait until ten-thirty which means I may just forget the whole thing. I walk back to my car, but as I put the key in the ignition a loud rapping noise startles me. Tapping on the passenger window is my tiny running partner. She waves and says something, but I can't hear her.

I turn the car off and get out.

"Hi there! I was hoping I'd run into you again. You kind of disappeared the other night, didn't you? Was that your family?"

I remember seeing her at the corner of the street, watching me, waiting perhaps, and I am embarrassed by the way I just left her. Alone.

"Yes, it was.  They were just getting back from their vacation. From Mexico," I add, although I doubt it mattered. "Sorry I just left like that. I should have said something."

"Yes, well, I wasn't sure if you were coming back for a few minutes there.  But I figured it out." She taps the side of her head and winks.

She claps her hands together.  "Tell you what, I had such a good run that night, and you are really easy to run with -- so, let's do it again, okay ? I mean, I see you have your family, and other stuff going on probably, but I am pretty flexible with my time. I can work around your schedule. How does that sound?"

She stands in front of me with her eyes bright and wide and a hopeful hint of a smile, and I am not sure if she is nervous or over-caffeinated but she bounces slightly from the ball of her foot.

"My name is Gracie by the way," she says, sticking her hand out to me.

I reach out to her. "Eva."

"Okay, Eva, so when are you running next?"  Persistent.  Not surprising.

"I don't know.  I just started, really.  This is all pretty new to me," I confess.

"Really?" she asks, cocking her head to the side slightly. "Hmm.  It doesn't seem like it. You must be a natural." She winks at me again, so I guess she's kidding, but it feels kind of good to hear those words once more.

"How about Thursday?" she asks. "Will this time work?  Or are evenings better?"

There's no avoiding it. I sigh. "Well, now that the kids are back, it's better if I run once they go to school. So, I guess this time is good. Nine, or nine-thirty. Whatever is better for you."

She bounces even more. "Great! I'll meet you at the corner of your street at nine o'clock, okay?"

I agree, and then get back into my car.

"Eva, this is going to be good," she says, looking intently into my eyes. "For both of us."

As I fasten my seatbelt, she is wiggling her keys into the door of the storefront where we were standing. It is only after I pull away that I see it is a running store.

My phone is ringing as I walk into the kitchen. I can see that it is Michelle, and although I don't want to, I answer it, trying to sound as normal as possible. After all, I did miss her big party.

"Hi Michelle! The kids said they had a great time with all of you. Thanks so much for helping out!"

"Eva." She gets right down to business. "What happened to you?"

"I thought Ben told you. I had to rest. I needed the rest after the-- after I --"

She interrupts me, "Oh, I don't mean the...the... miscarriage. Of course Ben told me about that. And I am sorry." Her voice takes on a sympathetic tone. "I don't mean to be insensitive, but Eva, it's probably a blessing in disguise. Life is tough enough for you guys."

Life can be tough for many reasons. Sometimes it is because the people in your world are too emotional or too removed. Sometimes it is because there are more bills than there is money, or more bodies than there is space or more noise than there is silence. Or sometimes the people you resent point out just how lousy a life you have, and the fact that it is true causes you to deny it even more.

Dismissing her insult, she continues. "That's not what I called about anyway. I thought you were going to help me this morning. I've been waiting at Christopher's for over an hour."

Ugh. Christopher's. I look at the hand-written to-do list that is still stuck to my refrigerator door. Christopher's is an interior design studio that Michelle has been dying to work with for so-o-o-o long. For her birthday Tom has given her a blank check to redecorate the main living areas of her home. And Michelle really needs my help because, as she says, I have a great eye for art. What she really means is that I have nothing else to do and she needs someone to agree with her choices, so I am the best qualified for the job.

Of course she doesn't know about Ben and me. Not entirely, anyway.

Our family business has remained our business, as usual.

"Oh my god, Michelle, I totally forgot, but I can leave in two minutes. I'll be there in twenty."

A complete lie-- it will take at least an hour at this time and Michelle knows it.

"I already moved the appointment to noon Thursday. So don't forget. I need you for this."

I am waiting for Gracie at the corner of my street. Yesterday I went to the bargain department store and bought a new pair of running shorts. They don't quite look like the ones in the cute little boutique, but they are better than the stretched out cotton shorts I've been using, to Katie's embarrassment. These shorts are basic black, silky nylon, and they have a little pocket inside where I can put a key. That's convenient.

"Eva!" she is calling me from a block away, so I wave to her and jog out into the street to meet her. As I check the oncoming traffic, I see a flicker of shadow from the corner of my eye, and I know what it is before I look again.

Standing in the street, I keep my eyes fixed to where I know the shadow moved out of sight. I can feel his presence. I can feel his fear and his worry and his pain. It's Ben. At least, I think it is.

But nothing moves and a car has blasted its horn at me, threatening to run me over. I cross to the other side and Gracie jogs up to me. We turn east together and run through the park.

"I need to be back in an hour," I tell her. "I have to meet my sister-in-law to help her with some redecorating she is doing." I roll my eyes and groan. "I don't know why, but she thinks she needs me there to get this done. Honestly, I don't see how I can help her at all. I've never decorated anything more than my kid's birthday cake."

"Well, she needs you there for something, right?" She smiles at me.

Gracie smiles a lot. She smiles when she runs, when she's tying her shoes, when someone else is angry or rude or an emotional, self-centered mess. She smiles. She points out the obvious, the things that the rest of us ignore in order to maintain our grudges, our judgments, our reputations.

It's easier for me to resent Michelle if I think she is using me, instead of actually needing me. I push back.

"Oh, you don't know Michelle. She doesn't need anybody or anything. She's got it all. House, husband, money, career...money."

"Everybody needs something," Gracie says. "Most of us have no idea what that is, so we keep looking and looking for it. One thing after another, maybe it's this person or that person, or some title or recognition, money, fancy stuff, new stuff, somebody else's stuff. Or a big insulated bubble to block out the world." I look out over the waves to my left, making sure she is out of my vision.

"Everybody needs something," she repeats.

We run quietly.

A quarter mile stretch of gravel trail opens up in front of us. Gracie slows down so that she is jogging in place.

"You ready to see what you're made of? Let's do a few of these, okay?"

We had already run at least four miles. How could a quarter mile, even a fast quarter mile, demand that I be made of anything at all?

"Sure," I agree, and toe the line next to her.

"It's a quarter mile to the next drinking fountain. You ready?"

"I am."

She drops her voice to a whisper, a deep intensity settling into her jaw line. "One...Two...Three...go!"

I leap away from our starting line but I am already a few steps behind her. Gracie isn't just running fast, she is pounding her feet into the ground like a rabbit, turning over each stride so quickly that I can barely see her feet touch the ground. I am running after her but my long stride and deep breath aren't enough. Somehow my feet must pull from the earth faster, must kick forward faster, must barely hit the ground before they are hurling themselves down the path again. It's just a quarter mile, but before I am halfway to the end my legs tighten into blocks and are flooded with a burning sensation that seems to spread along my legs and deep into the muscle.

I slow to my comfortable quick, long, even stride and meet Gracie at the fountain, where she is pacing with her arms above her head, regaining her breath.

She grins at me. "How'd you do?"

"Well, obviously not as well as you. Something happened to my legs though."

She squats down to poke at my legs. "What's wrong?"

"I don't know. My thighs started to feel like they were on fire or something."

Gracie stands up, grinning at me.

"Oh, Eva," she says, "that's nothing to worry about. It just means you're running hard. Get used to it."

"Why?"

"Because running is about to get tough! This time, you'll stick with me, okay?"

I have no desire to "get tough", but I line up next to Gracie anyway.

This time, when she counts to three, we both take off quickly, but I can tell she is holding back for me. I work my legs as quickly as I can to keep my stride even with hers, but her feet can move more quickly than mine. The burning starts sooner this time, but I try to follow Gracie's direction to get used to it. It hurts. I hate it. I refuse to get used to it.

And then the fountain is just steps away, and I finish without my legs bursting into flames. This time I need to pace with my arms over my head too, and I can't tell Gracie how much my legs burned because I am breathing too hard. And just as I am finally feeling better she calls to me to line up with her again.

We run four more like that, and while the burning continues, and I am pretty sure I run slower at the end, as we jog home I feel stronger than I have in a long while.

Back at our meeting place, Gracie turns right to continue her jog to wherever she goes. She lifts a hand to wave back at me.

"Thanks!" she calls. "I needed that."

"Me too!" I call back to her, not sure what I mean.

Is this what I need? Legs on fire? Lungs nearly choking? Why would anyone need that kind of pain?


I'm at Christopher's and Michelle and I are leafing through page after page of fabric. I've recommended a teal and sand palette with accents of deep brown and moss green. I like the way the colors float together and soothe the mind.

Michelle likes it. Then again, maybe it's too dark. Then again, maybe Tom will like it. Then again, it's her birthday gift, so she should get what she wants, right? And she really does like the idea of soothing colors. Life can be so stressful, so hectic, what with the job and the house and everything.

"So, about your...um...miscarriage. I guess all that heaving and vomiting meant you really were pregnant, huh? I told you so."

I drop the fabric in my lap, amazed that she is going to bring this up again.

"Oh?"

"Well, whether it was a miscarriage or ... something else...I'm glad you're ok now. I was worried there for a while." She pats my hand, softly, condescendingly, somehow distracting herself into silence. I want to pull my hand away but she keeps at it, until suddenly her eyes fill with tears and in a blink or two they are rolling down her cheeks.

"Yes, I'm okay now. We are all okay now. Gosh, Michelle, please don't cry. I'm ok." She sniffles and pulls a tissue from her pocket.

"It's just tough to see Ben working so hard and you seem so tired all the time, and, well, let's face it, I know it's hard for you guys to make ends meet. No offense." She moves her hand to my cheek to somehow soften the sting.

"And when Ben said it was better this way, well," she continues, sniffling into her tissue, "I just started thinking, it's so unfair that you don't even want more kids but you go and get pregnant like that!" She snaps her fingers, looking at me for the first time, almost accusingly. "And for five years we've been trying and trying and I…I just…can't!" she wails. Now it makes sense. Her tears are for her pain, not mine.

"Michelle, I didn't know. I mean I thought you were still waiting. I thought you were too busy, or weren't ready. You never said anything…"

She slumps onto a pile of fabrics on the table in front of us, her shell of perfection momentarily suspended. "I just don't understand! We did everything right! We have a fantastic home, a great income, plenty of savings. But nothing! And now, at my age, it's probably too late." A new round of tears soaks into the brocade and silk tweed squares.

She lifts her face and stutters quietly, "I need this! I wasn't trying to be cold. I just need to be pregnant, to build a family, like you and Ben. I hate that I get so…so.. jealous of you!"

I'm stunned. How could this woman, who has everything, be jealous of my pathetic life? It almost makes me laugh. But then I picture Maddie's sweet blond curls, Jake's round cheeks, and Katie's sharp eyes, and it all fills my heart. Nothing else could fill that space, and Michelle must have that same heart-space too. Empty.

"Oh, Michelle," I say. "But it's not too late. There are plenty of doctors who can help you, or other ways to build a family." I try to hug her, to pour some of my motherhood into her heart, but of course, it doesn't work that way.

"If there is one thing I have learned from having kids," I continue, "it's that you have to give up a lot of control. Kids, and families, don't grow from a plan in your head. They grow from love in your heart."

My voice catches and starts to break as my words ring in my own ears. I am not sure how to pull myself out of our unintended closeness, but Michelle, the epitome of poise, certainly does. After a few minutes of sniffles and then a quick mascara clean-up, Michelle is back in action, and I am taking down notes for her wonderful birthday present, all talk of babies folded neatly away.

I run more days than I sleep now. Not a nervous, get-away-from-here run, but an open-eyed, look around and see who else is here kind of run. I almost feel happy when I run. Almost.

It is June, and Katie is graduating from eighth grade. She has been asked to write a graduation speech, which she is working on every evening after school, starting from scratch each time.

"I just want it to be meaningful!" she explains to me.

I listen to variations that include a touch of humor or a sentimental tone or quotes from the great thinkers in life.

"It's not quite right," she sighs, disappointed in herself. I want to tell her that each one sounds amazing, that they are beautiful and moving and sweet. But that won't do anything to help because she wants it to be meaningful and she is the only one who knows what kind of meaning she is looking for.

Ben and I are back to normal again, if mutual avoidance is normal. He plays with the kids and plans weekend schedules based on piano lessons for Jake, ballet for Maddie, soccer for all three of them, and then chaperoning Katie and her friends as they go to bowling parties and pool parties and dance parties.

So, as far as making plans for the weekend, or catching up on Jake's trip to the dentist, we are completely back to normal. However, our normal now includes nights full of empty spaces and irrelevant mumblings. Sometimes he stays at work late, but most nights he just comes home and takes over with the kids while I disappear into my room, my run, or a long shower. We pretend that we are sharing the responsibilities of parenthood, and smile without looking at each other when we explain this to our neighbors, who admire our relationship so much. But sharing implies a togetherness that we don't have. Dividing or segregating might be better descriptions for how we parent. Like two sides of an aisle, two shifts in a factory, two poles of the earth.

I am waiting in the kitchen for Ben to get home. I will meet Gracie tonight so I am already in my shorts and tank top, my feet slipped into my untied shoes. They are not very comfortable. I have run in them for the past four months, and before that I have worn them for everything from running errands and carrying kids to the park, to hauling boxes of toys up and down the stairs as we moved in here six years ago.

Ben jiggles the keys in the door, almost a signal for me to get out of the way. I squat down to tie my shoes as he walks into the kitchen, Katie mid-sentence as she practices her speech. She stops with a squeal, "Daddy! Listen to this!"

"Gimme one minute, Katie, and then I will be all yours! Where's your mother?"

Katie points at me and Ben looks a little disappointed, like he was hoping she would say, "Oh, Mom fell into Lake Michigan."

"Hey." My non-emotional greeting confirms my presence, his presence, and our mutual desire to get away from each other. I have one hand on the door when Katie calls us out on it.

"Daddy, why don't you ever seem happy to see mom anymore? It's like she's barely there and you guys are avoiding each other. It is seriously worse than Kaitlyn and her stuck up clique at lunch. And it is super uncomfortable to be around."

I stop with my hand stuck to the doorknob. Ben isn't moving either. But Katie keeps looking from Ben to me, back and forth, as if she is expecting a response.

Ben gives her one.

"I am always happy to see Mommy. I am always happy to see all of you guys. Mom just has something to do, that's all. She runs. Alone."

"Well," Katie folds her arms over her chest, professor-like, and narrows her eyes a bit. "then you should go with her."

Ben looks at me, asking silently for a little support.

"That's okay," I tell Katie, "running is something I do for myself. Daddy isn't interested in doing that."

"Is that true?" she turns to Ben.

This is a trick question, and we all know it, but Ben answers in his most upbeat lying voice he has.

"Of course not! I'm always interested in what Mommy is doing. But I just got home and I need to stay with you kids while Mommy goes for her run."

He seems satisfied with the believability of his reasoning, and turns to walk up the stairs.

"Oh, that's okay. I'll hang out with Maddie and Jake. Go change your clothes and Mom will wait for you." She glances back at me, as if to make sure I heard her.

Ben's jaw tightens into a forced smile. I shrug and motion for him to get going.

Katie leaves me in the kitchen as she calls to her siblings.

"Okay, you guys, Mom and Dad are going for a run and I am in charge! Who has homework?"

I can't decide if she will be better suited for government or business when she grows up. Either way, she is going to be a ball-buster all right.

I can see Gracie waiting for me on the corner. I don't know how she will feel about having an extra body lumbering after us, or in front of us. I realize I have no idea if Ben can run at all, or if he will sprint past us both. Maybe he'll just run with us far enough to make Katie happy, and then he can return home.

Ben bounces down the stairs, motions to me with his head and calls out, "Okay, kids, we'll be back soon!"

To me he mumbles a quiet, "Ready?" as he opens the door.

I follow him, but he turns the wrong way, so I redirect him. "This way."

I can see that he doesn't give a shit which way we go, so he sighs and turns back around. Instead of running next to me, he runs behind me, like a confused puppy. It bothers me.

Over my shoulder I point out, "So, we are meeting Gracie, that lady up ahead. I run with her once a week."

This surprises Ben and he leaves my shadow to peek out at her.

"Well, just one more thing I didn't know, I guess," he says as we cross the street.

Gracie has been watching us and has figured out we are running together, despite the gap between us.

"This must be your husband, right?" Gracie grins and sticks out her hand to Ben.

Ben returns the handshake but says, half joking, "Well, I could just be a friend, or her brother, or her lover, couldn't I?"

Gracie lifts her sunglasses and looks from Ben's face to mine and back again.

"No, you're married. It's written all over your faces."

We turn to look at each other, trying to see what she sees. It's not a gaze that either of us can hold for very long.

"Well, let's go!" Gracie turns to the path and we follow her, like ants in a row.

Once we get to the lake, Gracie picks up the pace again.

"Tempo run, okay?" she calls over her shoulder.

I call back to Ben, "Tempo run."

"What does that mean?" Ben asks.

I don't want to explain. "Just keep up."

I think Gracie might have been ready to tell Ben what a tempo run is, how it pushes you to the edge of your aerobic threshold. How even a little bit faster will suddenly have your muscles burning and your breathing out of control. Running at tempo pace is like walking on a tightrope. As long as you stay focused and relaxed and completely aware of your body you can run for a good hour without stopping. But one distraction, one complaint, one moment of weakness or arrogance and your run falls apart.

But she doesn't say a word.

Instead we move like a wave together, picking up the pace until we are skimming past families on bikes, easy joggers, and beach-bound kids. I am aware of Ben behind me for a few minutes, but soon I become focused on my own breath, the cadence of my steps, the strength of my back, the ease of my arm swing. I keep scanning these parts of my body as we move mile after mile. My legs start to tire and it becomes more difficult to hang on to the pace, but I have done this before and I know I can do it again. We have turned around at the harbor, but the pace stays strong. Locked in rhythm, my legs move automatically now. At this point I can look out over the lake, at the white sailboats dotting the horizon. The evening sky shimmers on the lake and the whole city seems to take in a deep breath and relax.

Gracie holds up her hand, fingers spread wide, meaning we have five more minutes. I look behind me and see that Ben has, in fact, kept up, as I told him to. He seems to be staring at something straight ahead, but I know that his gaze is actually turned inward. I know it because it is how I have spent the last few years looking at the world.

Four more minutes. She picks up the pace and now I am breathing hard, running hard. Ben moves next to me.

Three minutes.

Our stride is even, step for step.

Two minutes. He is starting to fall off, fatigue floods his brow.

"Come on --" I grunt. "We got this."

He lifts his shoulders a bit and pulls beside me again.

One minute.

"We...can...do...this..," he gasps, repeating it over and over until Gracie lifts her hand one more time, slowing gradually to a light jog. She moves beside Ben and me and gives each of us a high five.

Ben is grinning, although he can't speak, and as he lets his breath slow down, he grabs me around my shoulders in a giant one-arm hug.

"Holy crap, Eva! Why didn't you tell me you can run like that?" He looks at Gracie. "Are you her coach?"

She just smiles and shrugs her shoulders.

Is that what she's been doing? Coaching me?

We are jogging side by side now, shifting every now and then to accommodate a passing bike or group of runners.

"Are you training her for some race in particular?" Ben asks Gracie.

She shrugs again.

"Are you?" I ask her.

She just throws it back at me. "Do you want me to?"

"I don't know. "

"That's Eva for ya," Ben grumbles, exasperated. "She never knows what she wants."

Gracie puts her hand on Ben's arm. "Then we will wait until she decides."

I can tell Ben feels bad now. He doesn't mean to be critical or impatient. I don't exactly make it easy for him.

"No, you don't have to wait," I say. "I'd love to train for something. What do you have in mind?"

"Well, I am helping to organize a half marathon race as a fundraiser for a local charity. Wanna try to win that one? It's not until next spring, so you have lots of time."

I look at Ben, wanting...his approval? his permission?

He just grins.

"Win?" I think that's a little far-fetched.

"Eva, do you have any clue how fast you are?" Ben shakes his head at Gracie, still grinning. "She has no clue, does she?"

Gracie shakes her head too.

"Well, then, alright," I agree, "let's see what happens."

Ben punches the air. "Nice!"

"Looks like you've got Ben's support, don't you?" Gracie observes.
Support.
That's it.


Katie's speech was splendid. Emotional. Dramatic. Inspiring. And yes, meaningful.

Too bad most of her classmates were talking, texting, or sleeping throughout the whole thing.

She wails into my shoulder as we wait for the rest of our family to arrive for her graduation party.

"They didn't even look at me! They didn't even pretend to be listening! I am so glad to be getting out of that school!"

I pat her gently on her back, like I did when she was a baby, wailing with colic or just plain orneriness. It's just as ineffective now. She moves her catastrophic dismay to the kitchen table, burying her face in her folded arms.

I take my hand from her back and turn her face to look at me. She is half child and half adult and I am not sure which one I should talk to. The gentle soothing I've been trying only diminishes the time and effort she put into her speech, fueling her tears.

So I speak to the adult-Katie.

"You're right. It was a fantastic speech. Your classmates are juvenile miscreants who are lucky to have recognized their own name when called to the stage. And while I know you were speaking to them, to your class, you did not write that speech for them. You wrote it for yourself. You wrote it because those thoughts and ideas and values live inside you, and you have no choice but to give life to them. After that, it is out of your control. It is for every other kid, or parent, or teacher in that room to listen or not, to agree or not, to change or not, to become a better person or not."

She has stopped whimpering and the self-assured Katie that I have known for fourteen years is reappearing before my eyes. She straightens her back, brushes her hair out of her eyes, and sets her jaw with the same determination that I have seen in Ben before.

"Thanks, Mom," she whispers, hugging me. Ben steps into the doorway, but pauses and watches us together with that, Is everything okay? kind of look. With her hands still on my shoulders, Katie looks into my eyes. "I am so lucky to have you as my mom. You always know what to say to make me feel better."

I kiss her on her forehead. "Well, you make it pretty easy by being an awesome kid!"

She grins. "I guess we were made for each other, right? Probably most families are. Even the miscreants!"

She pops up from the chair and bounces into the living room as her grandparents, aunt, and uncle arrive, tears left in the past.

I'm still sitting at the table when she dashes back into the kitchen with my running shoes in her hand. "Oops," I say, "I meant to move those before company arrived."

She grins. "I figured you'll need them tomorrow. Maybe I'll go with you," she declares. "Yeah, I'm gonna start running, too. Just like you!"

Katie hugs her Aunt Michelle who is standing in the kitchen doorway, then she returns to the living room before I can answer. Michelle looks at the shoes dangling from my hands.

"Don't you think you've gotten a little obsessed with all that running?" she says, rolling her eyes. I throw the shoes into the broom closet and shrug my shoulders at her as she continues. "That's all you do anymore. I see you limping around half the time. And you're a sweaty mess the rest of the time. What about your job at the cafe? Don't you think you should do something productive with yourself?" She unpacks plastic containers of salsa, guacamole, and cheese dip. I grab a large bowl from the cabinet and she hands me the bag of tortilla chips to open.

I start to answer, "But I feel so much bet--"

Her voice softens as she continues, guacamole in one hand, a spoon in the other. "Eva, I'm worried about you. I don't know what you are trying to do to yourself, but now you're dragging your kids into it. And Ben, too, I hear! Really, Eva, if you won't think about all the damage you're doing to your own body, at least consider your family. Benji's knees won't last long if he keeps it up. And I hear that too much running can make teen girls sterile, too!" She stares hard into my eyes. "Do you really want the guilt of that someday?" I shake my head. She raps the spoon against my forehead, harder than I admit. "Sometimes I wonder if you ever think about the consequences of your actions!"

Grabbing the chips and dips, all balanced perfectly along her arms, she heads back toward the family, my family, the one I keep trying to destroy. She passes Ben. I'm not sure if he witnessed that, but I am ashamed nonetheless.

He walks over to me. "You okay?"

I nod quickly, swallowing the knot that has grown tight in my throat.

"Really? Well, that didn't look okay to me," he glances over his shoulder at his sister who is loudly organizing the placement of snacks. He comes close to me, tipping my chin toward him.

"How about that speech of Katie's?" he says proudly. "What an amazing young lady she's become!"

I run my fingers along the edges of his face, the strong lines that are reflected in Katie's profile.

"Sometimes I'm just blown away by the fact that...that...we *made* her," I whisper, barely believing it myself.

"Yep, her and two more like her!" He is smiling but then he remembers, which makes me remember. He stammers, "Well, three...I mean...never mind."

I dip my chin and mumble, "Don't..."

And like a cannon ripping through my gut, I am suddenly curled up and crying, quiet streams of tears pouring down my cheeks, and Benjamin is holding me in his arms. He picks me up, cradling me, and quickly slides past the living room doorway. No one calls my name or cries for my attention. He carries me up the stairs, kissing my neck, my arms, my hair.

He takes me onto the bed where he holds me even tighter on his lap, letting me cry, and when the tears slow down, between shuddering breaths, I say the only words I can, "I'm so sorry." My words are empty and overused. I use them to hide my true feelings, the ones that make me so ashamed, so unfit to be a mother at all. Not about the abortion, but about everything leading up to it. About all the feelings that I've kept locked inside for almost fifteen years.

Ben's embrace becomes tighter and I feel like I can no longer breathe. I push his arms away, but the tightness is still there, crushing my chest. I feel a scream, long stifled, clawing its way out. I throw myself facedown on the bed and let the scream finally escape, muffling it in the pillows around my head. Violent convulsions expose the festering pain of my lost youth, lost dreams, lost love, and most of all the pain of silence that has dug its claws into me for years. Over and over I scream until I am too weak to scream again. And now I just cry. Ben has held his hands lightly on my back, letting me scream and wail in my self-induced torment. Now that I am calm, he strokes the back of my head, curling beside me on the bed. He turns my face toward him and I see fear in his eyes.

"I'm sorry," I whisper again.

"Eva, stop saying that," he says gently. "I think there are a lot of things you want to say, and probably some things you need to talk about, but apologizing is not one of them. I don't even know what you are apologizing for. Maybe you could start there. So I don't have to walk around so afraid of what you are thinking or feeling. So I can be a part of your life again."

He picks up my hand, cradles it in both of his. His lip trembles as his eyes shimmer with controlled tears. "Is it me?"

For the first time I realize how much more hurtful my silence has been than any tirade or argument I have so painstakingly tried to avoid. Now my words spill more easily and truthfully.

"I'm apologizing for a lot of things I guess. And it's a lot more than the...the...abortion." I take a deep, shaky breath, having finally said the word aloud. "And it's not you, or rather it's not just you. It's us, it's the way I've kept both of us struggling for so long. From the time Katie was born." This I say in a whisper of shame.

A fresh spring of tears well up, but I keep going, staring at Ben's chest, afraid of seeing more pain in his eyes.

Ben's voice grows tense. "That's over fifteen years, Eva. That's a lot. A whole lot."

I'm about to say, Never mind, when he pulls me closer. "I'm listening," he says.

My words have no calculated beginning or sequence or logic. From a deep well of feelings harbored over days and months and years, I spill.

"Oh, god, Ben, it's just that when I got pregnant with Katie, well, I never dreamed how much it would change my life. And yours, too! So much has been out of my control for the past fifteen years. I didn't want to drop out of college, but what else could I do? I didn't want to let go of my dreams. At first, I thought I would just be postponing my future. But then, our family kept growing — and I love the kids! I love being a mom! But this," I wave my hand around the room, "this was never my dream, my plan. I didn't want to live with your mom, or move into your sister's house or stay at home cleaning baby spit-up all day. I didn't want to make you work more. I didn't want to be a self-centered mom who didn't want to have kids. But now I have them and I can't imagine life without them! You've worked so hard to make us happy, to make me happy. I'm so lucky to have you, but I'm so sad, too, and I haven't been able to figure out why. And, then, when I found out I was pregnant, and you had lost your job, and I saw the look in your eyes, well-- I just couldn't lay all that on you...on us... all over again. I'm not saying it was a good decision. Decisions like this are never good. I thought it was right at the time, and now I can't change that. I don't know if I'd want to change it, but I also hate it, and that makes me crazy. I want to a good wife, a good mother...and Michelle is such a great help to us, but sometimes...sometimes," My voice drops to whisper. "Sometimes I hate her too."

Ben listens. I can feel his chin pressing into the top of my head, and he nods slightly. I am surprised by the calm that has settled within me, the relief of letting go. But now it is Ben's turn, and I am afraid once again. Afraid that the freedom I once so flippantly desired would now be just moments away. I brace myself for the truth of his response.

He takes a deep breath before speaking.

"When you told me you were pregnant with Katie, that you had missed, what, three periods, right? When you told me that, I have never been so scared in my life. Nineteen years old and I thought I was pretty tough shit until that moment. Football, scholarships, college, big lawyer dreams, just evaporated as soon as you said that word. I know I acted like it was no big deal, that I could handle it, but I am telling you, I was terrified. I hung up the phone and started bawling right in my dorm room. David and a couple of his dumb-ass buddies were in there, and they were completely freaked out. I told them what you had said, and their advice to me seemed like a lifesaver at the time.

" 'Cut bait,' David had said. 'Tell her you can't deal with that. Tell her it's not yours. Tell her to get an abortion. Tell her to leave you out of it.'"

I sit up, not sure I want to feel Ben touching me anymore.

"All I had to do was walk away. The door was wide open to me and I could just turn around and never look back. The end."

Now it's Ben who is crying.

"You didn't tell me that," I mutter.

"It would have been so easy for me to just turn away. But I realized that no matter what decision I made, it was you who had to make all the real choices and you would have the consequences to deal with. Have a baby, give it up for adoption, raise it on your own, get an abortion, get married. All of those choices meant you had to hand your body over to someone. All I had to do was delete your phone number."

"You told me you wanted to get married. You said you wanted to have kids. You said you didn't like college anyway." Why have I been so oblivious to this? "You lied to me. And it changed both of our lives forever."

"No, Eva, I didn't lie. I thought good and long about you, about what it would mean to be with you and what it would mean to lose you. I couldn't lose you, because you were my best friend, my biggest supporter, and the light at the end of each day. I didn't know that by keeping you for myself, I would be forcing you to lose so much."

His hands are trembling, so I press them against my cheek, and feel his warmth blend with mine.

"And I love Katie. She looks like you; she's smart like you; she's beautiful like you. So, I am very glad we started our family together. It's not the way we wanted it to be, but like you said, look what we made!"

"What kind of mother am I?" I choke. "I know I couldn't have had another baby. And I know it wasn't right to hide this from you, but I just couldn't face you at that point. I know that sounds ridiculous, and I don't want you to think I'm making excuses. Everyday when I comb Maddie's hair or watch you play with Jake I think about that day, that decision. I just didn't know what to say." I feel stuck in a purposeless confession.

"Listen, I'm a part of this, too. I'm a part of those kids down there and I'm a part of the frustration you feel with my family and with Michelle. I am a part of your sadness and your anger and your happiness. I am a part of you because we took this on together. I guess it's easy for me now, to tell you what you should or shouldn't have done. Or to pretend I know how I would have reacted. But it's in the past, and I can't change anything. So the bigger question is, what happens next? Because if we want to keep hiding and pretending and lying, then that's a problem for all of us."

Something in my heart unclenches its grip, letting old memories of love and idealism resurface.

"We were so confident about all this in the beginning weren't we?" I say.

"Yep. Stupid kids. Young love." He smiles and twirls a strand of my hair around his finger.

"I remember thinking we'd get a farm, out in the country, and I'd grow all our own food and Katie would run around barefoot and free. Our mantra was *Who needs money?*" My reminiscence seems so immature, so unrealistic.

We laugh. "Oh, god, Katie would hate us!" Ben says.

I realize we've been in here for a while, and certainly someone will be looking for us pretty soon. On cue, a sharp, "Mommy!" shouts up the stairs.

"I'll be right there!" I call down, rushing into the bathroom to wash my face.

Ben walks in behind me and looks at me in the mirror.

"Eva, I am really glad you finally told me how you were feeling, and all the things that you didn't want for your life. But starting today-- starting now-- can you do me a favor? Can you think about what you do want? You are an awesome mother, a beautiful wife, and you do deserve to have what you want. Those are things I can actually help you with."

He kisses me on the back of my neck, and then heads downstairs, shouting, "Who's ready for hamburgers? Get me my grilling apron!"

I wash my face in the bathroom, removing the mascara streaks from my cheeks. I bend close to the mirror to stare into my eyes, puffy and red.

I am reminded of the day I vomited at work. Someone had called up to Michelle's office, and she squeezed her way into the tiny bathroom at the back of the cafe. She had stood behind me, her hands on her hips, while I leaned over the sink, washing the stench from my face. We locked eyes in the mirror, a string of saliva still dripping from my lips.

"You are, aren't you?" she asked, scowling at me. I shrug.

"Maybe," I reply.

"What are you going to do?"

I stared back at her. Finally I shrugged again.

"Oh my god, Eva! How do you not know? You have to do something!"

Then, very quietly and deliberately, "You have to *do* something. And soon."

I shook my head at her, as another wave of nausea swept into my cheeks and throat.

Michelle drove me home, the threat of spreading the flu firmly planted in everyone's mind. As I got out of the car she shoved a napkin in my hand.

"Here, in case you need it."

I held it to my lips as I went inside. The next day I saw the number she had scrawled across the bottom, along with the message, *For Emergencies.*

Ben jogs with me to the track where we are meeting Gracie. She is waiting already, like usual. Sometimes I wonder if she does anything other than run. I know that she owns a running store with her brother, and she says she is always busy with that, but to me, she is always running.

Today, she is leaning against the fence that surrounds the track, so she doesn't see us approach. Her arms rest on the top of the chain link, making her look like a little girl, trying to peek over the top of the fence. Her chin is resting on her arms, and even when I think she might be able to see us, she is still caught in some other time or place. It is only when we are close enough for her to hear our feet that she realizes we are there. She jumps slightly, and turns away from us briefly, wiping her hands across her face. Then she is smiling up at us again, the same Gracie I am used to running with, but with moist eyelashes this time.

We jog out onto the track together while Ben drops off to the side to do his own workout of push ups, jumping jacks, squat jumps, and lunges. He says that I've inspired him, that we should all spend more time taking care of ourselves. I'm not sure Jake agrees with him, since that means giving up his daily chips and soda, but his complaining stopped after a few weeks. And now that he is back in school, he has less time to whine about it anyway.

Habits are tough to break and tough to create but they are super easy to maintain, whether they are good or bad. I think we are creating some good habits lately.

Gracie gives me her plan for the day. "We'll do a two-mile warm up, then two by four hundred, two by eight hundred, two twelve hundreds and one sixteen hundred at ten seconds faster than race pace. A five minute break. Then we'll walk it back down the ladder, okay?"

I smile at Gracie. I barely understand her, with all the hundreds and paces thrown in there. But I will do what she says and trust that she knows what she is doing. The race is still six months away, but both of us are excited. And every day Ben asks me how my training is going, so he may be the most excited of us all.

Half way through our warm up I ask Gracie, "How did you know Ben was my husband when you first met him? You said it was all over our faces, and I have to be honest, we were not in a good place at that time. We could barely stand to be around each other. I can't imagine that we were glowing with marital bliss."

"I didn't say you were. I just know how people look who love each other, who are tied to each other, but carry the pain for each other too. That's what you looked like. You and Ben shared the same burden on your face, whatever it was."

She doesn't ask what it was, and I am glad, because we are healing from that and I don't want to go back to it. So I tease her a little bit instead.

"How did you get so smart about people? Are you a psychic in running shoes?"

She laughs a bit. "I guess that's what happens when you work with that many people. You start to read them better. They remind you of people you've met or people you competed against or trained with…" Her voice trail off, like she has more to say, but then our warm-up is over and she switches to coach mode.

Ben jogs to the starting line with a stop watch in his hand. Gracie heads across the field to coach me through the tough parts, and Ben shouts out the time splits after each lap, until I finish the first sixteen hundred in five minutes and fifteen seconds. Gracie jogs back over with a bottle of red juice in her hand.

"Here ya go. This will help you recover for the next set."

We sit in the grass, the October sun on my back, sweat beads rolling down my arms, my face, and my chest. Gracie has her arms folded across her chest and she nods at me with a knowing smile. "Yep, just like I thought. You got what it takes!"

"Oh really?" I call back to her, grinning. "I suppose you know that because of someone you trained with or competed against?"

Gracie's smile disappears. She turns to cross back over to her spot at the halfway point. Ben looks at me, and I shrug my shoulders. Whatever I said, it hurt her, and I have no idea why.

We finish the work out, and by the end my calf muscles are cramping and my lungs are having a tough time keeping the oxygen flowing. Our cool down feels impossibly slow, but both Ben and Gracie jog with me in silence. Gracie sets the pace by jogging in front of me, to make sure I don't start running fast (no chance of that I tell her) or drop down to a walk.

After a couple laps like this Ben whispers in my ear, "You need to ask her. Don't pretend it didn't happen. You need to face it. You can do that." He grabs my hand and squeezes it, then drops back to a shuffle.

I pull alongside Gracie, who is still jogging silently. She flashes me a huge smile, and swallows hard.

"I said something that upset you," I begin.

She waves her hand at me, indicating I am over-reacting.

Before she could brush me off completely I continue, "You don't have to tell me what it is, but please don't pretend it didn't happen. I'm tired of pretending. So I just wanted to say that, whatever it was, I am sorry."

She nods, still quiet. I take that as an acceptance of my apology. We both slow to a walk as we return to the starting line. Ben picks up my bag and walks back to us.

She grabs my hand and looks into my eyes.

"You were right. You do remind me of one of my training partners. Someone I trained with a lot, who worked as hard as you, who had no idea she was as good as she was, who ran because it made her feel alive.

"Her name was Julie. But she's gone now, so it is nice to have a new running partner. In fact you were the first person I ran with since Julie, aside from group runs at the store."

"She's gone? What do you mean?" I ask carefully.

Gracie nods, confirming my hidden question. "She was hit by a car two years ago. She was running with me, and we got to the intersection at LaSalle -- you know how crazy it is there? Well, I stopped, but she kept going. A car was accelerating toward the on-ramp. I grabbed her hand, but I didn't grab on tight enough. That car tossed her straight into oncoming traffic." Gracie's eyes have filled again, and I want to tell her to stop, but I remember Ben telling me to face it, so I take her hand and keep listening. "She died.

"Her husband is furious with me. He blames me for pushing her too hard, for making her run too fast, too much. He blames me for her death. And I blame myself too."

"No!" I protest, "it's not your fault! How could you have known that she'd keep running, or that the car wouldn't stop? It was an accident! How can he blame you?"

She nods. "Ron loved Julie very much. And when she died, they were going through a rough patch, like most people do when the honeymoon is over and real life sets in. I think in addition to blaming me for her death, he blames me for preventing their reconciliation. He blames me because he was angry with her when she died. And that is something that neither of us can undo."

We walk off the track together, heading back to our homes, to the rest of our lives. Ben has his arm around me now, and I can feel him squeeze me just a little bit tighter. He reaches out with his other arm, gently patting Gracie's shoulder.

"I'm sorry, Gracie. And I'm sure it is awful for this Ron guy, but if he is making you feel worse, then you need to just tell him to leave you alone. You don't need that grief laid on you."

Gracie smiles at him.

"Thanks, Ben, I appreciate it. But you see, it's my grief too. Julie wasn't just my running partner.

"Julie was my daughter."

There is nothing Ben or I can say after that.

Silently, we all let the tears flow, grieving and releasing together.

As we walk home, for the first time since I've met her, I begin to see Gracie as more than a crazy runner-lady, more than a hard-driving coach. I begin to see the effect that love and pain and unconditional support has on just one person. I learn what it means to love someone, to stand by them no matter what happens, because we all need that at least once in our life. Every one of us.

Running through the cold of winter has made my body strong, but my soul stronger. I have learned to accept the biting winds that course across the lake, picking up speed and ice before they slam into our faces no matter which way we run. I've learned that despite the cold, I will survive. Despite the wind, I will make it home. Despite the ice, I can return to warmth.

This year, for Michelle's birthday, I ran a cold five miles with my husband and my three children. We all bundled up and took turns running in front, or slowing to look at the frozen waves along the shoreline. When we got home, we wrapped ourselves in blankets and played LIFE and drank hot chocolate.

When she asked why we couldn't go to Florida with them this year, I wanted to blame the kids' schedules, or Ben's work, or some other safe excuse. But instead I told her the truth.

"I need some time with my family," I said.

"But, I'm your family! In fact, Eva, I am the one who practically runs your whole family! Your job, your house, your kids!" At this she paused. "The least you guys can do is celebrate my birthday with me. After all," she murmurs, a tear shimmering in the corner of one eye, "after all, I don't have kids like you do."

"I know," I said, patting her hand. "And I do appreciate all your help. But I think it's time I started making the decisions for my family on my own. I need to run my own life, Michelle, and right now, that means spending more time with Ben and the kids."

Before her frown imbedded itself permanently, I teased her a little by saying, "Maybe you and Tom could use some time to yourselves as well. You know, to get romantic!"

She continued to pout, but I could see she liked that idea.

And it eventually proved to be effective, too. Michelle and Tom are expecting twins in November.

As the spring thaws and my runs get longer, I try to imagine Michelle as a mother. Will she be organized and punctual and decisive, the way I have always known her to be? Or will she, like so many of us, discover a path all its own, unheeding any schedules or demands we place on it.

Katie waits for me on the stoop of our new house in Rogers Park, stopwatch in hand, a cold sport-drink on the steps beside her.

"Nice job, Mom! That was fifty-six minutes! Did you run the full 10 miles? Did you stop at all? Oh, wow. You are going to totally kill this half-marathon!" She falls into an easy jog beside me as I cool down, her chatter slowing only slightly. She throws one arm around my waist and tugs me close to her, giving me exactly what I need.

# 11  GRACIE

I have always loved watching the change that occurs in women as they begin running. Most of the women who come to Run the World are hoping to lose weight. Some are looking for some time to themselves, or with their friends. More recently I've had women with a competitive spirit looking to see how hard they can push themselves. All of these women are running toward a goal of some sort. I used to be like that. Focused on the goal — for my dad, for my school, for myself, and finally for Julie, my daughter.

The 1970's was a great decade for women in many ways, but the two greatest impacts it had on me was my running and my marriage. And those two mixed like oil and water.

Jeff Matthews was "the boy next door" who went away to Vietnam at a time that I was just trying to run faster circles around a track. By the time he returned I was a Business major and a store clerk for my dad. Jeff was slim and muscular and cute and cocky. At first he applied to work at our running store, but Dad didn't need any help, so Jeff would just hang around and talk, telling us stories from Vietnam. Some of them were pretty scary, but he also told us of exotic landscapes and shorelines and the many guys he had met from around the world. Each time though, he'd end his stories with, "it was just tough being alone through all that." Whether it was good or bad, it was the being alone that bothered him the most. And I could see why. Never knowing if you were living your last moment, seeing your last sunrise, eating your last meal — that's got to mess with a person's mind. Well, it did with Jeff anyway.

It didn't take long for me to start listening to him, more than to the customers, so finally my dad told us to get out of his store and go on a real date. This made me blush a little, but Jeff just cocked his head and said, "Yes, sir," to my father. "Pick you up at seven tonight," he said to me.

We'd known each other since Jeff was in high school and I was the skinny girl running around the track with the rest of the boys. Jeff didn't talk to me much back then, but he'd ask my dad a lot of questions about his running days. You'd think Jeff would have joined the track team with all that interest, but he didn't. He wrestled a little, and sat on the bench a lot at football games. But he seemed most interested in running.

On our first real date he told me the truth.

"I was never into sports. I'm just not that kind of guy," he admitted. "But there was something about running that I was really into." He smiled at me and took my hand. "You."

My heart pounded against my chest and I prayed that my hand wouldn't sweat.

"Gracie, I could watch you run all day! Your hair bouncing, your legs and arms swinging, your.. your.. well, the rest of you just swaying like the prettiest thing ever. I'd talk to your dad for hours just to watch you running." Then he stopped. "Does that sound creepy?"

I laughed and then so did he. It was easy to fall in love from that point on. We already knew each other, and he had professed his long-held fascination with me. Jeff got a job working in computer sales, and was making a great salary, which he lavished on me. What girl would walk away from that?

So we did get married, the next summer, right after I graduated from Loyola. The red flags popped up almost instantly.

At the reception, we stood in line, greeting our friends and relatives. A few of my college friends came up and hugged me and then Jeff.

As Jeff shook hands with the guys he leaned over to me and said, "I guess you wasted your time focusing on an M-R-S degree, didn't you?"

I was more confused than anything else, and I was enjoying the wedding so much, that I forgot about it completely.

I was pregnant within a few months of our wedding day. Jeff insisted that I immediately stop running, as did my doctor. I was sore and crabby and I started to resent this pregnancy that had brought my life to a halt, while Jeff's life became more social, more lavish, and more demanding.

He fell into the habit of calling me his "good soldier" when he asked me to do something.

"Hey, Gracie, be a good soldier and take my suit to the cleaners for me, okay?"

"Hey Gracie, grab a few beers out of the fridge for my buddies, would ya? That's a good soldier!"

When he told me to stop working, he had me tell my dad that it was doctor's orders. Jeff was scooping the pictures and calendar off my desk and into a small box. He confirmed my lie by adding, "You know how stubborn your daughter is, Billy. But the doctor knows what's best."

"Yes, I know my daughter well," my father answer him, staring straight through my lies. But he held the door as we left. Jeff put his arm around me until we were back to the car. As he shoved the box into my arms and walked himself to the driver's side door, I looked back at the store, my second home for the last ten years. My father had his face pressed against the glass of the entrance door, watching.

The day Julie was born, Jeff was nowhere to be found. My dad, my mom, my brother and sisters, all took turns beside my hospital bed or on the phone, calling his work, his friends, his local hang-outs. Finally they just gave up and waited.

When it was time to push, my Dad excused himself. "I'll leave you with your momma," he said. His eyes betrayed the anger he was holding back.

I grabbed his hand. "Please don't leave," I asked him through clenched teeth as another contraction waved across me.

He turned back to me. "Never," he said, giving me that smile of his that always let me know things would be alright.

So Julie entered the world with her grandparents on either side, her aunts and uncle bursting through the door as soon as they were allowed in and her father passed out in a hotel room, robbed by the hooker he had indulged in the previous night.

My father was a patient, forgiving man, but Jeff's behavior had diminished Dad's seemingly endless stock of both.

"No daughter of mine is going to be treated like this," I heard him grumble to Mom outside my hospital room. "Not my Gracie. Not by that.. that... lousy..."

Mother hushed him, but she stood by his side to block Jeff's way in to see me as I was resting peacefully with my newborn little girl. They were quiet about it, but the nurse let me know how bad Jeff smelled and how bold my father was, just inching him back a little at a time until he was backed right into the elevator. Jeff didn't even try to come back.

When I was released from the hospital, Julie and I moved back home-- to my parents' home-- and Jeff disappeared from that day on. Eddie told me he's seen him around once in a while, but he hasn't changed much.

As my strength returned, I started bringing Julie into the store to visit, then I started to help with check-outs behind the counter again. The next thing I knew, Julie was as much a part of the store as the rest of us, running to get different sizes, or hanging up displays, or rallying her school friends for a girls' only run. Her passion for running grew directly out of the soil in which she was planted — our running store.

It has taken me a while to tell this story to anyone other than Hera. But it seems to flow easily as I tell Ben and Eva on our walk back from the track this evening.

"When I think back on it, I have so many doubts. Maybe I should have moved out of my parents' house sooner. Given her a different kind of life, instead of pushing her to be a runner like me. Maybe she didn't need me to be her coach, or her grandpa to be her coach, or her uncle to be her coach. Maybe, if she had found some other passion in her life…if I had given her a chance to be her own person, and not just more of who I wanted to be… maybe then she'd still be here. Maybe Ron is right, in some way. Maybe I did push her to her own death."

I look into Eva's eyes, doubting she could ever understand the ambivalence of motherhood.

Eva wraps her arms around me, and Ben wraps his arms around the two of us.

Eva whispers softly. "You know that's not true. You know that we make decisions based on the best person we can be at the moment. Gracie, you have literally saved my life by pushing me to run. You have saved my marriage, my family … all of it because you make me run. You help me run. You gave me a reason to run. If you did even half of that for Julie, then she was the luckiest daughter alive."

Ben gives us both a squeeze before letting go.

"Time to let go of the past, Gracie. Too many people need you up ahead." He grins and turning leads us back onto the sidewalks toward home. Eva reaches out. And together we cross LaSalle Street, hand in hand.

# 12  KRISTINA

*The first thing to do is to buy the right shoes.*

Isn't that the truth?

The right pair of shoes tells the world exactly who you are and what you want in life. Take, for example, a pair of four inch red stilettos. Those shoes scream, "I want your attention, and by god, you are going to give it to me!" I don't have any red stilettos.

Instead I own two pairs of brown "sensible" shoes. The first pair has a slightly thicker sole for days that I am chasing four-year-olds around at the Drop'n'Drive Day Care. I have been working there a few days a month, for the past two years. The kids are supposed to call me Miss Kristina, but they blend it all together into "Mista". And while I love the little tykes, they can really exhaust the heck out of me with all the running and chasing and taking them to the bathroom and getting them their snacks and picking up after them. So a pair of thick-soled shoes is an absolute must.

The second pair of brown sensible shoes is a modified high-top and is part of my employee uniform for my "other" job that I work at Joy's Jumpin' Jungleland, a huge arena of trampolines, air mats, tight-ropes, swings and ball pits that has become super popular with birthday parties for kids. It's as if their parents are daring them to make it through another year. The noise level is always a loud, reverberating scream, so there is a "quiet room" where parents can sit and watch their darling dare-devils hurl themselves through the air while the noise is muffled to a low murmur. As a Jumpin' Jungleland employee, I watch for impending injuries, shout out warnings, and call parents to the Safe Oasis when their kids are lost, tired, or crying. They are usually crying. At the end of the day I clean up snot, blood, and vomit that seems to cover everything, including me.

When I am not wearing one of those brown sensible pairs of shoes I am shuffling around in a very thin worn-out pair of gray flip-flops that I have had for more years than flip-flops were intended to be worn. My toes are frequently dirty, with cracked toenails and cracked heels a prominent part of their appearance. I don't bother with nail polish because, let's face it, who am I trying to impress?

I put my shoes on the floor of the closet and hang up my uniform. I pick up a large gray sweatshirt from off the floor and squirm my way into it. I've been rotating a few outfits for the past week. If you can call gray sweats an outfit. My apartment is still stacked with boxes that I haven't even thought about unpacking in the last six months.

There are no mirrors. No reflections. As long as I avoid looking down I do not have to remember why I am here.

Zachary Burns and I had been friends since fourth grade, when he moved in with his grandma across the hall from us on Princeton Avenue. In no time we became inseparable. We'd walk to elementary school together, just a block away. Then we'd walk across the street to church each afternoon for an hour of Bible study, then on to the drug store for some pop and candy bars or cheap potato chips to munch on while we did our homework together at his grandma's. Zachary would help me with my math and I would help him with his English because neither of us was good at both of them. Then we'd paint or draw something from our day. His pictures always involved a stick-figure dead guy with blood spurting out of him somewhere. I would draw my day based on how I felt. Some days it was a sketch of science class; some days it was a blurry mix of noise and tears and gum and fighting in the hallways. When I painted or sketched, I would lose myself and lose track of time. My mom worked two jobs, so once our homework was done I went back to my apartment and watched TV until she came home. Sometimes Zachary would come with me. But that only lasted until high school.

Zachary made the Junior Varsity football team as a high school freshman, and by sophomore year he was on Varsity. We still went to school together, taking the city bus south. We'd help each other study for tests or I'd let him copy my homework, but once we got off the bus he'd walk away with his football friends, and I'd walk away alone.

After school Zachary would go to practice while I pretended to go to church by myself, but instead I'd buy a snack of sliders and sit out in the parking lot eating and watching the team across the street. I'd catch the bus back home as he went into the locker room to change, so I'd be lying on the couch before he got home. Then he'd come over to my apartment with a soda and some chips, and eventually whiskey and soda and chips. He'd tell me about the plays his team worked on and boast about how sore or strong he was getting and which of the girls was hitting on him now. He dated girls for an average of nine days -- just long enough to get laid or to get turned down, so he'd move on to a new one. I'd complain to him about my math teacher, the obnoxious kids in my English class, and my steadily increasing size.

"Zachary, you gotta stop bringing those chips over here. I can't stop eating them, and look at me! I'm getting huge!"

He'd laugh at me, rub my flabby belly like I was a lucky Buddha, and say "So what?" But he wouldn't bring them for a few days anyway, and I would eventually go buy them myself. He was happier munching on chips with me anyway, and it was fun to watch him enjoy them so much. Of course, he was a guy, playing football, and I was a teenage girl doing nothing but sitting on my ass. So he could afford to like them more than I did.

We only had one class together all four years of high school, during our junior year. It was an English elective class on poetry that I took because I loved poetry and Zachary took because it fit best with his football practice schedule. I sat in the front of the room where I could hear Mrs. Wolfe. She always read those poems so strong and full of passion. By sitting up front, I could forget that there were twenty-five other kids sitting behind me, and I could get all caught up in the meaning of the poem. No one else seemed to like poetry as much as me, so I tried to act like I was bored or sleeping, but really, I would listen to every one of those poems and reread them at night, especially the ones I could really connect to.

One day she read a poem by Carl Sandburg-- *Chicago*-- her voice rough and urgent, the way a great big city would sound if it could talk.

*"Hog Butcher for the World,*
*Tool Maker, Stacker of Wheat...*
*City of the Big Shoulders:*
*They tell me you are wicked and I believe them,*
*for I have seen your painted women under the gas lamps luring the farm boys.*
*And they tell me you are crooked and I answer: Yes, it is true*
*I have seen the gunman kill and go free to kill again.*
*And they tell me you are brutal and my reply is:*
*On the faces of women and children*
*I have seen the marks of wanton hunger.*
*And having answered so I turn once more to those who sneer at this my city,*
*and I give them back the sneer and say to them:*
*Come and show me another city with lifted head*
*singing so proud to be alive and coarse and strong and cunning...."*

Even though Chicago doesn't butcher hogs or stack wheat anymore, it still gets a pretty bad reputation for a lot of the nasty stuff Sandburg talks about. But I liked how he turns that back around to show the strength and pride of the city, too.

I had just raised my hand to share this, when Mrs. Wolfe scowled toward the back of the room. I turned around to see three guys turning purple from trying not to laugh, and Zachary, in the middle, just smiling and shaking his head slowly. He didn't look at me.

"What do you find so funny, Mr. Burton?" Frankie Burton gasped for breath. "Nothing...nothing... just asking Burns here if he's ever poked any... any.. hogs!" As he doubled over in his laughter, I saw Eric Fischer pointing to the front of the room. I turned to see what he was pointing at, and with a sudden shock realized he was pointing at me.

Zachary lifted his head and when he met my eyes, any trace of a smile melted. I could see he felt bad for me, but what was he supposed to do? These were his buddies, his teammates, and I was just the girl who lived across the hall.

Mrs. Wolfe forgot to call on me, and I forgot that I had something to say. The next day I sat in the back row, closest to the door, and I never raised my hand again.

We never talked about it, but I knew then that Zachary and I had two different ideas about friendship. To me, it was a twenty-four/seven kind of thing. For him, it was part-time only. And I accepted that, because after all, it was better than nothing.

Until the night he proposed.

It was late May of our senior year, just two years ago. Zachary and I were hanging out as usual, eating Fritos and onion dip, drinking rum and Cokes, and watching TV in his grandma's living room. Zachary was on the floor, me lying on the couch, and we started having one of those "future" talks -- you know, "what are you gonna do after high school? after college? after joining the NFL?"

The dreams mixed with drink and pretty soon we had our whole lives plotted and perfected until we almost believed we were living it. Zachary would be an NFL star who drove a yellow Porsche and lived in a huge lakeside penthouse condominium. In my dream-life, I had eight kids, four boys, four girls, and a big house that was tidy but had lots of kids' artwork hanging around. I pictured myself with paint all over my arms and hands and when my loving husband would come home he'd kiss me and clean up all the kids while I took a bubble bath.

Zachary laughed. "I cannot picture you in a bubble bath! Unless your tub was filled with soda pop!"

Embarrassed, I just giggled a little. "Yeah, I know. Unlikely anyone is gonna marry me looking like this, anyway." And I nodded down at my large belly, my round thighs, my voluminous breasts.

Zachary probably felt sorry for me after that because he stopped his laughing and goofing around and got serious. "No, Kristina, that's not what I meant!"

This time I got serious. "It's alright. I know who I am. I know what my future is really gonna be like. And it sure isn't marriage and bubble baths."

Serious and drunk don't mix well, so when he waved me off with an adamant, yet slurred "That's bullshit!" I threw it back at him. "Oh yeah? Think you could marry someone like me?"

Zachary didn't respond.

I stuffed my hand into the Fritos bag. "See what I mean?" I shot at him, my self-pity soaring. "If someone who actually knows me isn't interested in me, I don't see how anyone else would be."

Zachary rolled onto one leg, swaying a little, and with an exaggerated flourish, took my hand. "Hold on, I didn't finish my future. To completely fulfill my dreams, I forgot to mention that I will have Miss Kristina Gomez as my one and only bride from now until the end of time. And we will have babies and bubble baths every night and lot and lots of Fritos!" I grinned. He grinned, and finished with "How does that sound?"

"Sounds awesome!" I said, and flopped back onto the couch.

He grabbed my head between both of his hands, like I was a big old dog, kissed my forehead, and then rolled back onto the floor, snoring into the carpet in no time.

The following day Zachary didn't say anything about his future or mine, so I didn't either. A few final exams, a boring senior prom, and a long graduation line later, we finally finished our senior year and could start making real plans for the future. Zachary had been awarded an athletic scholarship from Northern Illinois University, which meant he'd be leaving for summer football camp by the end of June. There was no money for me to go to college. No scholarships, no savings, no college applications showed up in my dreams. So instead I applied for jobs. Dead-end, low paying, mind-numbing, no-talent jobs. Perfect for someone with no future.

That is, unless I was part of someone else's future.

I started to imagine my life as the wife of an NFL player named Zachary, and suddenly my future seemed a bit brighter after all. He did say I would eventually be his bride, so maybe...just maybe...he actually was serious, that there was a part of him that knew we should be together. It made perfect sense!

So I started working the job at Joy's, and I thought I might be able to save up for a wedding dress. Just in case.

I gave up soda and cookies, so I could fit into that dress. Just in case.

I leafed through old issues of Big Beautiful Bride magazine for pictures of wedding cakes and invitations and the perfect dress. Just in case.

The day before he left for NIU, Zachary's grandma made a huge dinner and invited my mother and me and the pastor at our church to join them and say good bye. For the first time since I had met Zachary, I spent time in front of the mirror plucking my eyebrows, covering up pimples, and curling my long black hair. I needed to talk to him, and I needed him to like what he saw when he looked at me.

After plates of homemade fried chicken, French fries, coleslaw and brownies (my favorite meal!) I pulled Zachary outside on the patio where we could escape the heat and find some time to be alone.

Zachary put his arm around me. "So, this is it..." Silence followed and I so badly wanted to fill it with my request, my dreams, with the big question that had been floating in my mind for the past month.

"So," I responded slowly. "So, yeah, I guess this is the beginning, right?"

Zachary twirled, dropped to the ground, and flipped himself back up again, grinning. "You bet it is! Big things are heading our way!"

Why hadn't I noticed his dimples before? Or the way his throat curves down toward his chest like the slope of a mountain, the edge of a waterfall, the waves of Lake Michigan. Pulling me in, a few years too late. Unless...

"I've been meaning to ask you..." I was hoping he'd be thinking the same thing. Wondering about the same questions. When he turned to listen to me, his eyes lit up, and I charged in.

"I was just wondering, if...you know...those dreams of yours...you know...I could be in them if you want. I mean, I'd like that too. I can't imagine not spending our life together. I mean, we are practically family now, right?"

Zachary looked through the open door of the apartment where his grandma and my mom chattered away, the dishes flowing from table to sink to towel.

"We are, aren't we?" he said, throwing me into a headlock. I struggled and pushed to get him off of me, but per usual, he would only let go when he felt like it. This was why I never bothered to curl my hair or wear anything pretty. I would just end up in a headlock. He let go, laughing, and grabbed at my curls. I pulled the strands, now knotted, back into their place.

Then Zachary surprised me. "Kristina, I think that's a great idea!" He had one foot reaching back into the apartment, the other one still out on the cement ledge that doubled as their patio. "Great idea!"

And that's when I knew I was gonna marry Zachary Burns.

Over the summer Zachary came home a couple times, but he was always sore or going to work out or meeting up with the other guys from NIU. And once football season started in the fall he didn't come home at all. I was working long hours at the Daycare or Joy's Jumping Jungleland, and came home every evening exhausted, flopping on the couch. My days were busy and fueled by my infatuation with Zachary, as well as the convenience-food display down the street. I decided Zachary loved me for who I was, so there was no point in pretending to be anything different. Pretty much everything I ate was a shiny yellow-white color, unless it was coated in chocolate or cheese powder. They say "you are what you eat" so pretty soon I looked just like the Twinkies and donuts I consumed, although I considered myself voluptuous.

Voluptuous-- what a beautiful word! A word that means healthy, sexy, confident, alluring, somewhat of a vixen. Despite having none of these attributes, I attached that beautiful word to my lethargic heaviness. I decided that I had Zachary, and he liked voluptuous women, and that was really all I needed.

Sometimes it is so much easier to survive when you can just hang on to a lie or distraction or delusion, rather than face the ugly truth about yourself. My truth was definitely ugly, and Zachary was so sweet and handsome, so I simply clung to his drunken dream and secretly planned our future.

My twentieth birthday fell during Zachary's spring break, so he took me out for dinner to a funky blues club. We ordered battered catfish, hush puppies, big bowls of gumbo and a double order of onion rings. I was so glad to have some time with Zachary, to finally talk about our future together. I shifted my chair so I could face him.

"What are you doing?" he asked. "You can't see the stage if you move there. Do I smell bad or something?" He grinned that lovely wide grin of his, the one that never meant anything special to me, but on this day it meant the whole world.

I smiled back at him, and couldn't stop, even when his gaze went back to the stage.

The music was loud and smooth, a five piece blues band. The lead singer was a slim young black woman with a short Afro, bright round eyes, plump red lips, and a long neck. Her grey dress had a soft sparkle in it that brought out the shimmer in her eyes, and the neckline was low in both the front and back, so her neck looked like a delicate reed, so pretty and frail. She was a perfect little flower. She looked at us while she sang, and nodded at Zachary. I leaned towards Zachary and moved my fingertips closer to his. It was time we talked about our plans, our future, even if he was still caught up in his college life. So I spoke gently to his hands resting on the table, avoiding his eyes.

"So I was thinking, we don't have to rush anything, but maybe we could start saving up for...for when you...for when we get...married?"

Zachary didn't blink, didn't turn, didn't change a single bit of the expression on his face. I wanted to speak privately, quietly, but this music was too loud. He couldn't even tell that I was speaking to him. I agonized over the fact that I would have to say it again, and tried to remember exactly what I had just said.

A bit louder this time, I repeated myself, letting my fingers brush against his to get his attention again.

"Zachary, I don't think you heard me." Zachary glanced quickly at our fingers, touching, and I continued, my voice full in my throat. "I was saying, we should start planning our wedding."

As she finished her song, Zachary turned to me and said, quickly, "Kristina, what are you talking about? Wedding? " His eyes bore into me, confused, maybe angry.

Over his shoulder a girl stared at me over her cocktail, a smirk inching into her bright red lips. I watched her elbow her friend next to her, tipping her head in my direction.

Zachary pulled his hands away from me, resting his chin in the double fist he made. He stared away, then suddenly turned toward me. "Is that what you thought? All this time, is that what's been going through that head of yours? Did you think -- I was serious?"

"Well, yes. I mean, a little." My throat was getting dry and I felt like I might choke. "I guess I shouldn't have," I mumbled to him.

"Aw, Kristina," Zachary lowered his voice. "You'll always be a part of my family-- you're like a sister to me. Shit, if I'd known you were thinking all this time that we were gonna…" He stared at me like someone trying to decide whether to throw an old shoe into the trash or into the Goodwill box. In either case, it is no longer wanted.

I tried to focus on the singer, taking her bows, blowing kisses to the crowd. Zachary moved, almost imperceptibly further away from me. He applauded, but from the corner of his mouth he muttered, "Oh god, this is so awkward. Can we let it go for now? Can we talk about this later?"

I grabbed my glass of water and tried to drown the lump that was rolling into a huge stone in my throat. I nodded, water dribbling out the sides of my glass and down my chin. Zachary forced himself to grin again, his eyes pleading with me as he said, "Let's just have some fun like we used to, okay?"

He poked at my stomach, making me spill down the front of my blouse, too. "Sure," I agreed quickly, bobbing my head up and down. "Stupid… just, ya know, dreaming out loud again!" I tried to laugh, like it was all a big joke after all.

Then this little flower glided up behind him and asked, "Is this the birthday girl?" with a huge friendly smile across her face. Zachary's eyes did not leave mine as he introduced me to Violet (yes even her name is a flower!) who is a student at NIU and a musical prodigy as far as he's concerned.

She smiled and leaned over him, hugging him from behind and said, "Aw, he's always saying that!"

Always? Always?

I tried to keep watching them but their voices pounded my head and I couldn't stay focused. The girl with the bright red lips was giggling into her hand, whispering dramatically to her friend who wouldn't even stop staring at me.

Eventually Zachary stood up and I must have too. We put on our coats and Zachary left some money on the table. Violet-Girl was standing by the door, a wool cape wrapped around her shoulders, and she waved us over to her.

"Are we all ready?" Zachary asked. He put one hand gently on Violet's tiny low-back.

He threw his other arm around my neck and gave me a sloppy birthday kiss on the cheek.

"So are we cool?" he whispered in my ear. I nodded, wiped the smear of saliva with the corner of my coat, and grinned the biggest, stupidest grin I could as I walked behind them to the taxi waiting for us outside.

The next day I started looking for a studio apartment, one that would keep me from running into Zachary Burns ever again.


So, here I am today, standing in front of the wall of mirrors and stacks of shoes at Run the World shoe store. I am following Step One of the Seven Step Plan to go from *Last to Fast*. At this point I'd be happy going from Fat to Last, but I haven't found any program that sets such a low bar.

The slim paperback brochure showed up in the mail one day. I don't know if it was one of those advertisements that everyone gets or if someone was trying to hint not so subtly that I should lose some weight. So, since September, I let it sit on the counter while I sat on the couch. Eventually though, I decided to read through it, because I was coming up with a plan — a Zachary Burns plan.

The brochure is shoved into my purse. I pull it out and scan the cover briefly. It has a cartoon drawing of a large woman lying on the couch, her belly fat protruding from underneath a gray t-shirt, and a monster-sized soda in one hand, bag of chips in the other. Well, that was a familiar image. Turn the page, however, and a bright perky gal in a pink t-shirt and turquoise shorts is poised in mid-stride, grinning out at the reader to *Follow me!* Our chubby cover girl then follows Miss Perky from page to page, following each of her seven steps, and by the final page there are now two cute perky gals, one of them in a gray and pink t-shirt chugging a bottle of water instead of soda.

Well, it's worth a try.

"Hi, can I help you find something?" I am eye-level with a sliver of a man. His hair is peppery gray and wrinkles shoot from the corners of his eyes, but his body is that of a teen-age boy, slender and light and small. He is wearing blue warm-up pants and a Swoosh t-shirt, so I assume he works here.

"Yes, I am looking for a pair of shoes."

"Okay, great! We have lots of those here," he chuckles to himself. He seems to bounce lightly even when standing still. "My name is Ed. I'll take care of you! So, what kind of shoes are you looking for?"

I consult my brochure again and follow its advice. I repeat exactly what is written on page two, filling in the blanks.

"Hi Ed. I'm Kristina. I am a beginner runner. I will be running mostly on the sidewalks around the city." These are two of the three determining factors for choosing shoes -- level of experience (none) and running surface (concrete). The third is my weight and I am not about to announce that, although if Ed is at least somewhat intelligent he should be able to see that I am a big fatty.

"A beginner? Great! What's motivated you to start running?"

I look at him for any signs of sarcasm. There are none. He seems genuinely curious, so, I surprise myself and tell him my plan.

"I'd like to get in shape. I'd like to lose about fifty pounds. And once I do, I'd like to make my ex-fiancé jealous as hell. I figure running will do that, right?"

Ed shrugs his tiny shoulders at me and grins. "Maybe. It all depends. But you won't know until you try, and you can't try until you've got the right shoes. So....let's see..." Ed looks from my feet to the rows of shoes and back again. He asks me to step onto what looks like a welcome mat, but as I do, a screen in front of us lights up two foot-shapes. The feet have areas of red, yellow, and green on them.

"Cool, huh?" Ed asks me. "These are your feet!"

Cool alright. My feet appear mostly red, with a small yellow smear under the toes and a little green blob the size of a jellybean in the middle of my foot.

"The different colors represent the amount of pressure on that area so we'll know how much cushioning or stability you need. It recommends a few ideal shoes for you and also tells us the shoe size, depending on which brand and model you get. This technology just keeps getting better all the time!"

He stares at the screen for a few more seconds, then snaps his fingers. "I've got it! I'll be right back!"

I sit down on a bench facing the rows of shoes. There is one row of thin sleek slipper-like shoes that curve up at the toes. Next to those are a variety of thick soled running shoes that seem to vary only by their color and logo. Most of them are primarily white with colorful trim, but a few stand out as solid navy blue or red. Rugged, dark colored shoes that resemble hiking boots more than running shoes take up a corner space along with a wall of belts and hats and pins. I walk over to the wall and pull one of the belts off the rack. It is made from a piece of wide black elastic with hooks and pockets that I think could come in handy. It says it is one size fits all so I wrap it around my waist and pull the stretchy band but the two ends refuse to meet. I tug harder. I suck in my stomach. The ends inch closer and I nudge the plastic pieces together, hoping they will catch.

"Here we go, Kristina," Ed calls out. He bounces out of the back room with an armload of boxes. I release the ends and try to just look curious.

"Is this any good?" I ask nonchalantly.

"One of my favorites!" he chirps and he pulls over a chair to begin the shoe-fitting process.

Unlike other shoes, running shoes have almost nothing to do with whether you like them or not.

The first pair is a hideously bright orange.

"Those are hideous," I point out.

Ed doesn't even flinch. "Oh that doesn't matter. In here, the shoes pick the runner, not the other way around."

So I try them on.

Oh my gosh...

I have never felt so good in my life! These shoes are soft and cushiony, with raised arches that feel like a mini massage. I stand up and take a few steps in them. My feet are nestled in a thick cushy foam that springs back lightly when I take a few steps. I am so used to fighting with my body to get it to move. I am so used to feeling like I am sinking into the floor with each step and struggling to lift my legs to take the next step. I wouldn't say I feel light, but for the first time in years I forget that I am, in fact, over two hundred pounds.

We try a few more pairs of shoes but it was love at first fit for me and those orange sneakers. Ed smiled a little when I called them sneakers, but he didn't say anything.

"Should I put them in a bag, or do you want to wear them home?" he asks.

"Oh I'll wear them!" And eagerly I throw my old flat brown shoes in the bag and swing myself out the door.

If this is what running feels like, I think I'm going to love it.

I walk up the stairs to my apartment full of energy and inspiration, falling into a head-down, arms pumping sort of jog up the two flights. I am panting and huffing by the time I reach my door. A trickle of sweat travels down my back. That's okay. I kind of like it.

Plopping down on the couch, I kick my feet up and lay my head back. I dig into the open bag of goldfish crackers that I left here this morning and pull the *Last to Fast* booklet out of my purse again. I check off step one, and turn the page. The chubby girl in the booklet has put down her soda and is sitting upright on the couch. She looks pensive and uncertain, perhaps even somewhat sad. But I am impatient with her. I want her to get up and start moving and get skinny, but step two is telling her to first plot her route.

*Your new ambition will be tested many times in a variety of conditions. Always make sure you are prepared for any condition by dressing in layers, fueling properly, staying hydrated, and most of all, by planning your run in advance. Don't let the thrill of a new sport and fancy gear mislead you into thinking you have also trained to run. You can avoid many injuries common to beginners by taking your time, stretching appropriately, and by easing into a daily running program. Your first run may be no more than a mile, but eventually you will be trained enough to run 5 miles, or 15, maybe even a full 26.2!*

I fling the booklet onto one of the boxes that I've been using as a coffee table, then swing my legs off the couch, pulling myself up to sitting. My bright orange shoes stare up at me, pleading to hit the pavement.

Okay then. I am taking these new shoes out for a run and we'll see just how far I can go.

I pour myself a cold glass of water and gulp it enthusiastically, sliding my shirt sleeve across my mouth to absorb the dribbles. I bounce up and down a little and feel the weight of my stomach follow just a tad behind my movement. I reach my arms overhead and stretch out, bending first to the left, then to the right but it is difficult to return to standing, so I stop. Kicking my foot up toward my behind I reach desperately for my ankle, my toes, a shoelace even. No luck, since I can't reach that far around. Instead I head for the door, thinking I should have a banana for energy. But the closest thing I have is a cheese stick, so I take that instead, and go back down the stairs to my new runner life.

Clouds have covered the sunshine from earlier, casting a dreary shadow on the city streets. I walk to the end of my block to get the feel of moving and, confident I can pick up the pace, I turn north on Michigan Avenue. I lurch forward a step at a time, into a non-walk. I can't really call it a jog, because I think I actually move faster when I walk, but I am bouncing differently, my knees bending slightly, my elbows tucked alongside my stomach, and I am definitely breathing harder than usual. Despite the soft cushy shoes, the slower than slow pace, my throat begins to feel tiny and clogged. Breathe in, I tell myself, as if I'd forgotten how to do that. But my efforts are painful and fruitless. I try to slow down, but that really just requires stopping altogether.

This is ridiculous. I have only gone one block and my heart is pounding, my ears ringing. I look back at my starting point. I think I could throw a rock the distance I have traveled. Then I see the road ahead of me, the one that spears the city like a magnificent arrow, and I am overwhelmed by how long it is, how many blocks are stacked together to make even one straight mile.

Defeated, I walk home, stopping at the quick mart for a slushy and a wheel-turned hot dog.

Today is my birthday. I am twenty-one years old, finally an adult, but when I look at my life, my tiny little apartment, at the mess I see in the mirror each day, I don't feel even close. It seems so long ago that my "dreams" of adulthood were so bright and loving and complete. In just two years I have fallen into a hole of non-stop go-nowhere work and a routine of sloth and slop. Those shoes don't help.

Every morning when I leave for work my orange running shoes are staring at me from the floor where I kicked them off two weeks ago. After that first run. After my only run.

Today I pick them up and throw them in my bag in order to return them. I need the money, and I'm obviously not going to be using them anymore. Might as well buy something I can use -- like toilet paper and a month of electricity.

Happy Birthday to me.

My chubby friend and her paper-doll cheerleader are still lying face down on a box labeled Important Stuff. They obviously don't need these shoes either.

I have a list of errands ahead of me, the first being my new drivers license. Kind of a waste for someone who can't afford a car. But as my mother said, best to be prepared. No one likes the DMV, but Chicago's city clerk office is a nightmare. I take the Pink Line train into the Loop as early as possible. The doors are still locked, so I buy a large caramel latte and wait until a security guard finally opens up. By now there is a huge line behind me, and I would have liked to keep it that way but I am pushed out of the way as busy suit-and-tie guys bustle past me. I am looking for an easy way to get to the Vehicle Registration Department as a tall woman in a tight fitting dress and high red heels elbows her way past a crowd of people waiting for the elevator. I decide to take the stairs instead, which actually does get me in front of a number of people. Twenty minutes later I am smiling for the camera and my claimed weight of 154 pounds has escaped question. I figure by not using a round number it looks more believable. Despite the obvious.

The photographer, a middle-aged black woman, hands me my new license. "Happy birthday," she says. "Have fun tonight, but you better be careful. I'll bet you'll be out partying all night, wontcha?"

I just shake my head and put my new license in my wallet. There is no chance of any partying this year. I will spend my birthday working with sticky little kids, having dinner with my mother at my favorite restaurant, and then going to bed. Alone.

I step out onto Clark Street, preparing myself to tackle public transportation. I'll have to walk over to the El, a few blocks away, and then walk a few more blocks to work. I'm already tired, and my feet ache as it is. My bag is heavy and cumbersome, so I look inside to see what I can ditch.

I toss out an apple and bottle of juice. From the bottom of the bag a gleam of orange blinks at me. Hmmm. Maybe I can get one more good use from these shoes. They are pretty comfortable, after all.

I pull the sneakers out one at a time. I kick off my brown shoes, tie on these neon kicks, and head over to the Red Line station on Lake Street. My feet remember this feeling and they welcome the relief, and I am not too worried when I need to exit the train and start walking several blocks down Devon. The air is springtime crisp, that chill that has an undertone of warmth swirling through it, and with the sun out, I forget that I am running late, that I am a massive mess, and instead I am peeking out at the world, a person who is calm and happy. Who is this person? I have never known her, yet she is here, inside me, and knowing she is there makes me feel good.

I want to wear my orange shoes all day, but Joy and her uniform requirements won't let me. I put on the brown shoes I am so used to and they feel foreign and stiff.

After six hours of cleaning up kid crap, I head back to the El, my calm self having disappeared. I'm tired, sore, and crabby. The eight blocks seem twice as long as they did this morning. I debate skipping the shoe store, but since I am going right past them I make myself stop. At least I'll have some cash for a taxi afterwards.

The shoes are now back in their box, and they feel heavy in my arms.

When I walk in to Run The World the same man who sold them to me is ringing up a customer behind the counter. Ed. When he sees me his eyes brighten and he starts to bob up and down. His customer, a thin, tired-looking woman, rips open the package she has just bought and starts chewing on a gooey granola bar. Instead of leaving, she sits down in the back of the store and keeps eating.

"Kristina! Good to see you! How are those shoes working out for you?"

"Um, ya know, not all that well. I'm actually here to return them." And I offer up the box of orange sneakers, like a sacrifice to the gods.

"Oh, that's too bad. What seems to be the problem? We'll find a pair that's just right. Shoes are tricky -- it takes a while to find the right pair."

"It's not the shoes -- it's me," I say quietly. More people enter the store, dressed in black tights and bright t-shirts. They nudge past me to get to the back of the room.

Ed frowns sympathetically. "What do you mean, it's you?"

I lean in close and whisper, "I tried it. I can't run. I'm just too big."

He nods. "I think I know what you need." Ed walks me to the back of the room where the rest of the people are gathering.

"Mick!" he calls out, and a tall cheerful-looking guy waves at Ed. "I want you to meet somebody." Mick steps his long legs over and around to get to us. He does not stop smiling, even when he reaches us. He must be the happiest employee in Chicago. He grabs my hand and shakes it enthusiastically.

Ed introduces me. "Mick, this is Kristina. She's a new runner--"

"No, no," I interrupt Ed. "I am not a runner. I just bought some shoes and need to return them. I don't have the receipt. Can I get a refund, or at least store credit?"

Mick shrugged. "Don't know, babe. I don't work here. But I recommend you keep them so you can run with us."

"Kristina needs a newbie running group. I thought your group would be perfect for her, Mick. What do you think?"

Mick has been half-listening as he greets another woman who has just arrived, kissing her on the cheek and giving her a big hug.

"Great idea." He nods at the box in my hands. "Put those shoes on and let's go. We start on time--" a chorus of voices join him --- "every time!"

The woman whom he had kissed sits me down, grabs the box, and hands me a shoe. She is not like the other runners here. First of all, she is heavy, like me. Well, maybe not quite as big as me, but definitely fat. Instead of black tights, she wears loose nylon track pants and a bright yellow fleece. She is probably in her fifties, with a bubble of black curls topping her round head. She speaks to me in phrases and commands.

"Hi honey. Sara. Newbie once too. Put this on. Walk-run. That's the way. Next foot. One step at a time. Okay now. Don't 'but' me. Move out."

Before I know it I am being pulled out the door, Sara on one side, Mick on the other. The late afternoon sky is growing dim and I have no idea what I am doing, but I don't stop. The sidewalk has been overtaken by an athletic looking mob, who quiet down as they divide themselves somehow. A small group of skinny runners mumbles a quick goodbye and flies away down the street toward Lake Michigan. I notice that Ed is in that group. Then three more groups set off, each a mix of ages, sizes and gender. Their demeanor is less serious, and I can hear their chattering conversation long after they cross the street.

Then it is just Mick, Sara, two other women, and me. I am trying to get back into the store, to escape this impending disaster. But Sara keeps pushing me forward. Then Mick leads the way by doing something amazing. He walks. We follow. And just like this morning, a lightness creeps out of me as I listen to the women catch up on the days' big events.

"Maggie, how was your lunch with your mom today?"

"Sara, did you get that job you applied for?"

"Wendy, I swear you look like you've lost weight!"

And suddenly Mick calls out, "Run!" and our small group stops talking and starts jogging. Oh no, this is where it all fell apart for me last time. I consider turning around right here, but decide to give it a try. I move my body in that oh-so-uncomfortable jog, my breasts bouncing heavily, my ankles protesting the sudden assault. And then just as I am about to give up, Mick lifts his right arm into the air and shouts, "One! Wasn't that fun?" and the group falls back into a walk again, clapping and cheering, "Yes, Mick! Tons of fun!"

Wow. Their enthusiasm for this short jog seems a little over the top, but to be honest, it wasn't too bad. That does feel like a reason to celebrate. Sara eases back to walk alongside me.

"See, sweetie, this is how we do a fun run. Three parts fun; one part run. It gets us moving, a little sweaty, but no one keels over." She laughs, but I try to listen to my own heartbeat anyway, making sure it isn't about to explode.

We continue with this pattern of walking and jogging for about fifteen minutes, Mick keeping count after each burst of jogging. We reach ten before we stop for water. I am amazed by how long I have kept moving and figure we must have covered a mile by this point. At least it feels that way.

The water fountain is a huge circular stone with four spigots shooting cold streams of water. We gulp heartily, except for Mick. I feel a pang of hunger creep into my stomach and I realize I do not have a snack with me.

"Mick," I say, "I don't have any fuel. What should I do?" I'm proud that I at least know enough to call it fuel and not a snack. The skinny paper-doll runner would be pleased.

Mick smiles at me -- is he laughing?-- and says, "That's okay, Kristina. You won't need fuel until we start our long runs in May. When training begins for the marathon, okay?"

Is he kidding? I just moved for fifteen consecutive minutes for the first time in my life and he is talking about a marathon? What is that, like, a hundred miles?

"Mick, don't scare her like that," says Sara. "Kristina, you don't have to run a marathon. Just keep running with us. That's a great place to start." She scowls at Mick, and he shakes his head, grinning a cute little apology in my direction. Yes, I realize I think it is cute; Mick is cute.

We walk-jog back to the store, and I keep watching Mick's easy galloping stride that somehow pulls me along, pulls me into this group. We are back in another fifteen minutes but it feels like half of that. And Mick was right; I did not need anything to eat in order to make it this far. In fact, for the first time in a while I am not looking to eat anything at all.

The other groups are getting back to the store close to the same time we do. The only difference is how much path each of us covered. Ed's group ran six miles; most others were close to three or four; our little group ( little, ha! ) covered two-point-three -- an increase since their last run. Wendy and Maggie give me high-fives and claim that it was my presence that spurred them all to run faster. I laugh at that.

Then Mick gives me a hug, just like he hugs Sara, but that embrace sinks into me so strong and warm.

"Thanks for running with us, Kristina. See you all on Saturday!" he calls out to us, waving goodbye. In three strides, he has crossed the street and begins running again. This time he moves swiftly and smoothly, quickly becoming a tiny little dot bouncing along the lakefront path again. I watch until he disappears completely.

I decide to keep the shoes.


I meet my mother on 18th street for my birthday dinner. Even though I have moved out, she is my best friend, especially now that everyone else is either gone or doing their own thing. My mother, Lucia, is a beautiful short round woman, proud of her Cuban heritage, but tired from the struggle of surviving on her own since she was not much more than a girl.

When she was fifteen years old she was living in a lousy part of Miami, her family across the little strip of ocean, and gangs and drug dealers all around her. She finally got out of there and moved into an apartment with a middle-aged executive who worked in one of the buildings she cleaned. He had a house and a family in the suburbs, but he would spend several days a week "working late" so he'd stay in the city and buy her dinner and pretty clothes. But he would also drink too much, and he'd let all his midlife anger out on her, bruising her face and her body more than once. She had just turned seventeen when she learned that she was pregnant with me. He gave her five hundred dollars for an abortion. That's when she moved here, to Chicago, alone. Just packed her bag and left while he was at work, no note, nothing. She paid one hundred and fifteen dollars for the bus ride to Chicago, and started her new life in Pilsen, sleeping in a basement bedroom with three other girls, all newly arrived from Mexico.

Since then my mother has worked as a bookkeeper at the same South Side firm for twenty years now. But she is also a business-woman herself. She started Lucia's Office Cleaning Services and Lucia's Alteration Services and Lucia's Transcription Services at different times in my childhood. She worked so hard in order to rent our own space, to pay our bills, to take care of me. When I compare her twenty-one-year-old strength to my twenty-one-year-old slop, I cringe. Amazingly, she doesn't act disappointed in me, but she must not think about it as much as I do.

I want my mother to just relax now, and take care of herself. That is one of the reasons I moved out. At least that's what I tell her.

Another big reason is to escape the constant reminder of Zachary and the ridiculous fantasy I created last year. For a few months it was easy to avoid him because he went back to school, but by summer it seemed that every time I opened our apartment door, there he was, with that skinny little flower-lady draped all over him. No matter how friendly he acted toward me I could feel a knife plunge into my gut. I couldn't have him look at me, this blob that I am, without feeling the rush of humiliation again and again, that year-old shame of meeting Violet. I moved out to give myself time and space to become a new person. So far, nothing much has changed. Until today.

"Kristina! Happy birthday, *mi niña bonita*!" I am twenty-one years old, but to my mother, I am always somewhere around five. I don't understand it, because certainly I don't look like a little girl anymore, in any possible way. But that's how mothers are, I guess.

We hug and walk through the big blue doors of Nuevo Leon for homemade guacamole, tacos, enchiladas, and flan. My mother talks about her job, the new curtains in her living room, and her sore hip. I listen and smile, but my mind is still out on the lakefront. As I eat, I feel the rhythm of my jogging breath moving through me. I dig my fork into the cheesy enchilada on my plate. It is hot and greasy, dripping with mole -- one of my favorites. But as it hits my tongue I find the grease overwhelming and before I have finished even half of it, I am satisfied. My mother notices when I put down my fork and she responds worriedly.

"What's wrong?" she demands. "Is it too spicy? Too bland? Are you sick? Are you --" she softens her voice, "are you menstruating?"

So many options, yet none of them correct.

"No, Mama, I'm fine, the food is fine, I'm just not all that hungry. Maybe it's from, uh, from running today." I look away from her, afraid she'll laugh at me.

"Ah, yes? You were running today?" She nods cautiously, waiting for me to say more. So I do. I tell her about the orange shoes, and my brochure, and Ed, and the running and the walking and the girl inside me who is begging to do it again.

Now it is my mother's turn to listen and nod and smile. She does not laugh. She does not warn me to be careful. She does not tell me it's about time. And I can feel her pride in me as she says, "That's nice. Sounds like something you like doing."

Yes it is.

My mother and I walk back to her apartment, my old home. She has a huge cupcake waiting for me, with a candle ready to be lit. I sit at the kitchen table as she clicks off the light and strikes a match to light the one yellow candle. The flame dances shadows across her smiling, singing face as she carries the cupcake on its bright yellow saucer and places it in front of me.

"*Feliz cumpleaños!*" and she claps, a single echo of applause.

"Remember, make a wish!"

I close my eyes, and even though I want to wish for Zachary to love me, to marry me, to want me, instead, a completely different wish barges into my mind and takes over.

In a long sigh I mumble, "I wish I could be happy." And before I can take it back, that wish bursts into the air for my mother and I to both hear it. My mother bites her lip before taking my hand in hers.

"Oh, honey, you can be. And you will," she says, hugging me tight. Then we cut the cupcake in two delicious halves.

When my alarm slices into my dreams, I instinctively heave the blankets off my body and swing one leg off the bed, dangling it above the floor. Before my eyes open, however, I realize it is Saturday and I do not have to work, but I have for some reason set my alarm anyway. I search the curves and corners of my mind until an image of feet, and sweat, and orange shoes floats together to remind me that I was planning to run with Mick's group again. He had said, "See you Saturday" and that alone is reason to get out of bed.

I am sleeping in my sweat pants, so I just need to find a bra, a warmer t-shirt, and my shoes before I am out the door, munching on a very brown banana. I take the Red Line north. The train is pretty empty, aside from a few sour-smelling guys in the back who are sleeping or passed out. I like it this way. Fewer people to squeeze past, fewer people to brush against. Fewer people looking at me.

I walk past a donut shop, a warm sugary breeze grabbing me by the throat. My salivary glands have been triggered and my stomach calls to me for something gooey and powdered. I have one hand on the door, when I see my reflection in the glass. Just as big and blobby as ever, but I have cool orange shoes, running shoes, on my feet, and a purpose in my mind. I take my hand off the door and turn quickly away, quick quick quick, before I change my mind.

What's the point of hauling myself out of bed, putting myself through the trip to get here, the suffocating run I am choosing to join, if I am just going to undo it all with a donut that I can swallow in less than ten seconds. I wish I could run so I could get away from here faster!

I still have two blocks to walk to get to our meeting place, the running shoe store. The streets are already busy with people on bikes, young families strolling with coffee in one hand, pushing the stroller with the other. And seeming to pop out of nowhere, are runners. First I spot one jogging south toward me, then behind her a small group appears. Ahead of me, three people in black tights and shiny zip-up shirts step out of a car parked along the street, and are followed by another, and then another car, all of them releasing black tights and bright jackets coating skinny bodies. I see my reflection in a cafe window. The only thing that would make me stand out more than these big, heavy gray pants, would be tight shiny black pants stretched across my butt and legs. Oh, that would be a sight! The ridiculousness of it makes me laugh, which is just the thing I need to make the last few steps toward the runners.

Sara sees me first. She waves, and calls to me, and gives a little whistle, just in case I didn't notice her yet. Mick is there too. He is handling a long black band, stretching it out and adjusting something on it while Maggie models for him. Finally she gives the thumbs up and he leaves it snuggly wrapped around her waist and turns to the rest of the group. I'm pretty sure we make a collective sigh as he locks eyes momentarily with each of us. Even me.

"Kristina! You came! Awesome!"

His voice is like a giant bridge reaching across to me. There is no turning back now.

Our group is bigger today -- at least seven or eight of us, including a few guys. One of the guys isn't even all that heavy. But when he walks his left hip seems to collapse a little, giving him the look of a wobbly drunk. I worry that he will fall down, but everyone else seems unconcerned, so I try to be as well.

We follow Mick onto the path across the street and begin walking at a nice, quick pace. In just a few minutes I am breathing pretty heavy and I can feel my armpits growing sweaty. Mick, on the other hand, looks like he is trying to look like he is walking quickly, but he is chatting so easily and spinning back and forth to check on us every few minutes, so I am pretty sure this is, literally and figuratively, a walk in the park for him. Just like the other day, each group seems to have started in its own time, but also all at the same time. But we are still the last group, and the space grows larger between us and the next pace group.

Sara takes a few quick steps to catch up to me. "Kristina. Glad you came back. Good decision."

I look up at her and nod, finding it hard to actually respond right now.

"Oh," she says, her eyes widening. "Need a bandana?" She slides a blue gingham scarf off of her wrist and shoves it at me. I shake my head, not sure what I would need that for. Maybe to wipe the puke off my face when I throw up, which seems to be a strong possibility.

She wipes her other bandana-wrapped wrist across her forehead, dapping at the few beads of perspiration that have started to collect below her dark curls.

I grab the scarf out of her hand and mop my forehead, my upper lip, the creases of my neck and the line down from my ears to soak up the streams of sweat. This seems harder than the other day, and I feel slow and heavy and unable to breathe. And then, to really push me to my limit, Mick lifts his hand high into the air and calls, "Two minute run!"

The group shifts to a slow jog, but I am already breathing so hard that the thought of running makes my throat almost close up on me completely, so I do the opposite and slow my walk to a near stand-still. Mick has been scanning the group and he presses his lips together when he sees me lagging behind. He points to Sara and then takes a few long strides back toward me until we are walking side by side.

"Nope, Kristina, this isn't gonna cut it. You gotta run when we run and walk when we walk. That's how we stay together. That how we help each other."

"I can't breathe. I'm so out of shape that even walking is too hard for me." My eyes start to sting with the threat of tears and frustration. "I can't keep up. Even with the slowest group here -- no offense -- but this just isn't working for me. You guys go ahead. I'll just do my own thing, here."

Mick stops walking and puts his hands on my shoulders, turning me to face him.

"How long have you been doing this -- running, I mean?" he demands.

"Uh, I just started, I guess."

"I see," he nods his head, a little sarcastically, but with a cute smile in his eye. "Because I've only been running for fifteen years. And I've only been leading this pace group for four years. So I thought maybe, if you had more experience than me, well, then you would know, obviously, whether you should run with us or just do your own thing."

I try to be offended, but he is full out smiling now, and who could feel bad looking into that face?

"You need to trust me, Kristina," he says. "I know it's hard, and you feel like you are out of shape and you can't breathe and you feel miserable and a lot of those feelings are pretty true! But it's not because you can't run. It's because you don't run. And we are going to change that. Okay?"

"Oh...alright..."

"So, we will start by running the two minutes that the rest of the group is finishing. It will be uncomfortable and you will feel like you can't breathe, and you will think you can't do it, but you will breathe, and you will do it and when the two minutes are up you will be that much closer to having as much running experience as me!"

I laugh.

And as he starts to jog beside me, and I lift my body into as hard of a jog as I can, he says again, "Trust me."

And I do.

Saturday is my favorite day of the week. Wednesday is my second favorite. Tied with Friday, perhaps, but for a different reason.

I have met with the Run-Walk group every week since Mick demanded that I suck it up and stop whining. Every time I tell it that way he strongly protests my choice of words. I respond by saying, "Well, that's the way I saw it," and I just smile at him.

Wednesdays are a smaller group. Sara is the only one who is as consistent as I am, but the rest of the group shows up on occasion depending on their other commitments.

So, those two days have been the days I look forward to the most, that I have circled on my calendar and chiseled out of any over-time hours at work or TV hours at home. They are the days that make me feel stronger every other day of the week. They are the days I forget about Zachary, which seems backwards, since he is the reason I am doing this in the first place.

Running in the heat of June is a different challenge. First of all, there are more people, everywhere! In our group, in the park, out on the running path, zipping by on bikes and roller blades and skate boards. June brings more sweat, skin rubbed raw, and long lines at the water fountains. But Mick was right. As uncomfortable as it can feel-- heck as miserable as it can be sometimes!--finishing the run is always a matter of choice, not capability.

Now that the park is so crowded with people we run in two's along the path, hugging the right side as much as possible, and moving into a single line if we need to pass anyone.

Occasionally someone will shout a warning or a threat if we don't move soon enough or far enough. As the slowest group out here, we get yelled at a lot. That used to bother me, but now I just let it go.

Today I am up front with Mick, a testament to my consistency and discipline, he said. We are walking for two minutes and then running for four minutes. This is the first time I have spent more time running than walking, and although I am pretty sure it will suck, I know it will also be fantastic. Up ahead is the thirteen minute group. They only take walk breaks at the end of each mile for less than a minute. Mick says that by the time their training is over they will be able to run that pace non-stop for ten miles.

"That's impossible!" I scoff. "How could anyone run -- actually run, without stopping-- for ten miles, unless they are a professional runner?" Which made me wonder. "Do professional runners even exist? Is that something people do?"

"Sure," Mick answers. "Running is a competitive sport just like any other sport. You have people who run because it's their job; they run to win. Then there are people who run to see how fast they can get, or to be part of a team. They might win a medal now and then, but they still have a day job. Then there are people who run to have fun --that's the rest of us! It's like we are all on the same team but playing different positions."

I try to picture myself on the same team as Mick in any other sport. It would never happen.

"Well then, our group would most likely be the bench warmers," I say.

"No, you don't get it." Mick gets serious all of a sudden. "It's like playing baseball in Wrigley with the Chicago Cubs. We get to go out on the field with them -- out to second base or the pitchers mound or the left wall ivy. We are on the same field, in the same race, on the same streets as the guys who win. And the ladies. The women, I mean. They have gotten super fast over the last few years. But no matter how fast or slow, we can all line up at the same time and cover the pavement step by step for the same distance. We are running in the footsteps of legends. That is super cool. And that is why I race."

He lifts his hand in the air and the group moves into a run once again. I picture Mick racing down the streets of Chicago, a sea of people behind him as his long legs stretch easily further than anyone else's. He is a winner, in my mind anyway, and maybe in his own mind too. His pride in being a runner emanates from him and sweeps me up so that our four-minute runs start to define me, too. Maybe not quite as a runner, but definitely as a participant in this sport. Four minutes feels like the blink of an eye. And for a few seconds I even begin to picture a finish line ribbon beckoning to me, too. After all, Mick isn't the only one running in the footsteps of legends.

Perky runner-girl stares at me from the front of the refrigerator where I have attached the *Last to Fast* brochure that got me started. She glares at me when I fill my fridge with leftover pizza and pouts when I complain about the rain or the heat or the lousy sleep I got last night. She reminds me that habits are hard to break and even harder to start. She reminds me that Mick and Sara aren't the only ones helping me on this journey. After giving me tips on clothing, fuel, pacing, stretching, and safety, she has begun to nag me about the hardest part of all.

*Dedication requires a type of blindness that prevents distraction. As you commit yourself to a new routine and a whole new way of life, the most critical component is your own persistence. Your health does not depend on the support of friends, the style or fit of your shoes, the time of day or the current weather. Every day, your healthy habits come down to only one thing -- getting it done! On the rare day that all of the support you need arrives on your doorstep, well, that is a day to celebrate. But the many days in between -- when weather and friends and time and mood are against you -- those are the days that you put the blinders on and you do it anyway. Every*

pathetic weight I have become. I don't just mean my own body weight, which has been my struggle for the past ten years. I mean the dragging weight I have become to myself, my mother and now Mick. I picture him groaning silently as he tries to go slower and slower to keep me moving. He keeps himself just out of reach, and I realize why. From across the street and on each corner, as we shuffle past early morning commuters, their eyes are drawn to this slow and mismatched caravan. He must be so humiliated to be seen pulling along this slow-moving blob.

As tears blur my eyes I let myself fall back. I hate how much I drag people down. How can I be so oblivious! So stupid! So embarrassing!

Suddenly Mick stops and spins around, putting his hands on his waist as he waits for me to catch up. He is not exactly frowning, but a sheet of ice has fallen between us.

"Listen, if you...," he starts.

"Listen, you don't have to...," I interrupt.

We both stop, then start again. This time, when we stop we both laugh a little, but I can tell he is still upset.

"You go first," I say, hoping he'll just tell me the truth and I can just get on the bus to go back home.

He takes a deep breath. "Well, it's none of my business, but I guess I thought I'd come run with you because you, kind of, didn't have... I mean, I thought you weren't seeing anyone...like, romantically. And then when I got here, well-- I felt kind of humiliated-- kind of stupid, so that's why I've been an asshole, running ahead of you." He drops his head a little, then mumbles, "Sorry."

I stare at him, speechless for a few seconds. What is he talking about? And then I see it from his place on the bus. Zachary's hand on my ass, his arm around my shoulder, his early morning goodbye. Did he actually think that we were —?

"Oh my god, Mick! Do you think that that guy-- at the bus stop-- was my-- that we were together?"

Mick stared at me hard. "I saw how you looked at him. Some things are just obvious."

Wow. I guess it's obvious to the wrong guy!

"Oh, Mick. It's kind of a stupid story. But if you run next to me, instead of in front of me, as we go back I'll tell you about it. But I have to warn you, it's humiliating. Like, really humiliating."

It has taken three months of early morning runs to tell Mick the whole humiliating story about my engagement to Zachary. I may have stretched it out a little, you know, just to get all the details right. But I'm pretty sure he didn't mind.

*****

Sara waves me over to her as soon as I walk in the door.

"Here." She shoves a paper at me. "Sign up."

I am still not used to her abrupt orders that she barks at everyone, regardless of the intention. But I'm not intimidated like I was when I first started running with her, and I'm not as annoyed as I was shortly after that. I just have to ask for more information, again and again and again.

"What is this?"

"It's a race. We're all doing it. Sign up."

"Oh, no. No, no, no. Not me." I hand the sheet back to her.

From the corner of the store a woman's loud voice is calling for our attention. She is tall, with curly dark hair, large round eyes that seem to mirror her round hips and round breasts, tightly wrapped in a bright pink tank top. She wears pink and gray capri-length tights, gray shoes, and a bright pink cap. Even her long fingernails are painted bright fuchsia. She is standing in front of a large flip board that shows the same sheet that Sara gave me. She glares at me when she sees me pushing the paper at Sara, so I take the sheet back and look at it and away from her.

"Ladies and gentlemen, thank you so much for coming here today and for giving me your time as I talk to you about the very first Race Forward for Freedom! My name is Anna Rigaldo. I'm sure some of you recognize me from the running group, but I am here today to talk to you about something else, something very important."

Something about her seems familiar, but I honestly do not remember seeing her in any running group since I have started here.

"As you know, Ed and Gracie, the owners of Run The World and sponsors of so many running groups in Chicago, have partnered with the charity Go Forward, to help raise scholarship funds for their clients."

Behind me Sara whispers loudly in my ear, "Is this a board meeting or a charity event?" and chuckles at her own humor. The pink lady must have heard her because she adds a scowl to the glare she had for me earlier. She flips to the next card. The Go Forward title and logo are at the top of the page, and pictures of battered and tearful teenagers are scattered about the rest of it. Instead of names, a country is listed beneath each face. Cambodia, Darfur, Afghanistan, Columbia, Liberia, Sudan, Georgia, Cuba, North Korea.

"Go Forward is a Chicago-based charity that provides support to teen refugees, helping them to get acclimated to their new life here, providing academic, social, financial, emotional and in many cases therapeutic services to the young people who have fled the horrors of famine, persecution, and civil war."

She pauses to give us time to look at the faces, to look into their eyes, to see their pain and their fear.

Then she flips to the next card again.

A colorful chart measures the needs of the teenagers against the cost of those needs and it is obvious that there is a huge gap between the two.

"By signing up to run the Race Forward for Freedom, you can help close this gap in two ways. First of all, Run the World is covering the charity sign up cost for each one of you who join the Race Forward team. That is forty dollars that goes directly to the kids -- no external race fees or administrative costs at all. I made sure of that. Secondly, as part of the team, you will raise money for your own donation. We ask for a donation of one hundred dollars."

A tiny woman standing up front steps in front of Anna, interrupting with, "Really, any amount would be appreciated."

"No," Anna counters. "Gracie is a lot more charitable than I am and since I am in charge of this -- right Gracie? -- then it is my job to make sure the event is successful for Go Forward, and that Run the World doesn't get taken advantage of either. Right?" She looks to Gracie, maybe for agreement, maybe for cooperation. "So, just any old amount is not going to be appreciated. Any amount that is at least equal to the store's donation and the race director's donation is the very least that would be appreciated. More than that would be very, very appreciated."

The runners shrink back a bit, but the pens start flying and the papers are heading back to the front of the group where Anna is collecting them.

"Well. What did you decide?" Sara holds a pen out to me.

Anna flips to the last card of her presentation. This one has a huge Thank You scrawled across the top, and the same faces-- at least I think they are the same-- are now smiling and clean, with full cheeks and neatly braided hair or crew-cuts. Instead of countries, there are now names under each face. Magdalena, Soon Yu, Jason, Yeni, Farheed, Ahdme, Katherine, Gabriella. So, this is what a few dollars will do for these kids?

"Oh, okay." I fill out my name, address, birthdate, and emergency contact. I check the box that promises to raise one hundred dollars or more for the kids of Go Forward and sign my name at the bottom, releasing all liability and placing myself in the scariest position of my life.

Well, second scariest.

"Thirteen miles!"

Mama clasps her hands across her heart.

I only just realized how far this race for charity actually was last week, when we got our training packets. Both Sara and Mick assured me that I could do it, and how would I know otherwise, except for the fear in Mama's eyes. Suddenly I am worried.

"No, no Kristina, I don't mean you can't do it. I just mean, that is really far, and it seems so hard, and you are doing so well. Do you have to run it all? Can you do half of it, maybe? I don't want you to hurt yourself... or...something."

I think "something" might mean making a fool of myself. Again.

"Yeah, you're right, Mama. I'll find out more about it. Maybe I can do something shorter."

I don't want Sara to think I am backing out of this, so I ask Mick first. We are sitting curled up on the beach after our Saturday run. Saturdays in September are mild and relaxed and tease us into forgetting about winter. The sand is warm, the winds are calm, and the sun is soft and soothing. Our whole running group is here at North Avenue Beach, grilling up chicken drumsticks and corn on the cob. Anna, the woman in charge of the Half-Marathon, is treating all the charity runners to a training kick-off today. She and her father stand among a half dozen grills, flipping, turning, and filling the air with the most delicious smells. I am sprawled across the sand on my stomach, kicking my feet up behind me. I'm not skinny like the girl in my *Last to Fast* brochure, but I don't feel anything like the girl on that couch anymore. My clothes are looser and everything just feels a little bit easier. Easier to lie down, easier to get up, easier to laugh. The only thing that's not easier is the running. I might be running more, but it's just as difficult as when I started. Which is why I'm worried. Mick digs into his second plateful as I mention my concerns about the distance.

"Thirteen miles is so far, you know? I was kind of thinking," I say casually, "what if there was a shorter race I could do, instead of the half-marathon. You know, one that is more my speed?"

Mick wipes butter from his chin, smiles at me and says, "You know, I was just thinking the same thing!"

This surprises me, but I am glad to know that Mick is on my side.

"Hey, Anna!" he calls out. "Anna, Kristina wants to know if she could run a shorter race — something more her speed!"

I sit up and hit Mick with my empty paper plate. "Shhh! What are you doing? Don't tell Anna!"

Behind me, a thin teenager, with ebony skin and eyes, giggles, and scoots a few feet away.

But it is too late. Anna has handed the grill tongs to Ed and with her head down and arms swinging, she is marching over to me. I shift behind Mick, who simply rolls out of the way as Anna reaches us. She jabs her finger into my face.

"More your speed? More your speed? Is that what you want? A short little race — what, like a 5K? Would that be more your speed, Kristina?"

I knew she'd be mad, but I'm not sure where she is going with this. I nod cautiously. A 5K sounds a lot shorter than a half-marathon.

"Well, miss, I'll tell you what. You start doing some speed training, some intervals, some mile repeats, and then you put together a nice little race course and get a few thousand dollars together and invite all your friends who are more your speed, and then sure, you go ahead and do your little 5K! In the meantime, you are a part of this group, and we are training for a half-marathon, and we are going to do this together, because we do not let each other down!" She stamps her foot as she turns back toward the grill. Grabbing the tongs back from Ed she shouts across the sand to me, "Got it?"

The girl behind us jumps up and follows Anna, asking her something about running partners. Mick shoves an oatmeal cookie in his mouth.

"Mmm. Maybe not such a good idea after all," he mumbles. But I can tell he is laughing at me.

I guess I'm just going to tell Mama there's no way out.

Secretly, I am relieved.

I put out a handwritten sign at work. It says, "Please donate to my Race Forward for Freedom charity group. Together we can make a difference in the lives of refugee teens living in Chicago."

I tape it to an old plastic juice container that I have scrubbed and scrubbed until there is no more smell or stickiness. It placed it next to the pick up door at the DayCare Center and another one at Jumping Jungleland.

For a week, they sit empty. I don't think anyone even looked at it.

It's Wednesday now, and I have my bag of running clothes thrown over my shoulder, ready to sprint out of the Drop and Drive when Gwen, the manager, waves at me frantically from the pick-up point. It is her job to check IDs and verify authorization of drivers before handing over the kids. Parents need to pick up all kids by five o'clock pm. Every day, the last pick up is somewhere around six-thirty. And Gwen has to wait and wait the whole time, punching in phone numbers of people who either don't answer or apologize profusely while admitting they just had to stop for a latte on their way over.

Today, though, Gwen is not just aggravated.

"Kristina! I need you!" She is calling to me with panic in her eyes and faked calm in her voice.

I wish I hadn't seen her, but I did, and she knows it, so I retreat from my exit and head over to the driveway.

"I got stung," she splutters. Her eyes are big and a redness is peeking out from behind her collar. "On my neck. I need to go, now. Watch them."

She walks away unsteadily, hurrying, her hand tight against her neck.

I start to run after her, but five toddlers are sitting on the pickup bench, watching and as Gwen hurries away they start to sense the fear that she had tried to contain. Adam is the first to cry.

I want to run after Gwen, call 9-1-1, get the medical bag myself, but she left me with them -- these kids -- and they can smell fear as well as any dog. So I have to rein it in.

"Hey, Adam, what's up? Did you have fun today?" I wiggle his ears a little, trying to distract him. It works, and he pulls on my arm, and then on my stomach, and then on my bag as I try settling him back onto the bench.

Gwen taps on the window across the driveway and shows me a small pink bottle in her hand. She gives me a thumbs up, and I guess that's good, but I'd feel better if she called 9-1-1. I am trying to motion to her, asking if she called for help, when a line of cars pull in one after the other. Adam pulls on my bag again and it splits open, my bright orange shoes tumbling onto the sidewalk. His mother, having put the car in park and walked around to sign him out, picks up the shoes and hands them back to me.

"Are these yours?" she asks.

I nod my head, a little embarrassed to be sharing the one thing that makes me feel good with the people who ignore me every day.

She points to the juice container. "So, are you the one raising money for this race?"

I nod.

"Are you running in it?"

I nod again.

"Well, you should put your name on it. And your picture too. That way we'll know who this is for."

Maybe my silence makes her feel sorry for me, or maybe she is surprised that someone like me would claim to be running a race. But she drops a five dollar bill in the little money bucket, and picking Adam up in her arms, says, "Well, good luck then."

Gwen is sitting in the doorway where she can supervise the kids while waiting to see if she is going to die or not.

"Antihistamines," she says. I wait long enough to help the last toddler get into his babysitter's car, and for Gwen's husband to come pick her up. Just in case.

And while I wait, I write my name, big and bold, on my donation flier. Two more parents slip a few bills into the container.


I dump first one container, then the other, onto the table in my mother's kitchen. She dives in with both hands, laughing, letting the coins run through her fingers and cascade back into a shiny mound. I pull the bills out from the mound and start separating them by denomination. The stack of singles is the thickest, but there are plenty of five dollar bills as well.

Mama does the same with the coins, placing them in stacks of four quarters, ten dimes, and twenty nickels. The pennies get their own big pile that we will count through last of all.

Although most people consider pennies to be next to worthless, to me they are the most valuable of all. Once my picture was taped to the donation jugs, the kids started pointing and asking me why, and then they started bringing in their pennies to add to my fundraiser, to "help the new kids" as they said. Their addition to the fundraiser was always made with a tight fistful of coins that they carefully released into the jug. One little boy announced hopefully, as his pennies jingled to the pile, "Now they'll be okay, won't they?"

Those pennies aren't just money in the jug. Those pennies are the seeds of something much bigger, something that reminds me of the power of tiny actions. It makes my heart hurt.

Mama licks her thumb and then counts quickly through each pile, writes down the total, recounts it and double checks against her recorded total. She is never wrong so I don't know why she feels a need to do twice the work. But she is helping me, so I'm not about to complain.

Finally, she takes out her calculator and adds it all up, minus the pennies. Her eyes open wide and I ask her, "Well, did we make it?"

The race is on Saturday, four days from now, but all of the money is due at our last group run tomorrow.

"It depends," she says slowly. "Do you have to be exactly one hundred dollars?"

My heart sinks. I can see we have a lot, but if I do not have the full hundred I will have to add in my own money, which I suppose is only fair. But I had hoped that my share would be the running part, and other people, who weren't running, would do the money part.

"How much more do we need?" I ask her, trying to remember how much I have in my bank account and wondering if I can make it to my next pay day if I add some of that to the pot. Or if I should just hand over what I do have and step out of the race altogether.

"Oh, you don't need more," Mama says. "You have over three hundred dollars here."

"Three hundred dollars!" I grab the calculator from her hands. For the first time in my life I am doubting the accuracy of this numbers-obsessed woman. As I begin to add up the rows she has written down I feel her quiet, offended stare. I lower the calculator and turn to her.

"Sorry," I mutter. "That just seems like a lot."

She hugs me. "Yes, it is a lot! You have done good! Real good! But you count it. Go ahead, you should! That's ok."

So together, more for the thrill than the verification, we both count it all again, out loud, and laugh as the total grows bigger and bigger.

"Three hundred sixty-three dollars and twenty five cents!" I exclaim.

My mother nudges me and points to the mound of copper on the other side of the table.

"And that doesn't even include the pennies yet."

We dig in to the pile, making mini stacks of ten, and when we are all done we have an additional seven dollars and twelve cents.

*$370.33*

I think they'll let me run.


The money is organized and packed into a large plastic envelope that my mother had. I push it deep into my backpack, under my work clothes, cell phone, and wallet. I have changed into my shorts and running shoes in order to run-walk my way home. With the weight of my backpack it will likely be a pretty slow crawl, but I am so excited that I don't care if it takes me all night.

I jingle down the stairs, and start the slow steady pace that has become my new comfort zone. I walk past the school, the church, the store, the park where I spent years growing bigger on the outside, but so much smaller on the inside. Now, it's the exact opposite. My waist and butt and thighs have grown smaller over the past few months, but I feel like I am going to burst out of my skin. I think about those faces on the flip chart I had seen two months ago. I feel like I am a part of their lives, without ever having met them. And of course, all the people I run with now, who wait for me when I am slow, who cheer for me when I return to the store as one of the last in the group. How can I stay so small when I have so many people filling up my life?

Across the park I see a group of kids running, throwing a ball, diving to catch it, huddling together before they burst apart once again. They might be twelve or thirteen years old, at most.

I hope the "new kids" are playing ball, or swimming or hanging out with their friends too.

I look away from the kids to the path in front of me, just as a large body hurdles into me, knocking me over. As I flail to catch myself, my backpack is ripped off my shoulders.

"No!" I scream, grabbing at the air. I fall hard onto my belly and my face, but the panic of losing my backpack, losing all that money, is what scares me the most. I hear several feet skid and shuffle past me, one of them stopping long enough to land a heavy boot right into my ribs.

I cry out, "Stop! No! No!" and then, I just cry.

My bubble has burst once again, and I am in the familiar face-plant of failure. In a moment I hear them return, but I just lay on the ground, my face buried in the dirt, crying. I curl into a ball, preparing for another kick or worse.

Instead the bag is dropped beside me.

"Here, I got it." He's gasping for breath, but I recognize his voice instantly. I stop crying, frozen. Oh my god. It's Zachary. I don't know if he recognizes me, and suddenly I don't want him to.

"Thanks," I mumble. He reaches his hand down to me.

"Are you hurt? I saw them running toward you, so I tried to get to you first, but I couldn't."

I pull myself up to my knees. "I'm okay," I mumble again, still looking at the ground.

"Whoa, wait, is that you Kristina?" He ducks his face under mine so I have no choice but to look at him.

"Oh, Zachary, where did you come from?" I try to act like he is the one out of his element, but his confusion about me is clear.

"Wow. It is you. You've ...changed! A lot! Girl, I didn't know you could run!"

"Well, I don't really. I mean, I'm really slow."

"Well, that's obvious!" Zachary shoots me one of his cute, funny grins, and pokes my tummy just like he used to. But this time it feels like another boot kicked into my gut.

I try to picture what he sees-- a chubby wanna-be, a girl lost in delusions, a wheezing, dripping, mess whose only source of joy is his boyish laugh and big muscles. Embarrassment climbs onto my shoulders and swirls into my mind once again. I will never be the girl I want to be for him. A strong, smart, skinny, talented, beautiful lady for Mr. Zachary Burns. I can run ever hour of every day and I'll still be the fat friend who cleans up baby poop and spilled Slushies. The friend who can take a joke, a little teasing, a kick in the ribs.

"Hey, I gotta get back to my camp kids." He waves to the group of teens I watched earlier. "We should hang out. Me and my friends are gonna go get some drinks tomorrow night. You should join us! It'd be fun!" He puts his hand on my head, wiggling it like I'm a bobble-head doll. "Just like old times!"

"Sure. Maybe."

As he jogs away, he turns back and shouts, "Hey, careful with how much running you do. I don't want you to lose that booty! That's one of the things I like best about you!"

And in no time he's back to his kids, directing his group, and I am no more than a brief memory.

I put my backpack over my shoulders and this time snap the belt closed around my waist. I move into a slow walk until I am away from the park.

Ahead of me, that shining city stands large and proud.

The City of Big Shoulders -- isn't that it?

*Come and show me another city with lifted head singing so proud to be alive and coarse and strong and cunning...*

Carl Sandburg didn't see this city as dainty and sweet. And it's still pretty damn amazing.

Proud to be alive and coarse and strong. And cunning.

I like the sound of that. The feel of that in my bones. No wonder all those people come here to escape war and poverty and cruelty. Look at the power of this city, the faith of its people to survive, day after day.

Look at the people working, playing, living each day to make someone else smile, someone else breathe a little easier, someone else believe in their own strength. People like Sara, and Anna, and Mick. Mick.

My feet kick into a run, the weight of *$370.33* pushing me forward. I circle back, run past Zachary and shout out without stopping, through my gasping breath, "I can't make it tomorrow-- I have my final training run-- for my half marathon on Saturday -- It's important!"

And then back onto my route for my run back home.

I squeeze my way into the crowd at Run the World, my plastic envelope still secured in the bottom of my bag. I want to hand over the money as soon as possible. Sara is hunched over a table, two pencils stuck into a headscarf, tufts of black hair poking out in all directions, with a big metal cash register in front of her. She is even worse than my mom, because in addition to adding, re-adding, recording, and color-coding, her bossiness adds an edge of panic to the commotion.

I plunk my envelope on the table. She eyes it briefly and returns to shouting orders.

Finally she asks, almost in a whisper, "Full amount?" as if she expects me to say 'No'.

"Almost four hundred," I whisper back.

"Four hundred!" She is back in loudspeaker mode, so every one around us hears her.

"That's awesome, Kristina!" one of the fast girls shouts over to me. I don't know how she knows my name -- I realize I don't know hers -- but I say, thanks, anyway. Sara adds my total in, hands me a big square of paper with a number on it and a bunch of safety pins, then pushes me to move me out of the way.

"Have you ever seen a bib before?"

Mick is standing behind me, probably laughing at my obvious ignorance.

"Bibs? Plenty! I work in a daycare center. What the heck is this thing?"

He stoops down, taking the number from me. He puts one hand on my back, as he holds the square against my tummy with his other hand. His touch is so soft and warm that I think I'm going to faint.

"...and the pins go in each corner to hold it in place, okay?"

I nod or something.

"You nervous?" he asks. "You look a little freaked out. But don't be. You'll do great. You are so much more ready than you realize. You're strong!"

"And alive, coarse, and cunning," I add.

"Well, alive, for sure," he answers. "Do you remember how much you resisted this at first? You've come a long way, girl! You'll have to prove your cunningness out on the course itself. Come on, let's go."

So we leave behind the mob of runners and posters and money and bibs and the two us jog slowly across the street and out to the path once again.

The sun is sinking a bit later lately, as summer seems to be inching its way into the night sky. Soft grays and peach streak through the leftover blue of day. The path is still crowded and the beaches are dotted with frisbee-throwing kids, but tonight it feels more quiet than usual. Mick and I jog without talking, me waiting for his signal to walk. I picture Zachary laughing at my "obviously" slow pace and his quick retreat. I picture my dream coming true, marrying my childhood friend, and all I can see is my old self, on a couch with a bag of chips in my lap.

I am not angry at Zachary, exactly. It's not his fault I gained so much weight or lost so much faith in my future. I did that to myself, just as I am now changing myself. I may not be fast but I'm a hell of a lot faster than I used to be. But Zachary can't see that. And that is starting to piss me off.

"Turn around?" Mick suggests.

"Aren't we going to take a walk break?" I ask Mick.

"You ran through them," he says, smiling. "I guess you had something more important to think about than your next walk break. We've been running for twenty minutes straight."

I instinctively check to make sure my heart is still beating. It is.

"It's okay. I told you to trust me, didn't I?"

Mick grabs my hand, giving it a squeeze, and holds it for a few steps as we start back, letting go only as he moves back into a jog. We walk and run this time, with Mick giving me tips on what and when to eat to prepare for race day. I am trying to listen, but my hand has never felt this happy before.

And neither have I.

# 13  GRACIE

"I have a story to tell you."

The ladies pull closer to me, the way they used to. It's interesting how certain things never change. And other things change, well, everything. I haven't told any stories in a while, but it is hard to watch Anna deflect so many people with her observations and critiques and suggestions, so I decide to dig through my memory bank to pull out a story that will be engaging enough to quiet her need to talk. And indeed, she elbows her way to the front of our small group, tilting her head with an air of expectation and pausing her own personal dialogue long enough to hear what I have to say.

I've told stories about the early days of my running, about being the only girl on my high school track team, and the meets in which I could watch, but not participate. I've told the stories of my father's decision to quit his job so he could build my dreams of being a runner, and how that led to the Run The World store we own today. But those stories are still too close, too bruised, to pull out right now.

"I'll tell you a story about the day I became a part of history in the making, one of the early days of the New York City Marathon." Anna grins, her competitive spirit stoked, as I imagined it would be.

In 1971, New York City had introduced a marathon race that mostly looped repeatedly though Central Park. Less than two hundred runners entered that race. Due to AAU regulations, all of them were men. But the next year was different.

"Gracie, this is gonna be big!" my dad announced early in October of 1972 as the Women Run the World running group was gathering. My best friend Helen and I had just started our first year of college, but continued to train together at Run The World. At the time, our group was very small — maybe eight of us total, but we were consistent. We were tying up our shoes, shoes made just for women finally, and Dad was pulling new pairs just like them out of the boxes in the back room of Run The World. He set up a display in the store window in front of a big poster of New York City.

"What is?" asked Helen.

"New York's marathon has at least six women signed up to run! The marathon, Helen! You know how far that is?"

We smiled at each other. We both knew exactly how far a marathon was, but neither of us believed it was a distance for normal people to run. We ran a lot, and sometimes even ran for hours, stopping now and then. But twenty-six miles? That was like running clear across Chicago and back again.

One of the younger girls, Liz, questioned my dad. "I thought women weren't allowed in the marathon. I thought it was bad for us to run that far. That's what my mother says."

"Well, I'm not a woman, but I've known a few, and I have never seen anything bad happen when a female starts running. Have you, Gracie?" I smiled at him.

"That's cool, Dad, but I thought women were starting to run in marathons already. What's the big deal with New York?"

"Because I know something that other people don't. I got a call from out east, asking if I have any women marathon runners who want to be a part of a revolution."

Dad shot me down before I could ask. "No, Gracie, you're not ready for that. But one day you will be."

He huddled all of us girls together. "On Saturday, the women are scheduled to start the race ten minutes ahead of the men. This schedule is imposed by the AAU -- the Amateur Athletic Union -- and they decide if women can be in a race, and if they can compete with the men. So the AAU wants them to have a ten minute head start. Big deal, right? I mean, they will probably still be plenty far behind the lead guys anyway."

We all nod in agreement, since it sounded fair to us. After all, girls are slower than guys.

"Well, the race director, a guy I have only heard of in passing, but who is a huge supporter of women's equality, is staging a protest at the marathon start. Not sure what it will be, but oh, what I wouldn't give to be there!" My dad's eyes turned to that high-in-the-sky dream look again, which always meant one thing. He was a man on a mission and things were going to happen.

I held my breath. "Can we go, Dad? Can we go to New York?"

"Oh, please!" begged Helen. Together we pleaded. We offered to work for free, to double our track workouts, to wash the store from top to bottom.

Finally my dad scratched his beard, shrugged his shoulders, and mumbled, "We'll see."

Two days later we were packed in the car, a cooler stuffed full of food and drinks, heading east with my dad at the wheel and Helen and I in the back seat.

We took turns driving, making the trip in just under twenty-four hours, arriving early on Race Day morning.

We parked the car somewhere in Upper Manhattan and then the three of us jogged over to Central Park. The park is huge, like a city within the city. Even for Chicago girls, this place towered over us. Rolling hills and twisting paths made our legs ache and our hearts soar. And in the middle of it all, rich green trees and cool lakes. What a beautiful venue for a race!

My dad checked his watch. "One more hour. Let's get some food!"

The park had some quiet cafe carts packed with round bagels and tubs of thick white cream cheese. We each got one, along with some juice and followed the small stream of pedestrians to the race start.

We knew we were getting close when we saw trucks and camera crews set up under a row of tall trees. A banner was hung from a tree announcing this spot as the starting line for the New York marathon. Runners with bib numbers pinned to their shorts bobbed up and down without too much force.

We found a spot several yards away, beyond the starting line. A thick white line was painted across the wide curving path. This would also be the finish line in a few hours.

As eleven o'clock approached, a man shouted into a small microphone. "Ladies, to the starting line, please!"

My dad nudged me. "That's him. That's the guy I was telling you about. He's got something up his sleeve. Just watch!"

I nudged Helen too, and we were both frozen in place.

"Runners on your mark!"

Six women stood about three feet in front of the crowd of male runners who were still relaxed and waiting their turn.

"Runners, get set!"

From the crowd, a series of posters were passed to the front, almost to the women.

"Go!" A loud blast of the starting horn signaled that the runners should leap into action, but instead a hush followed the horn, and all six women sat down.

Some of them held up the posters that had been passed along to them, demanding that the AAU "WAKE UP" to 1972 and to Women's Equality.

Helen whispered loudly into my ear. "They're not running!"

I burst out laughing, as did my dad and the few people surrounding us who heard her.

The cameras flashed as one voice after another started to scoff the AAU and their archaic reasoning.

A woman jogged past us, going in the opposite direction of the race. "Oh, no!" she called out, looking at the ground around her feet. "Where's my uterus? I hope it didn't fall out!"

The crowd laughed, the seated runners laughed, the race officials laughed, and most importantly, the news reporters laughed.

The minutes ticked by, and then the women stood up again as the men moved up to the starting line. There were no arguments or debates or insults as I was expecting. Instead, a whole community lined up together, and as the horn blasted once again, they moved together past the Tavern on the Green to the scattered cheers of those of us who came to support this moment.

Forty-five minutes later the leaders circled passed us again, and in the distance we saw the lead women as well. Every few yards a woman would pop out onto the path and run behind or along side these marathon women, for just a little while, creating a constant ebb and flow of female power.

I looked to my dad and he nodded. I grabbed Helen and as two women ran up to us we jumped out onto the path and ran alongside these trailblazers. We were not going fast at all. Slower than most of my easy runs at times, but the electricity was palpable. Helen and I ran side by side behind a tiny brunette who was probably only a few years older than us. But she looked tough and confident, not excited and impatient the way I felt.

At one point she looked over her shoulder. She sent us an easy grin and held up her hand in a peace sign.

"Thanks for the support," she said, as easy as if she were sitting still. "Next time, I want you to be out here with us, okay?"

Helen and I nodded, and then fell back to let her continue her own race, as we dreamed about ours.

And that's how I became a part of history.

"That's it?"

I knew Anna would not be satisfied with that ending. There is something about her brazen honesty that makes me like Anna. I guess it's the same thing that makes the rest of the women drop behind or stop for water whenever she joins us. But her fire gives me an energy I need, and to be honest, I like throwing in some kindling now and again.

"What do you mean, That's it? I think that's plenty!"

Anna stops running, her hands on her hips, as she glares at me.

"You said you made history. No offense, Gracie, but there's a big difference between making history and watching history."

I am jogging in place, having turned to face her. Part of me is offended by her assumption about how history is made, and the other part of me -- the greater part of me-- knows that she is too young to understand. It is too early in her life to see the ripples of one tiny action. I am sure that in her mind, as in the minds of many, history is made through sweeping declarations, bold rebellions, and shocking obscenities. But those moments are fleeting and meaningless without the slow, quiet wave of change that follows. That is the rest of the story in "history." It's not what happened, but the result that matters.

The fact that six women sat on the starting line of the New York City Marathon is only historical because of the wave that followed. And even that event itself was just another ripple in the effort to bring women's sports in line with men's. And that is just a ripple extending from a much larger series of events working to bring equality and fairness to women at work, at home, in politics, in education, in leadership. That ripple isn't contained in the 1970's New York Marathon. It stretches to Oregon and Arizona, to South Africa and Liberia, to Finland and Syria and India.

How do I tell her that the only reason she is standing here today, tapping her Reebok foot and demanding a better ending to the story is because she is part of the story? And it hasn't ended yet. How do I tell her that running day after day, is mostly the same monotonous ritual, but that ritual becomes the definition of an entire person? Most of our runs aren't stories at all. But every once in a while...

"Alright, Anna. Let's keep going. I'll tell you about my first marathon. Would that be better?"

She sprints up to me, and keeps jogging alongside.

"Maybe. Did you have to push your way onto the course, or run with a body guard too?" she asks, hoping for more dramatic detail.

"Oh, Anna, it was so much more exciting than that!"

We finish our run as I tell her about the small size of the field, the minimal cost to sign up, and the lack of support along the course.

"Did you win?" she asks.

"I can't give that away yet! You'll have to hear the rest of the story first."

She shakes her head at me, knowing I am stringing her along, but apparently not too bothered by it.

She grabs her bag from the storage area in the back of our store, a large pink duffle, and hurries out the door, waving to me as she goes. "See you on Saturday!" she calls. "We can finish the story then!"

I turn down the lights in the front of the store and begin to tidy up from the day's sales. Business has grown dramatically this past summer, which is good. It keeps me busy. Keeps me preoccupied. Focused.

I line up the boxes on their shelves, readjust the mannequins and their clothing, pick up stray receipts, tissues, and food wrappers.

It's quiet. But the remnants of life are still clinging to every part of this store. From earlier today, and from forty years ago. From the first simple Run the World poster on Opening Day to the heart-wrenching beauty of the Race Forward poster hanging over the sign up table. I can sense my past in every part of the store. I can hear my father's gentle but determined call for action. I can smell the dust from the track, the back alley oval that we couldn't stay off of long enough to pave with proper asphalt. The energy of running clubs and teams and trophies and tears still buzzes in my ears. I can feel the tug of my daughter's hand on my shorts as I leave for another run, her uncle Eddie pulling her onto his back, until she is old enough to join us too. And I can feel her hand ripped from mine as she is thrown into the street, no longer a child, but my baby, Julie, nonetheless.

Maybe this is where the story ends. It certainly has felt that way for the past few years.

I remove the bib numbers from a large box and stack them neatly next to the printed out list of charity runners who are running the race on Saturday.

Anna's binder and flip chart are behind the table. Her call to action. To help a new group of kids find their way through this big city, this big world, this huge life.

The picture of Yeni on the first page startles me. I have seen it so many times, as part of the presentation Anna has made over and over again. But today I see more than just a seven-year old girl. I see the pain of a nation, the strength and love of a mother, the faith of a child.

She is part of this story too. Which means it absolutely must go on.

# 14   THE RACE

In any city, on any race morning, there exist both individual rituals and collective determination. Each runner, man or woman, may arrive via different paths, and their goals might vary, but today the intersection of Clark and Addison is the starting point of a shared journey for them all. Today, their journey will be long. A half-marathon is just over thirteen miles long. It demands patience and perseverance more so than speed. It requires preparedness, certainly, but more importantly, it requires faith.

The sour beer smell of last night's revelry lingers in the air hovering above the small group huddled on the corner opposite Wrigley Field. Silence is the unannounced norm, as bodies function separate from minds at this early hour. Tables and fences and banners are unloaded along the street and slowly brought to life as the entry point of this inaugural race. Run The World has supported many local races over the past 35 years, but this is the first one that it has personally spearheaded.

Gracie Carlson Matthews is a spark of energy that drives into every aspect of the race organization. A shock of blond-silver, she bounces across the street, among the piles of supplies, under the banners and into the tents as they are erected across the wide span of street.

Remarkably, it all takes form in less than an hour. Gracie stands in front of the large map of the racecourse, visualizing each street and every turn.

Gracie has created the route to highlight some of her own favorite running paths. The race begins in the shadows of Wrigley Field and then heads north on Broadway, through the young eccentric neighborhood known as Boystown. At Lawrence Avenue they will turn west, through Ravenswood, a section of Chicago known for its ethnic restaurants and home to the Go Forward Foundation. This is where languages and skin colors dot the streets like a beautiful mosaic. They will cross the North

Branch of the Chicago River and head down Kedzie, a street she conquered as a teen. At Irving Park Road the runners turn east and head back toward the lake, dipping under Lake Shore Drive to meet the path that she and so many runners have followed all summer. At Fullerton, they cross back under Lake Shore Drive, to Clark Street, passing Run the World, for the last two miles north. It is a course filled with different terrain, and a changing atmosphere. But for Gracie, it is also a journey of her past.

Anna Rigaldo inches her dark green Impala through the barricades on Addison, ignoring the shouts behind her.

"Hey, lady, you can't drive down there! Street's closed!"

She rolls her window down, hangs her head out, and scowls. "Hey, I know!" From the passenger seat, Ron places his hand softly on Anna's shoulder. She takes a deep breath, then pulls her car over and leans farther out, smiling wide, if not ingenuously.

"I mean, I do know this street is closed. Thanks for your help. I'm actually the one who's organizing this. I'll be out of the way in a few minutes." She looks at Ron, whispering a small, "Thanks." He shoots her an understanding grin.

Her forced patience pays off, as three men hurry to move the barricade she is squeezed against.

"Not a problem, ma'am. Just didn't want you to get stuck in here."

She gives a little wave and pulls her car into a spot just beyond the alley, but a good distance from the proclaimed starting line. She checks the rear view mirror-- first for traffic, then to apply a quick swipe of red lipstick. She presses her lips together, sealing the color. Ron leans over and kisses her hard on her freshly painted mouth. She laughs to see his messy red smile, and then the two of them swing open their doors.

A block away, Eva Flanagan is carrying her eight-year-old daughter on her back. Maddie drapes herself across her mother, still sleepy, her head bobbing from side to side. Behind them, Benjamin has one arm wrapped around Jake and a huge duffle bag hangs from the other one. Katie carries a rectangular Tupperware container full of homemade energy bars. She is explaining to her grandparents, who walk on either side of her, how important it is to refuel after a race, and how important it is to choose the right kind of fuel, and how everything she put into these energy bars is organic and wholesome and healthy. "Because Mom runs really hard, so she needs a lot of energy!"

The sun is just beginning its climb above the horizon, transforming faceless shadows into familiar friends. Gracie waves to Eva from the Results and Awards tent, then bounds across the street to help her ease Maddie off of her back and into a lawn chair.

The early morning chill is both exciting and startling for Kristina Gomez. She exits the Addison Red Line train along with a large stream of people with paper numbers pinned to their shorts, t-shirts, or stretchy belts. Behind her she pulls her mother, who is carrying rolled up posters and flags to wave at the runners as they go past her. She has one poster especially for her daughter, which she will hold up as she nears the finish line. She had found the words in a running magazine, and it made her cry when she read it. So she made it into a big poster as a surprise.

"You go ahead, Kristina," she says. "I'm going to find a good spot up front so I can see you start and finish." Then before Kristina gets too far away, she calls out, "Good Luck!" She throws a kiss to her daughter, then squeezes through the crowd. She finds space next to a man slouched into a folding chair. A Go Forward t-shirt is stretched across the round ball that is his stomach.

"Excuse me, may I squeeze in here?" Lucia puts her bag of posters on the ground next to his chair. He jumps as if startled, and then heaves himself out of the chair, smoothing his hair back as he clears his throat.

"Oh, yes, of course, signora. Please, take my seat." He insists that she rest, as he has been sitting here for over an hour already, ever since his daughter dropped him off.

"You see, she is in charge of this whole race!" he beams. "I am very proud of her, but I did not realize how long this would take! Do you have someone running too?" Lucia smiles and shows him the posters and the flags and the one made just for Kristina. The man pulls out a handkerchief and wipes his neck and his forehead and while Lucia looks away he wipes his eyes, too. She gives him a sign to hold, and together they wait for the starting gun.

Kristina drops off her bag at the Gear Check and then looks around for her running group. She sees Mick first, towering over the rest of their small group. They are huddled together around Sara who is handing out special bibs to pin to their backs. These bibs all have the faces of some of the kids they are running for. Mick chooses a girl from Columbia -- Magdalena -- to pin to Kristina's back. Then he squeezes her shoulders before taking her hand and leading her towards the starting line. He points to the crowd gathering in front of them. "In the footsteps of legends," he reminds her.

Japlo Umunna clamps her hands over her ears. The voices seem to be shouting at her from only a few inches away. But there is too much motion swirling around her in too many unpredictable ways, so instead of moving away from the voice, she grinds her fists deeper into her ears. A tug on her left arm tells her to follow, but she freezes until the hand returns and takes hold of her arm, and leads her slowly away from the loudspeaker.

And then she can hear Yeni, mid-sentence, describing the scene. "--so try to stay to the right. And there are a few checkpoints that are like small raised areas that you'll need to cross over. Here, come feel how this one is to run across. It goes up for one step only, then back down. So Gracie will say 'checkpoint!' and you'll know, ok?"

"Okay," Japlo answers, trying to remember the slight but distinct bump that will rise up from the street.

Yeni stops abruptly. "I change my mind. I will lead you. You are worried, I can see. I would not want you to miss the bump and then fall."

Japlo smiles sadly. "You will run with Anna. You will run fast and have fun with the other teenagers. I will not fall. Do you think Gracie would let me fall?"

She knows she has Yeni trapped, for she cannot possibly doubt Gracie's ability to guide her safely. But Yeni's worry is still very real. It is not an easy thing to let go. For either of them.

Japlo hugs her daughter, now taller than she is herself, and assures her. "And if I do fall, you know what I will do then?" Japlo can feel Yeni smile.

"That's right. I will just get back up!" She pushes her daughter gently away. "Now go. Find your running friends. I will find mine, too."

A dark, thin man slides closer to Japlo's side, murmuring softly before wrapping his arm around her waist. She lifts her cheek to him, nuzzling into his chest and taking in a deep breath of his scent. Tambo has promised himself he will let her run with this woman, but fear claws at his heart. He does not forget how lucky he is -- truly it was luck or the guiding hands of angels themselves who plucked him from the agony in which he'd fallen. For three years he had searched Liberia, and then two years he had lived without hope. Until the letter arrived from his brother. A five year-old letter.

*Japlo is here.*

And now that he is in Chicago too, how can he ever leave her side again?

"Go Yeni!" he calls to his daughter. "Let the wind carry you! I have your Ma. She is too bull-headed to fall, anyway." He covers her thin shoulders with the extra jacket he has been carrying. "Just until you start to run," he whispers.

"Is Saa here?" Japlo extends eager fingers, expectantly. Saa has barely talked to her since he has arrived, and when he does there is cold resentment in every word.

"No, Japlo, he is still sleeping. At least, I think he is sleeping."

He does not tell her that Saa cannot sleep anymore, not like you or I or anyone who is not plagued with memories worse than nightmares can. But he lies in bed and stares at the wall, and occasionally slams his fist into the wall to make the pain less horrible. Japlo might know this, but she pretends he is not broken anyway. Maybe to her, he isn't.

Anna's voice carries over the bustle of organizing and arriving, so it is easy for Yeni to find her way. She is happy to be running with Anna. She loves Anna's bright outfits and matching fingernails. And although she can be a little scary, her bold, bossy personality makes Yeni feel safe and proud. She wants to talk to Anna about her brother. About his anger and bitterness and violence that scares Yeni and saddens Japlo. She wants to find out how a happy little dove can become so mean. But more importantly, she wants to find out how to turn that around. And Anna is the person who can help her, she is certain.

The starting line vibrates with the various levels of nerves and determination that fill most races. Ready to pounce at the first blast from the gun, the elite runners stretch and hop and stare straight ahead, like meditating jackrabbits. Behind them are the strong and steady runners, who are challenging themselves to a new finish time, and doubting the quality and extent of their training. Beyond the curve of pace groups, promising respectable finish times, are the run-walkers, whose energy is less urgent, but whose nervousness dwarfs any others, because they are not just accepting a challenge. They are accepting an entire truth about themselves, about running, and about survival.

The streets are lined with the friends, families and supporters of these runners. Their cheers are fuel to the apprehensive.

A large poster with huge bright letters proclaims: *The miracle isn't that you finished. The miracle is that you had the courage to start. Go Kristina!*

The finish line might declare a winner, but the starting line defines the victorious.

Ed Carlson checks his watch, preparing to announce the start of the race with a loud horn that dangles from his belt. Fifteen more minutes. From his angle, perched above the crowd, he watches the clouds grow gray and full in the distance. But the sun has risen over the lake, so it is bright and warm right now. This is the thing about Chicago. One minute the winds blow calm and easy, and the next minute they pull together a storm from nowhere, which makes it impossible to plan races like this.

Ten minutes to start time and Ed announces the names of sponsors and benefactors and the President of Go Forward, who is surrounded by her flock of teen-age refugees. They cheer loud and long when Ed announces that one of these teens, Yeni, and her mother are also running in this race.

Five minutes to start-time and voices fall quiet as the National Anthem is sung by the Chicago Children's Choir. The crowd softly joins in until a tunnel of national pride surrounds the runners.

One minute to the start. If you could measure the heartbeat of an entire crowd it would match the power of that anthem. A scratchy countdown from ten begins over the loudspeaker.

"...Three!...Two!...One!..."

The long loud blast of the horn rips steady feet from the earth, urging them forward for a little more than thirteen miles.

Ed cheers as a tall, skinny blond shoots ahead of the crowd, her face relaxed but focused. He waves to his sister, Gracie, as she jogs along the side, Japlo's hand resting lightly on her shoulder. A sea of color and movement rolls toward him and past, filling the street like a dam broken open.

It takes fifteen minutes for the last person to cross the starting line. Ed smiles and heaves a relaxed sigh, relieved to have most of the work over with. Now, he will move to the finish line and wait.

Eva was so tense when she heard the blast of the horn that she burst out in front in just two steps. She can feel the line of runners on her heels in just a couple breaths. In a few more steps a group of men ease past her. If she knew more about running and competition she might have been embarrassed by her own brazen start. But she does not know that her rabbit-like start caused her to lose credibility in the eyes of the local elite women, the women who have raced against each other and compared their paces and counted their awards. These women are serious runners, who have nothing to worry about from this over-confident, ill-paced lady that no one has ever seen before. She doesn't know, and therefore, she doesn't care. She doesn't know that the women hold back to see when she will fall apart after her fast start. So when she floats past Mile Five and the gap continues to grow wider, there is a sudden confused urgency behind her to catch up. She doesn't know this, either, so she keeps running and maintains her lead.

Adrenaline fuels most runners at the start of every race. Anna is no exception. But Anna is used to this feeling. It has been her source of fuel for the past ten years. This is a race, and that means competition, and that means everything she has been working to control is being thrown out the window. This is not a time to be polite or patient. This is a race, after all. She knows that she cannot keep up with the fastest runners, so she ignores those who fly past her with ease. But there are other runners who try to edge by, stepping a bit too close or bit too abruptly in front of her path. She turns to Yeni, who is pumping her arms and legs with the ease of youth.

"Come on, Yeni," Anna calls. "Let's stay with the crowd. Just follow me. I'm pretty tough when it comes to moving ahead!" Yeni nods her head and lengthens her stride.

"I'm right behind you, Anna! Don't worry, I'm tough, too!"

Anna runs just ahead of Yeni, calling back instinctively every few minutes.

"Still there, Yeni? — Whoa, look out! Coming through!" she warns. Anna swings her elbows out, making room for herself and Yeni. She glances over her shoulder and sees skinny Yeni pushing her way through as well. On either side of Anna, the runners step out of her way, the familiar parting of the sea that makes her feel in control. And it is only Mile Three.

Japlo's hand bounces lightly on Gracie's shoulder, instead of resting unnoticeably as usual. They have run together so many times, but today their rhythm is off. Gracie does a little skip to switch lead legs, hoping that will help, but the slight bounce only confuses Japlo, who also changes her lead leg. Then as the crowd begins to push past them, edging too close for Gracie's comfort, she shortens her stride, slowing down a bit. Japlo's toes scrape against Gracie's heel, and they both stumble a few steps, pulled apart momentarily. Japlo stretches out her arm, waving her small hand up and down and over, searching for Gracie. Gracie grabs that hand and holds it, tight. The two women continue, hand in hand, as the crowd thins out and there is more space. Eventually Japlo asks, "Do you want me to run like this the rest of the way? I can, you know."

Gracie pauses. They have practiced running together for over a year now, always with Japlo's hand on her shoulder. But today that does not seem secure enough, safe enough. She doesn't answer Japlo, but grips a bit tighter. They pass the Mile One marker in rhythm at last. It is Japlo who picks up the pace. She feels Gracie tug slightly on her hand, but does not slow down.

"I know you are worried," Japlo says smoothly, "but you needn't be. You do know I have run through worse, right?"

Gracie smiles. "Yes. I guess that's true. I just don't want anything bad to happen to you."

Japlo wriggles her hand free of Gracie's and follows her arm with her fingertips until she reaches her shoulder. Japlo smiles sadly, but pushes Gracie lightly, indicating that she is fine. "Everything bad has already happened. From now on, it is only good. Now, let's see how fast we can move like this!"

Kristina crosses the starting line ten minutes after the clock starts. Mick has told her that her official time is recorded through a chip that is tied to her shoe, so she shouldn't worry about the numbers on the clock. She just needs to stay focused and stay strong. So she keeps her eyes glued to Mick's back. Focus is not a problem when he is leading her. It is very easy to keep her eyes on him, to feel as if she is a part of him. It's the staying strong that has her worried. She has never actually run thirteen miles —

her longest run being twelve miles just two weeks ago. Mick has assured her that one extra mile is not a problem, but he doesn't realize how hard those twelve miles were. He didn't see how much she cried afterwards. Staying strong has never been one of her best qualities. Thirteen miles of strength might not exist in her.

They run past Ed, the man who sold her that first pair of orange running shoes, and he gives her a thumbs up. "You got this!" he shouts to her. As she follows the stream of runners, her eyes focused on Mick, a wild waving from the side catches her attention. Her mother is waving and shouting, and holding one side of a huge poster, while a chubby dark man holds the other side. He is watching her mother and echoing her shouts. "Kristina! Kristina!"

As she gets closer she can read the message on the poster. "...*the courage to start.*" Mick turns back to her. "Is that your family?" Before she can answer he points to the poster and says, "See? The Start Line is behind us, so you've already done the hardest part! If you can do that, you do anything." Mick's smile relaxes Kristina's fear.

She follows him into the rest of their journey.


Thirteen miles of running can take anywhere from a little over an hour to more than three hours. But it's thirteen miles all the same. Thirteen point one, to be exact. And in that time, each person will reach a point that urges her to stop. Each runner faces this internal demon in different ways, but it is a demon common to them all.

Then there are external demons that force a different kind of perseverance. Today, that demon is the storm rushing toward them across the flat plains of Illinois and smashing into the swirling winds over Lake Michigan. Depending on where the runners are when the storm clouds hit the wind, there might be different levels of fatigue or fear. But the storm hits everybody at the same time.

A wild wind tore down Addison, knocking over the signs and small tents set up along the way. Each gust brought the smell and taste of rain closer. Ed unplugged as many speakers and lights as he could. His team of volunteers grabbed papers and computers and piled them into the trucks lining the alley behind them. Heavy drops of rain fell ahead of the downpour, a final warning to take cover. The crowd of spectators squeezed into coffee shops and drugstores. Ed needed to stop the race, to pull all the runners in, but he had no idea how to find everyone. So he started up his van, inching it down Addison in the fifty-minute wake of the last runners. He hoped that the participants would use their common sense and seek shelter until this thing passed.

The rain exploded from the sky with a simultaneous crack of lightning and thunder. The runners screeched and bolted off the racecourse to dart into the lobbies of condominium buildings lining Broadway or to flatten themselves against locked storefronts. Anyone who has run in Chicago long enough knows that storms are to be respected and feared.

However, Eva hasn't been running in Chicago long enough.

Anna has stopped in the middle of the path just past the turn at Fullerton. She has run through ten miles and her body is growing rapidly fatigued. Every time she had asked Yeni how she was doing, Yeni pulled up closer to Anna and shouted "Great! Just like you!" As she'd drop behind Anna again, tears had pinched her eyes, and she scowled away any complaints. When the downpour began, Anna had already turned south onto the lakefront path with Yeni just a few steps behind her and the wild waves of Lake Michigan to her left.

But now runners stream past her, cutting in front of her, lunging back toward the shelter of the underpass, and Yeni is nowhere to be seen. "Move it!" screams a skinny brunette, pushing Anna out of her way.

But she won't move. And even though the pushing and screaming is making her bristle with anger, she can't get distracted by that now.

"Yeni!" Anna cups her hands around her mouth and calls into the crowd huddling under Lake Shore Drive.

"Yeni! Yeni!" Anna turns and calls behind her, then to the right, then up ahead, then to the lake on her left. The waves are crashing furiously onto the cement harbor, showering everyone still on the path with a cold spray of lake water before dragging itself out once again. Anna's shouts begin to carry with it the clawing of desperation and fear. She draws a shaky tear-laden breath and realizes she has done exactly what she promised Japlo she would not do. She has lost Yeni.

The sky has grown very dark and combined with the wind and the rain and the blur of people it is almost impossible for Anna to see anything. A wave crashes against the pier, flooding the path and soaking her shoes. The power of the receding undertow knocks her off her feet. Her stomach lurches as she realizes how easily Yeni would be pulled off this path and into the lake. She is just a girl, a little girl who trusted her. A little girl who just wanted to run with her. She just wanted to talk to her. She just wanted to be like her.

Anna groans to herself. "Oh, Yeni, you don't want to be like me. Stupid, selfish, self-centered idiot! Please don't be like me. Please don't be —." Her prayer, too difficult to utter, disappears in to the storm.

Anna drops to her knees and crawls carefully to the side of the pier. A wave towers above her and then slams its weight onto her prone body. She holds onto the edge of the pier as the wave grabs at her. She searches the edge of the pier for any sign of Yeni — a leg, a braid, a flash of color.

"Yeni!" Anna screams helplessly into the lake as the waves pull back for another attack. "Yeni!" This time the wave grows tall from nearly twenty feet out. The crowd by the underpass sees it, and pushes farther in. Then one skinny dark girl wiggles out from the crowd and screams, "Anna!" just as the wave crashes, lifting Anna's body off of the pier, pulling her legs toward the lake, while her fingers dig into a tiny ridge along the edge. Yeni grabs the hand of the person closest to her. "Hold on!" she calls. Without any further direction, the runners link arm-to-arm and hand-to-hand, creating a human chain, and before the next wave can hit, they have pulled Anna out of the lake and away from the edge of the pier.

Anna ignores everyone as she wraps Yeni in her arms, burying sobs of fear and relief in her soft braids. One of the ladies standing nearby puts her hand on Anna's shoulder. "You're a brave woman," she says admiringly. A rain-drenched man adds, "And that's a brave girl you got there!"

Yeni smiles and holds Anna's face in her hands. "See, just like you!"

Gracie and Japlo had already crossed the halfway mark when the storm hit. Gracie had watched the clouds approaching from the west and timed her run perfectly. As the first few raindrops fell she led Japlo carefully up the front steps of a large brick bungalow. And now, they sit together on the covered porch as Gracie describes the movement of the storm and the beauty in its trail. Dark swirling clouds dip closer and closer to the earth, layers of black and purple and green. And then just behind that, like another world entirely, a slab of bright blue, pushes the storm away. Japlo smells the rain, feels the wind, and hears the pounding of raindrops on the porch roof. A moist wind curls around them, but they are safe from the lightning and can remain primarily dry. Even so, it is now Japlo that shakes with panic.

She grips Gracie's hand and for the first time since she has met her, Gracie sees fear in Japlo's eyes.

"Where is she? How can we find her? Can you call someone?"

Gracie assures her that Ed is bringing the race to an end, that he is looking specifically for Yeni and he will call as soon as he finds her. She taps the cell phone that is tucked away in a waterproof running belt.

"You know she is going to be fine. She is with Anna. And if there is one person stronger than this storm, it's Anna!"

Japlo smiles and relaxes her grip. Gracie's phone vibrates and she checks the message that appears. Smiling, she pats Japlo. "That's Eddie. She's safe. But they want to keep running, once the rain passes, if you say it's okay."

Japlo hesitates, then nods her head. "But only if it stops raining!"

"The clouds have already passed over us. In another ten minutes we can get back on the course too. That is, if you want to. Or we can get a ride back to the start if you'd rather."

Japlo grins. "And let Yeni think that I was too afraid to finish a little race? No, we will keep running. Besides, we aren't running to win. We are running to help a lot of people. People who helped me, too. We will run it all."

The front door creaks opens, and a slow-moving gray-haired man leans into the screen door.

"One more lap," he orders. "One more lap. One more lap."

Gracie stands up and stares with wide, hopeful eyes at the man. Behind him, a soft female voice calls out.

"Daddy, come away from the door, now. There's a storm out there."

His stare is blank and unexpressive. But he doesn't go back in, either.

Still looking into her father's eyes, Gracie calls out, "It's just me, Kelly. We were running when it started to rain, so we stopped here while it blows over."

Kelly comes to the door, standing behind the old man, peeking around him.

"Daddy, look, it's Gracie here for a surprise visit. You remember Gracie, right, Daddy?" His expression does not change, but he holds Gracie's gaze as she walks closer to the door.

"It's okay," Gracie says. "He remembers the important stuff." She lifts her voice. "Right, Dad?" She reaches up and through the screen, taps him on the nose. A quiver shoots across his lips.

She calls into the house to Kelly. "We're leaving now, but I'll be here tomorrow morning, as usual, Kel."

Kelly waves at her. "Well, go finish your darn race then, so you can tell Dad all about it tomorrow!"

Kristina's group is not worried about the storm. In fact, most of them are relieved that the storm cut their race short. Instead the group is happily ordering hot chocolate and coffee and muffins as they sit around tables in Cafe Villa. Each of them relays exactly what they saw, and how close they were to the first lightning strike, and they gasp and exaggerate and congratulate themselves on finding a cozy place to escape.

Except Kristina. She leans her forehead against the window at the front of the store, watching the rain diminish its intensity. Bluish-gray clouds replace the dark green sky, and a small river floods the gutter alongside the street. Despite her initial fear, or maybe because of it, Kristina wants to finish this race. Otherwise, she will have to tell all those children and all their mothers that although they held up their end of the bargain, she could not. She closes her eyes and tries to push the clouds away with her mind.

Mick walks up behind her and places his hands on the window, one on either side of her head, leaning over her shoulder to peer at the sky. His thinly covered body pushes against her and Kristina freezes against the window as well. She is trapped between this cold pane of glass and his warm, hard body. Maybe trapped isn't the right word.

"Hey, it looks like it's gonna clear up!" he calls back to the crowd of relaxing runners. No one responds, but a few more people order doughnuts and coffee.

Mick brings his lips close to Kristina's ear, his breath tickling her neck and back and breasts. "What do you say we ditch these guys?"

Kristina stiffens. How could Mick suggest bailing on something she had worked so hard to do? Her building desire for him instantly deflates as he tugs on her elbow, whispering, "Come on!"

"No," Kristina says, pushing Mick's hand away. "I like you, Mick. I really do. But I came here to run, not for you, not for this group, but for myself. I want to finish this damn race, if I have to wait until midnight to run it!"

Mick smiles, pulling Kristina begrudgingly toward him. He dips his face low to hers and whispers once again. "These guys are done with their race. I meant let's leave them here and get back on the course. You and me."

Kristina's face blushes deep red, as she mumbles, "Oh. I thought —" Mick pushes her away from the window before she can finish.

Kristina's embarrassment dissolves when they quietly slip out the door and Mick pulls her back to the spot along Lawrence Avenue where they had dodged into the Cafe twenty minutes earlier.

"Just seven more miles to go. Are you up for that?" She nods.

He pushes Kristina slightly ahead of him, and taps her lightly on the butt.

"There ya go, Kristina. This time you lead. I'm pretty sure you know the way."

Eva runs because that is what she has done for the past eighteen months. She runs because it is the one thing that makes her feel alive. And today she runs because she wants to win. Gracie expects her to win. Ben expects her to win. She needs to win, so she keeps running. She runs because she doesn't know that everyone else has stopped.

Eva turns north onto Clark Street amid an electric storm that criss-crosses the sky above her. Windows are slammed shut and a few people stand huddled under store canopies, clutching their coffee or grocery bags. She splashes through puddles that have appeared quickly and have not yet found a way to the drainage sewers. The rain and wind sting her eyes and scrape her cheeks. She does not notice the group of men who had been leading her, suddenly duck together into the open door of Run The World.

Eva pushes against a wind that keeps her nearly frozen in mid-stride, unrelenting in its power. She lowers her head and pushes harder, the rain pelting her from all sides. She passes a police station, where red and blue sirens blare and add to the light show around her. This is where she started her run many months ago. And now she owns this street. Day after day, mile after mile, she has taken possession of this asphalt ribbon. Maybe Michelle thinks it's an obsession, but it's obsession that breeds passion, and it's passion that gives life to a dull and dying soul.

She sees the Finish Line banner, flapping wildly just ahead of her. But there is no one standing next to it, no one on the stage, no one at all.

"It's over?" she mumbles to herself through gasps. "It can't be over! It can't be over!"

Eva slows to a walk just a few yards away from the finish. The downpour ceases almost as quickly as it began. The thunder and wailing wind hush. Eva stands in the middle of an empty street, with strands of hair clinging to her cheeks and her neck.

The door of a large van suddenly bursts open, and Benjamin jumps out, running to the corner, just beyond the finish.

"Eva!" he calls to her. "Oh my god! I — I can't believe you ran through that! You basically just ran through hell! You need to finish!"

As the spectators peek out from the trucks, stores, and doorways, Eva jogs forward the last few yards, dipping under the half-ripped FINISH banner, and into the arms of her husband.

Maybe Tambo is right, that we are all here by pure luck. The odds seem stacked against us for most of our lives, don't they? But when we know the power of the will, the unbending faith of the spirit against odds of survival, then how small a leap might it be to restore a bit of the family, or to heal a bit of the pain, or to bring love a bit closer to us all? Maybe it doesn't take luck at all. Maybe we just need to do it.

Each step may be our own, but together we rise above challenges great and small. There is no finer metaphor for this life than the journey of the runner. When she runs, she shows us the strength that lies in each of us, if only we keep our feet, and our hearts, moving forward.

~

# ABOUT THE AUTHOR: M. RAE

M. Rae was born and raised in the Chicago area, where she spent many years running through city streets, across suburban trails, and along lakefront paths. This is where she met the many women and men who have inspired her running, her writing, and her belief in the power of a community. M. Rae has played a supportive role in leading both children and adults to a healthy and harmonious lifestyle as a coach, a mentor, a teacher, a training partner, and now as a writer.

M. Rae has run fourteen marathons, ten half-marathons, and several shorter local races. Regardless of the distance, racing has always been an opportunity for self-reflection. It is her greatest hope to continue to run, and race, for many years to come.

M. Rae currently lives in a suburb of Chicago, where she teaches Middle School English, coaches Cross-Country and Track, and runs as often as possible.

*With Grace Under Pressure* is M. Rae's first fiction novel.

CPSIA information can be obtained at www.ICGtesting.com
Printed in the USA
LVOW06s1623100915

453651LV00011B/783/P

9 781502 838162